ALSO BY LAUREN BLAKELY

The Caught Up in Love Series (Each book in this series follows a different couple so each book can be read separately, or enjoyed as a series since characters crossover)

Caught Up in Her (A short prequel novella to
   Caught Up in Us)
Caught Up In Us
Pretending He's Mine
Trophy Husband
Playing With Her Heart

Standalone Novels (Each of these full-length romance novels can be read by themselves, though they feature appearance from characters in Caught Up in Love)

Far Too Tempting
Stars in Their Eyes
21 Stolen Kisses

The No Regrets Series (These books should be read in order)

The Thrill of It
Every Second With You

The Seductive Nights Series

Night After Night (Julia and Clay, book one, includes the
   prequel *First Night*)
After This Night (Julia and Clay, book two)
One More Night (Julia and Clay, book three)

Nights With Him (A standalone novel about Michelle and Jack)

Forbidden Nights (A standalone novel about Nate and Casey)

The Sinful Nights Series

Sweet Sinful Nights (Brent and Shannon, June 2015)
Sinful Desire (Fall, 2015)
Sinful Longing (2016)
Sinful Love (2016)

The Fighting Fire Series

Burn For Me (Smith and Jamie)
Melt for Him (Megan and Becker)
Consumed By You (Travis and Cara, August 2015)

This book is dedicated to my daughter,
who helped brainstorm the plot. You are brilliant, my dear!
And, as always, to my dear friend Cynthia.

CHAPTER ONE

Ten years ago

I'd go anywhere with you.

People said those words, but they didn't always mean them. Brent was sure Shannon did though. She'd go anywhere with him.

As he gunned the engine on his bike, all he could think was that in less than ten minutes it would be happening. He'd be walking through the front door and giving the woman he loved the best news of their lives.

Weaving through the late afternoon Boston traffic, he fast-forwarded to the next few weeks—they'd go to the land of sunshine. He'd take her far away from Boston, and keep her far away from all the other places she didn't want to be. He could see them holed up in a little one-bedroom apartment in Los Angeles, spending their nights fucking, their days working. Fine, she didn't have a job yet, but there had to be work in Los Angeles for an injured-dancer-turned-entry-level-choreographer, right?

With equal parts excitement and anticipation radiating through his bones, he darted through the stalled cars. Up ahead, maybe five hundred feet, was the exit that would take him to his apartment, where she'd been living for the last two weeks since her lease ran out after they'd graduated. His was up next week. Perfect timing to leave town together.

Flipping on the blinker, he turned off the highway, then jetted down the road to his building. Soon, he pulled into the asphalt lot, shut off the engine, and unsnapped his helmet. He headed to the concrete stairwell, taking the stairs two by two, up to the third floor.

He unlocked the front door quickly and tossed his keys on the entryway table. The late afternoon sun shone through the dirt-streaked window, but the living room was empty, the gray, rumpled couch missing his pixie-sized woman. Then again, he'd never known Shannon to sit still or lie down. Unless her legs were wrapped around his waist, and hell, that was where he'd like them to be in about three minutes, because this called for a celebratory round or two in the sack.

He turned into the kitchen, looking for her.

"Babe," he called out.

The home was still.

Their apartment crackled with silence.

It was the tiniest apartment in all of Boston, and for a split second, maybe more, his heart stopped beating, and a rabid fear swooped down out of nowhere. But then, it wasn't entirely from nowhere. It was born from the life she'd lived before she came to college.

A door squeaked—a sliding glass door badly in need of oiling. He spun around, returning to the living room and the tiny balcony that he hadn't thought to check. There she was, walking inside, the widest smile in the world on her gorgeous face, her bright blond hair, short and sleek, pushed back in a slim silver headband.

"I have something to tell you," she said. Her eyes lit up as she held her flip phone in her hand.

"I have something to tell you, too," he said, and roped his arms around her waist, easily lifting her lush, limber body. Instantly, she wrapped her legs around his waist and dropped her mouth to his, kissing him hard. She darted out her tongue, sliding it between his lips, and he groaned, wanting to take her right there against the wall, on the balcony, on the floor. Or hell, just standing up like this would be fine. Being madly in love with a woman who could bend and move in hard-on inducing ways was pretty much the greatest thing in the world. Yeah, he was a lucky bastard.

"Ladies first," he said, setting her down, then gesturing for her to talk.

"No. You go," she said, her forest green eyes twinkling. "I want to hear all about your big interview." She reached for the collar on his shirt, tugging both ends. "I bet they adored you. I bet you already have your second interview lined up."

"Better than that," he said, and dipped her, her back arcing effortlessly as she looked up at him from that position.

The last thing he'd expected when he walked into his job interview today was to be hired on the spot. That wasn't even in the realm of possibility. It was an informational interview. Besides, the job he'd originally gone in for was based in New York. But the post that *Late Night Antics* offered him—a gig with more money, more cred, and more opportunity—was in Los Angeles. At twenty-one, he'd landed a comedian's dream job.

"Tell me, tell me!" she demanded, laughter in her voice.

He raised her up again and parked his hands on her shoulders. "We're moving to L.A. next week!"

Her sweet laughter stopped, as if he'd turned off a switch, but the eerie silence made no sense to him.

"What?" she asked, her voice small.

He nodded, letting the enthusiasm he felt roll off him. Surely, she'd catch it, too. She'd have to be infected with his excitement. Their future was unfurling before them. "I got the job. They offered me a job on the spot. For *Late Night Antics*. This never happens, Shan. I'll be the youngest comedy writer in the history of the show, and you know what happens to the youngest writers."

"They go on to have the biggest careers," she said, repeating what he'd told her many times before, but she sounded monotone, as if she was merely parroting him.

"This is huge, babe," he said, keeping the conversation upbeat.

"I know. It is," she said, sounding hollow.

"What's wrong?"

"I thought it was for a job in New York. That we were trying to find work together in New York so we could be together. You know, Mr. and Mrs. Nichols, and all," she said, trying to smile but her lower lip quivered the slightest bit.

He shook his head. "Well, it was. But they loved my work so much they offered me a gig and want me to start next week in time for the new fall season. It's an amazing opportunity. Top late-night TV show in the country. *In the world.* And you are looking at the newest writer. And he is looking at his bride-to-be."

He thought for sure that would return the smile to her face, the kind that made her crinkle her nose, with its constellation of freckles. He loved nothing more than making her smile, making her laugh, especially considering what she and her family had been through that wasn't the least bit funny whatsoever. "We're going to L.A.," he added, because the silence was too much.

But there was no smile. Her eyes were glassy, wet maybe. Then she seemed to draw in that flash of sadness and replace it with a hard fierceness, and a tight line across her lips.

"Brent," she said carefully. "Did you say *we're going to L.A.?*"

He nodded eagerly. "I start next week. We're moving to L.A. I took the job."

She stepped away, pushing her hands against him. "You. Took. It?" she repeated, each word needing its own longitude and latitude.

"Hell yeah."

"You never thought to discuss it with your *bride-to-be?*" she asked pointedly, holding up her hand and flashing her ring at him—the diamond he'd given her, set in her grandmother's band that her brother Michael had helped him track down.

"No." But he was too surprised by her question to even try to figure out why she was asking.

"What about me?"

"What about you? You don't have a job."

"But we agreed to look for work in New York. That was our plan. I thought the job you were interviewing for was in New York. That's what you told me, and that's the only place I've been looking. I turned down an opportunity in Tucson last week because you were worried it was too far away."

He shot her a look. "Shan, that was with a tiny little dance company."

Her stare could burn a pinhole through him. "Don't put it down now. We both know why I said no. Because you said you couldn't bear to be apart from me. That's what you said, so don't act like it would have been the wrong career move for me. I did that for you. You said you weren't going to find work as a comedian in Tucson. And now you just went and took a job in L.A. without even talking to me," she said, holding her hands out wide, waiting for his answer.

"I didn't think I needed to," he said, raising his chin up, holding his ground. "It's the perfect gig for me. So I said yes." He planted his feet wider, as if they were two gunslingers ready to do battle. She crossed her arms, the next move in the dance of their anger. Familiar choreography for the two of them.

"Well, I got a job, too," she tossed back, arching an eyebrow.

"In L.A.?" he asked, hoping wildly.

She shook her head. "In New York. Like we talked about. Then it goes to London."

He wrenched back and narrowed his eyes. "You didn't tell me you were looking for work in London."

She huffed. Oh, she breathed fire. That woman knew how to be angry with him. She'd mastered it. She pointed a finger at his chest. "No, I didn't tell you, because there was nothing to tell, and now I am telling you that my modern dance teacher called me today to tell me Lars Branson just lost his assistant choreographer for the West End production of *West Side Story* and asked did he know anyone who could fill in at a moment's notice? He mentioned me, since he knew I was looking for work, and the job starts in New York and then moves to London at the end of the summer. I didn't say yes because I wanted to talk to you about it first. To see if you'd even want to go to London with me."

"But I thought you were looking for work here," he said, his arms spinning in circles, as if she'd understand he meant all of the United States of America. "Not overseas."

"I wasn't looking, Brent. Don't you get it? And unlike you, I didn't take the job. *Yet.* I said I'd need to check with my fiancé, which is evidently more than it occurred to you to do."

"I thought you'd be happy for me. I thought you'd want to come with me. C'mon, Shannon. I said yes because it's the opportunity of a lifetime. And you'll come with me, won't you?" He stepped closer and slinked his hand around her waist, her body under his fingertips sending that electric charge through him that only she had the power to do. Since the moment he laid eyes on Shannon Paige-Prince two years ago, in the audience at an open mic night at a local comedy club, he knew he had to have her. He'd nearly forgotten the next line in his bit. He'd barely been able to look away from her, from those jade green eyes and those ruby red lips, slightly parted as she'd watched him on stage, and laughed at the punch lines. His friend Hal had told him in advance that he was bringing along someone he had to meet, since both Brent and Shannon grew up in Vegas.

The second his bit had ended, he'd jumped off the stage, made a beeline through the crowd, and introduced himself to her, and asked her out one minute later. "*I'm going to say the one thing that I hope doesn't make you laugh tonight. Go out with me, please,*" he'd said, and she had laughed, but she'd nodded, too, and said yes immediately.

He called up that lifeline now, tried to recreate the success that had won him his first date with this fiery, fierce, intense woman. "Go with me, please." He had to convince her. Make her see that Los Angeles was where they belonged. Where they could start their life together after college. "There must be tons of choreographer gigs in L.A."

She narrowed her eyes. "No. Choreographer jobs are a lot like jobs for comedians. They're hard to come by. So maybe you should come with me."

"To London?"

She nodded. "Yes. Would you like to? Because, see what I'm doing right now?" She gestured from him to her. "I'm discussing it in advance with the man I love." Her voice softened then, as she seemed to strip away the anger for a moment. "We could try long distance."

The look on her face was so sweet, so hopeful, and it nearly made him say yes.

But he couldn't bear to be apart from her. He shook his head vehemently. She had to go with him to Los Angeles. "No. I can't do long distance. It'll be awful not seeing you. Besides, you've always been there for me. You always came to see my shows. This is the same idea. You're my rock. You're my woman. I've got to have you with me."

"So you want me to turn down *West Side Story*?"

"Shan, can't you put it aside?" he said, then the next words tumbled out before he could stop them. "You can't even dance anymore."

She closed her eyes and pursed her lips, red clouds billowing out her ears. "You ass. You know that hurts. You think I *wanted* to tear my ACL and never be able to dance again? At least you can write jokes no matter what."

"But it's true. Doesn't it make more sense for you to go with me? This is a big deal for me."

"And *West Side Story* is a big deal to me. This is my chance to have a career after dance. To do the only thing I might possibly be able to do and still be in the dance world. And at least I didn't accept it. I waited to talk to you."

"I thought you'd go with me. C'mon, you're my wife."

"Not yet."

"But you will be."

"Not if you keep making decisions without asking me."

Shit. This was bad. This was the jet spiraling from the sky. This was an engine spitting out fumes and spinning out of control. He had to lean on the one thing they'd always done well. He cupped her cheeks in his hands, his six-foot frame towering over her.

"C'mon," he whispered, as he kissed her neck. "How about some fucking and fighting? That's what we do best."

She banged her fists against his chest. Yup. That was how it started. That was how they played this game.

"Yeah. Like that, babe. Just like that," he said, as she squirmed in his arms. It was the moment before. Before she let go. Before she gave in. Before she was consumed with the same desire he had—to fuck it out. To fuck out their anger. To turn all their frustration into a coming together.

He nuzzled her neck, kissing her furiously, looking for the reaction this always elicited—the almost instantaneous melting into his arms, the way she molded to him, responding to kisses that turned a moment from bad to good. She shuddered and gasped, and those twin signs drove him on, reminding him that he and Shannon were unbreakable, that no matter what they did or said, no matter how hot-headed she thought he was, no matter how secretive he accused her of being, at the end of it, they were a chemical reaction that couldn't be denied.

She kissed him ferociously, threading her hands in his hair and pulling his top lip through her teeth. He groaned, loving her roughness. Loving how she gave as good as she got. She bit down hard, and the temperature inside him shot sky-high. He backed her up to the wall, ready to strip her clothes and have her.

Then, he felt her hands on his chest, and, harder than she ever had before, she pushed him off, so hard he stumbled and nearly lost his balance.

"What was that for?" he asked, shock echoing in his bones.

"There isn't any fucking and fighting today, Brent Nichols."

"Why?"

"Because you think everything can be solved with your dick. You think it's okay to just make choices for us. It's not. All you had to do was ask me first and I'd have said yes. But you didn't even think about talking to me. You think you can just tell me how it's going to be."

His chest burned with frustration. He could not lose her. Would not. Hell, he was ready to toss her on his shoulder and carry her across the country if he had to.

"I'm not telling you how it's supposed to be. I'm telling you that I need you with me. I have to have you by my side."

"Which means you're not really giving me a choice, are you?"

"What choice do you want me to give you? I took the job, and I need you with me."

"You already made it clear that your career is more important than mine. And you know what? I'd have gone with you. I'd have called up Lars and turned down the chance to work on *West Side Story*. But you taking this job on the other side of the country, when we'd made plans to look for work in New York, shows me that I will never be number one to you."

She swiveled around, grabbed her purse from the living room table, and marched to the door. He swore a cloud of angry smoke swelled behind her.

"Where are you going?" he asked, following her.

"I'm going out," she said, biting out the words.

"You're telling me you won't even consider going to L.A. with me?"

"Are you telling me you won't even consider going to New York with me?" she asked, countering him.

He said nothing. He let his mind cycle through his options. They were being squeezed thinner by the second. This job was the biggest opportunity he'd ever have. It could make or break his career. He had to take it, and he had to keep her. He imagined himself at the tables, laying down his bets, taking a risk. He was going all in, and he was doing it with a big bluff.

"If you don't go with me, there's no point staying together," he said, making his Hail Mary pass. He had to do something. He couldn't lose her. He had to let her know his way was the only way for them. "You've got to go to L.A. or we might as well be over."

Her nostrils flared. Her eyes widened. And her fingers started working. She reached for her left hand, twisting the silver ring.

"That's how it's going to be? This is what we've come to? You make threats to keep me?" she said, and she didn't shout, she didn't raise her voice. She whispered her vitriolic words and they sliced him.

"Shannon," he began, trying desperately to backpedal. "It wasn't a threat."

She held up her hand, her eyes like ice and her lips a firing squad. Then she tugged on the diamond ring. His stomach dropped. He might have been bluffing. But she was not.

"You made this choice. *You*," she said, her eyes narrowed and full of fire, her fingers shaking. "Here's your hardearned diamond. I want my band back. Send it to my grandmother's house."

"Please. I didn't mean it," he said, trying to claw his way out of the hole he'd dug.

She pressed her finger against his lips. "There's nothing you can say to me now. You already said it all with your ultimatum. So, allow me to have the last word." She peeled open his fingers one by one, and dropped the ring into his palm. "I might be the one leaving right now. But you are the one walking away from *us*. You just made the biggest mistake of your life."

A black cloud engulfed him. He had no clue how the day had gone to shit so quickly. He reached for her shoulder, trying to figure out how the hell to take his foot out of his mouth. "Shannon—"

She held up her hand, then walked out the door and out of his life.

As the latch clanged shut, he knew she was right. He was the one walking away, but there was no going back now.

CHAPTER TWO

Present day

"He's not going to be there tonight."

Colin spoke as if he were a soothsayer, as if he'd peered into the oracle itself and been granted a view into the future, three hours from now when they were to meet with the Edge nightclub to seal the deal.

"How do you know for sure?" Shannon asked as she rested her ankle atop the barre in the studio at the Shay Productions offices, a few miles from downtown. Effortlessly, because she'd been doing it since she was four, she reached for her ankle and stretched. She'd just finished putting some of the new girls through their paces, and they were fantastic—sexy, gorgeous, enticing—everything her dancers were hired to be at clubs around the country, and the world now, too.

The late afternoon sun dipped in the sky, blasting its blinding light through the floor-to-ceiling windows that looked out on, oddly enough, sidewalks and trees. It always shocked outsiders that her Vegas-based company was actually located in an office park, not in the glittering sky-scrapers and hotels that greeted visitors with neon and lights. No need for spark and dazzle during the day.

"Because the meeting is with James, his business advisor and main investor. James is the guy at Edge that I've been working the deal with," Colin said. A venture capitalist, Colin ran his own firm but also handled the business part-nerships at Shay Productions. He'd been in talks with the second-in-command at Brent's nightclubs about integrat-ing Shannon's choreography. Shannon hadn't followed her ex's every move, but she was well aware that after a wildly successful career in comedy, he had transitioned to the business world and opened a string of popular nightclubs. Those clubs needed dancers.

"So it's just James going tonight?" she asked, triple con-firming what she hoped would be the line-up at the meet-ing. She didn't care if this dude brought his poodle if he had one. As long as Brent wasn't present, she'd be good to go.

Colin nodded. "Just James. Besides, he said Brent's not even in town. He's in the Caribbean or something, and I have a date at nine, so it'll be short and it'll be done," he reassured her, as he tugged at his wine-red tie, which was already close to unknotted.

Shannon rose. "Stop it," she said, tsking her twin brother gently. "You always do that."

"Do what?"

"Tug at your tie."

"I hate these stupid things."

"Then why do you wear one?"

Colin shrugged, and ran a hand through his dark, nearly black, hair. Funny that she and Colin were the twins in their quartet of siblings, but they couldn't have looked more different. Not that fraternal boy-girl twins should look the same. It was just ironic that Colin, the one closest to her, had the darkest hair and darkest eyes of her three brothers, while Shannon's natural coloring was fair.

"It's expected," he grumbled, as she straightened the knot in his neckwear. "I swear sometimes you treat me like I'm still the baby of the family."

"You always will be," she said, as she finished her task and held up five fingers to remind him. Five minutes younger.

"Anyway, James wants to meet you, since you're the face of the company. You're the star."

She scoffed, as she stretched her neck from side to side. "I'm absolutely not a star. Does this investor guy know it's me, though?"

Colin arched an eyebrow. "As in, does he think he's contracting entertainment services from Shay Sloan or from the woman who's the object of Brent's desire in 'King Schmuck,' one of the most popular viral videos in the last year?"

She rolled her eyes as she walked to the other side of the room to grab her water bottle. "I presume he knows the first," she said, taking a sip. "How about the second?"

Colin laughed. "I'm guessing no. That's what's so funny about it. Brent has no fucking clue that you've been under his nose all these years."

"Well, I had no clue he was here, either, until you started talking to his business guy. I didn't go looking him up," she said, though that wasn't entirely true. For the first few months after they'd split, she'd Googled Brent nearly every day. Hungry for breadcrumbs, she'd gobbled up each and every bit of information she could find, reading posts here and there in the entertainment trades about his show. But then she'd stopped searching for him regularly, because what was the point? They were through, they were over— they were done. She'd sent a friend to pick up her things from his place, and though he had called a few times in the days after he took off for L.A., she hadn't answered. After she'd left for London, she'd tried him once or twice from overseas, but had never reached him.

Then earlier that year, the *King Schmuck* video had surfaced, making the rounds online and catching Colin's eye. One evening when he was meeting her for dinner to discuss Shay's expansion in Europe, he'd instead marched into her restaurant, slid into the booth, and thrust a phone in her face.

She'd eyed him inquisitively. "Why are you showing this to me?"

"Just watch," he'd said insistently, and she'd zeroed in on the small screen.

Someone in the audience at a comedy club had recorded Brent. He strolled across the stage during a bit, looking far too handsome to be believed. Broader, sturdier, and older. A decade older, and she liked the way he'd aged. He shoved his hand through his hair—all that dark, soft hair.

He brought the mic to his lips. "Ever been that schmuck in a business meeting? You know which one I'm talking about. The one who has all sorts of shit up on his computer screen? You've seen this guy, right? He goes into a business meeting, he talks a good game, he flips open the laptop—he's about ready to share some really key business point. Like, some *big important thing*. But he forgets he was watching 'Hot, Horny Girls Who Get Off to Comedians'—wait, not that, that's a good site." He smiled briefly as the audience laughed. "So this guy, he forgets he was watching 'The Postman Always Comes Twice' or 'Hot Girls Who Like Ugly Guys,' and then his laptop gets plugged into the overhead. The guy is about to present at a meeting, and bam. There's his presentation right there. On screen. Splattered for everyone to see."

Laughter rippled through the crowd.

Shannon had craned her neck to stare at her brother. "I'm here to have dinner with you. Why do you think I want to see him talking about porn on his laptop?"

"Just trust me. I swear that's not what the bit's about," he'd said, as if he'd had a naughty little secret up his sleeve, using that same kind of voice he'd relied on as a kid, when he'd tried to trick her into touching a frog or a worm. She didn't trust that voice one bit.

But Brent had stage presence. He had that intangible quality known as charisma. Maybe it was the looks, maybe it was the charm, or maybe it was the sexy gravel of his voice. Who knew? Or maybe it was just that he was hot as hell, and he was funny. Rarely did those two traits exist in one man, but they resided in Brent, and she'd had a hard time looking away from the screen.

Brent had continued, pacing the other direction across the small stage. "So that was me. Yeah, me," he'd said, pointing at himself, stabbing his finger against his chest. "So, I'm meeting with the head of this hotel chain, and I'm suited up, right? Got the tie, the jacket, the tailored pants," he'd said, then glanced down at his jeans and loose T-shirt, as if to say *I'm still casual when I moonlight on stage from time to time.* "And we're talking about moving my nightclubs into his hotel, and I said 'let me show you the plans.' And what do you think was on my screen?"

He'd stopped, shaking his head, utterly bemused with himself. That was the self-deprecating tone and expression that he alone had mastered. The one that had worked its way into her heart in seconds when they were younger and made her fall in love with him. He was so damn charming, so utterly irresistible like this. When he owned every second of who he was.

"No, it was not 'Hot, Horny Girls Who Like Comedians,' though that would be a fucking awesome site. Someone needs to make that if it doesn't exist. And I will gladly sponsor it, bankroll it, whatever. Anyway, it was my ex's Faccbook profile. Yeah. I'm that guy. That idiot. King Schmuck. That asshole who Facebook stalks his ex," he'd said, then he'd stopped pacing and tapped his chest, the look on his face one of utter disdain for his own antics.

She'd grabbed the phone from Colin's hand and pressed end on the video.

"It was just getting to the part about you—"

She cut him off. "I don't want to see him. I certainly don't want to hear about him Facebook stalking some girlfriend."

"Um, Shan. That 'some girlfriend' is you," he'd said, sketching air quotes.

"I don't care," she'd said, and then gritted her teeth and tapped the menu. "Let's order and talk about Europe."

Colin had never brought it up again. While she knew the popular video was about her, she'd resisted every single urge to watch it. She didn't care to hear anything he could possibly say about her that was uttered in the same breath as 'porn on his computer screen,' no matter how funny, or how trendy the video had become.

Brent was an asshole, and the way things had ended between them was entirely his fault. He'd had the choice to have both her and work, but he'd picked work and ditched her. Case closed, in a classic stone cold fucking of her heart. Maybe that was why she couldn't deny her delight in the wild goose hunt he'd taken himself on via Facebook. He might have found Shannon Paige-Prince and been checking out her profile, but she wasn't that person anymore, and she barely maintained that page. Hell, she didn't maintain any profile because she didn't want to be known, or to be found. She preferred her new name, and new life, and living it off the Internet.

When she'd started her company four years ago, after amassing several high-profile choreography jobs following *West Side Story*, she'd already switched her hair color from bright blond to dark brown. Next, she'd jettisoned the last name she had growing up. She'd needed a sleeker and sexier name. Companies wanted to hire Shay Sloan more than Shannon Paige-Prince. But she also didn't want to see that look, that furrow of the brow that came when someone heard her last name. "Are you one of the Paige-Princes of..."

Nope.

Those questions needed to be cut off at the knees.

She'd taken her cues from Michael, her oldest brother. They all had. They always did. He'd been the first among them to change his last name to Sloan, and had suggested they all do the same. Sloan was an everyman name. It had no history, no notoriety. They could slip easily through this town and live free of all those questions from people who remembered who they had been long ago. With new names, their old life faded away, receded far into the rearview mirror.

"Anyway, *Shay*." Her twin brother lingered on her business name, mocking her playfully as he said it. "The guy you hate won't be there."

"I don't hate Brent," she said quickly. But she did. Oh, how she did some days. She hated him with all she had.

"Yeah, yeah, yeah. And no, I didn't tell James you were engaged to King Schmuck back in college." But even those words and the weight of their promise— *engaged*—seemed like a terrible understatement of what she and Brent had shared. They were everything to each other. "It's just not germane to the business deal we're striking. It's a private matter. Like a million other things that are private."

"A million things," she echoed. Things the four siblings would take to the grave.

"Then let's go to this meeting tonight and seal the deal to bring the hottest dance show around to the hottest clubs worldwide," he said, holding up his fist.

She banged her fist to his. "See you in three hours."

Shannon left their offices and headed to her nearby home, driving past a billboard of The Wynn, the place that had put Shay Productions on the map three years ago when she'd choreographed a sultry extravaganza of the senses for the theater housed inside that upscale hotel. The show has been called "lush, sensual, and a feast for both the eyes and the loins." That production had enabled her to quickly build her business, to take her routines and choreography well beyond one stage and on to worldwide venues.

She'd come far from *West Side Story*, but that first gig after college had led to the next one, then the next one, then to this.

She turned onto her block, a trendy street not far from the Strip, with an organic breakfast cafe and a hipster coffee shop, then pulled into the parking lot at her condo. As she locked the car door, she reminded herself that if she'd chased Brent to Los Angeles, she might never have had the chance to become who she was today. Her career had given her freedom and distance from the past, and that was a dream come true.

On the way upstairs she snagged her mail, slapping it on the kitchen table to look at later. She showered, blow-dried her hair, and applied fresh makeup, twisting her long chestnut hair into a neat updo. She slipped into a sleek black dress that zipped up the side—the whole damn side from hem to sleeve—then into a pair of four-inch red suede shoes that tied up her ankles and to her calves. Vegas nights could be chilly, so she grabbed a shimmery, silver wrap for her shoulders.

She looked the part. She *needed* to look the part. She might not be the one on stage, but she still looked like a dancer.

Hell, she *still* was a dancer, even if she'd never dance again the way she wanted to.

But she'd gotten over her injury.

She'd gotten over her loss.

She'd gotten over Brent.

She knew how to get over stuff. She'd done it since she was thirteen.

CHAPTER THREE

One thousand feet.

That was when the plane started getting service again, so Brent tapped the screen on his phone, ready for the barrage of messages to load. Wireless had been down on the return flight from Saint Bart's, and he was antsy to know what he'd missed. Edge had been expanding rapidly in the last year, so these days his company was like a busy airport with jets lined up, taking off and landing every fifteen minutes.

As his plane dipped closer to the runway in Vegas, the emails poured onto his phone. He scanned quickly for James's name, since his right-hand man was tasked with keeping him apprised of the latest deals, problems, and opportunities. Brent was the front man in their 70/30 partnership, but James was vital in helping guide the business and find the right opportunities for Edge.

Fortunately, the email that awaited him was of the opportunity variety.

"Meeting tonight with Shay Productions. Should be able to sign that deal."

Excellent news.

That deal had come together in record time—less than one week. Brent had been traveling to Ibiza earlier that month to check out the club scene there, and see what best practices he could adopt for his business. One of the clubs he'd visited had featured background dancers on pedestal stages throughout the club, dancing seductively all through the night. Some had circulated on the dance floor too, and the club owner had dropped the name Shay Productions. Brent had passed it on to James, who'd assembled the pieces quickly while Brent had traveled to Saint Bart's for the launch of his club there.

Brent hadn't slept in his own bed in ten days. He was damn tired, and ready to crash.

The Saint Bart's club opening had gone so smoothly that he'd returned one day earlier than planned. Hearing that the next deal was falling into place was music to his ears, especially since Edge's expansion into New York had been hitting roadblock after roadblock. He had a meeting in Manhattan later that week to deal with the latest challenges in that city.

He yawned as he began to reply *good luck*.

But then he covered his mouth, stifled the yawn and re-minded himself that businesses didn't grow if the CEO made sure he got a good night's sleep. Edge had thrived when Brent had burned the midnight oil and kept his laser focus on the company. That included meeting all their business partners when he was in town and making sure everyone was on the up and up.

The second the wheels touched down in the city he called home, he dialed James.

"Hey, where's the meeting?" he asked, as they taxied. He'd flown commercial and had enjoyed the first-class seat.

His brother Clay had taught him that early days were not the time for frills like a private jet; those would come with growth. Or better yet, make nice with people and they might loan you their jets. That was how his brother had flown the friendly skies in style.

"Mandarin Bar at the Oriental," James said. "You gonna join us?"

Brent nodded. "Yeah. I want to meet them before we sign off."

"Excellent. See you at eight then. Oh, and this deal kicks ass. Their dancers are fuck-hot," he said.

Brent laughed. "That's what we want, my man. That's what we want. I'll see you in two hours."

Soon he made his way off the plane, shouldering his bag from the overhead and heading down the escalator toward the terminal exit, where his regular driver waited for him. The black town car zipped along the highway as the sun fell below the horizon, and twenty minutes later he'd reached his home.

After a quick shower that both perked him up and washed off the remnants of cross-country travel, he pulled on jeans and a button-down. He tucked it in and considered a tie. There were plenty of times when he needed to go full suit, and that had been one of the biggest transitions for him in his new job. How the hell his brother wore a suit every day and liked it, he had no clue. Give him jeans and a T-shirt any day of the week. But this gig required a classier touch, so he added a tie, leaving the jacket behind.

He grabbed his helmet, locked the door, and hopped on his Indian Dark Horse, the new bike he'd bought last year to celebrate Edge's growing success. As the engine purred to life, he fast-forwarded to the meeting tonight with the entertainment services firm that choreographed dance shows around the world. Naturally he thought of Shannon, and couldn't help but wonder what she was up to these days. Was she still in choreography? Had she moved beyond *West Side Story*? Had she found a boyfriend? A husband? The thought curdled his stomach and made him gun the engine and ride faster, the cool evening air whipping past him as he drove to the hotel.

He'd tried to keep her in the past, where she belonged, because there was no room for her in the present. Especially since she didn't seem to exist anymore. He hadn't gone to the extreme and called a private detective to dig up a phone number. But he'd done enough when he'd Facebook stalked her nearly a year ago.

He'd learned nothing. Zilch. Nada.

Shannon was one of the rare breeds who'd managed to live most of her life off the Internet. That wasn't surprising. Given what had happened to her family when she was younger, it was no surprise that she'd learned to navigate the world under the radar.

He'd tried valiantly to move on from the biggest mistake of his life. Because she'd been right—she'd been absolutely right with her last words. Hardly a day went by when he didn't regret having walked away from being with her. As he covered the final mile to the meeting, he replayed some of the moments from their time together.

Like their first kiss outside a record store in Boston when he'd been riffing on how only old, angry record dudes listened to vinyl anymore, and she had laughed so hard she'd clutched her belly. He'd wanted to pump his fist from having made her crack up, but there was no time for that because she'd placed her hands on his cheeks and made the first move.

In seconds, he'd spun her around, backed her up to the brick wall, and kissed her as if his life depended on it.

The first time they'd slept together was only a few nights later. Neither one could hold back. The chemistry between them was too electric, too intense. They went to dinner at a Thai restaurant near campus, and the second he'd paid the bill he'd grabbed her hand, walked her out, and taken her back to his place. As soon as the door had fallen open, they were both nearly naked.

Then there was the evening he'd run out of gas in his motorcycle when they were on a date. They'd been one mile from his apartment. Still, he'd told her he'd carry her the whole way home. He'd hoisted her up and draped her over his shoulder as she'd swatted his back and shouted playfully, *Put me down.*

There were so many memories from their two years together. Smaller ones, slices of moments, but ones that he remembered just as fiercely. The way she looked as snow fell around her face when they walked through the city. The sweet, sexy smell of her neck when she fell asleep in his arms. How she went to nearly all his shows, and threw her arms around him and kissed him hard after each performance, even the night she gave up her tickets for them to see her favorite dance company, Alvin Ailey. She'd saved up for them, but he'd told her he landed a gig that night and needed her desperately at his show, so she came to see him instead.

Then the fighting—they fought over everything and nothing. They fought over their schedules, whose apartment they'd sleep at, and what they were going to do on a

Friday night. They argued about petty jealousies and fears. Every now and then they argued over money—she'd gone to school on a full scholarship, so he never wanted her to pay when they went out, but she didn't like to feel "indebted," she'd said. They fought over secrets held too close. He was an open book; she was hidden. But some things she'd shared freely. Like the letters. With crystal clarity, as if it were happening that moment, he could recall kissing away her tears every time she got one of those letters in the mail. The letters tore her apart, and soon he started opening them for her because she couldn't bear to read them, but she couldn't bear to throw them away either.

He wondered if she still got them. If they still ripped her in two.

And who kissed her tears away.

The notion that someone else was there to do that was like a fist in his gut.

When he reached the Mandarin Oriental, he kicked her out of his head once more, said hello to one of the valet guys he knew, and headed to the elevator, ready to turn his focus back to business and away from the past. The Mandarin Oriental was one of the few hotels in Vegas without a casino. While Brent enjoyed a game of slots or a round of cards, he also savored the calmer, classier atmosphere of this hotel—that was what made it a great spot for meetings with other locals. When you lived in town—and he'd grown up in Vegas and spent most of his adult life there— you had to find the hidden oases that let you conduct business away from the jingle of clanging slot machines, the slap of cards from the table games, and the eye-numbing parade of bare flesh in sequined tops serving drinks to tourists. God bless the visitors; they made this town run, and they powered his clubs with their energy and night-owlish ways. But sometimes, you just needed to be part of the engine and operate under the hood rather than as the ornament.

This hotel was one of those spots that let him do that.

The sleek metal elevator shot him up to the twenty-third floor, and as he checked his phone, he saw he was early for the meeting. When he reached the Mandarin Bar, the hostess greeted him, and said that James Foster was already there. Exactly as Brent had suspected. James was beyond punctual, and Brent was grateful every day to have such a steady guy as his lead investor.

The hostess escorted him to James, who was seated in a oversized red leather chair by the floor-to-ceiling windows that overlooked the city. He rose when Brent walked over, and reached out a hand to welcome him back.

"Good trip?" James asked as he sat down again, gesturing to the booth on the other side of the table. James was older than Brent by a few years, and had a long pedigree in business. While Brent had the vision and the guts to build Edge, James was the solid, reliable rudder who made sure they stayed the course.

"The best," he said, and recounted a few key details. When he was through, he glanced around, scanning the room for the waitress.

"The waitress should be right back. She'd just stopped by before you arrived," James offered.

Brent tipped his forehead to the square bar in the middle of the space. "I'll just grab a drink myself. You want something?"

"Vodka tonic."

Brent threaded his way around the leather chairs and chrome tables to the towering shelf of liquor that framed the bar. A guy he knew, Miles, was working behind the counter, and nodded a hello. "Hey, Brent. What's the latest with you?"

"Not much, just working on my tan," he joked, holding out his forearm to show the color he'd nabbed while in the Caribbean.

"Haven't I told you to quit the tanning bed juice?"

"This is all natural, man. Saint Bart's color."

"I'm working on my blue-light tan," Miles said with a laugh, as he glanced up at the tinted lights in the bar. "Anyway, what can I get for you?"

"Scotch on the rocks, and a vodka tonic."

"Coming right up."

Brent drummed his fingertips against the steel counter-top as Miles headed to the other end to pour. Turning around, he leaned against the bar and stared out the window, where the entire city stretched far beyond the glass. City of sin. City of secrets. City of endless opportunities. Whatever bout of exhaustion had threatened him when he'd landed had vacated the premises. He was wide-awake and energized, ready to sign deals, to grow Edge, to keep on building the business.

Glass clinked against metal, and he turned to grab the drinks and start a tab. A minute later, he had a glass in each hand and was making his way back to their table when he stopped short.

His pulse pounded.

His throat went dry.

The floor tilted and loomed closer. The glass walls zoomed in. He blinked.

He was seeing a mirage. Either that or he'd slipped back in time, because there was no other explanation.

After all those years, there she was, in the flesh. A vision in black and red, and a brunette now. He stared from across the room, trying to process what he was seeing.

Shannon Paige-Prince.

The biggest regret of his life, more stunning than she'd ever been, and she wasn't alone. She was with one of her brothers, and they were both focused on James. Heading for his table. As she turned in his direction, she looked up and they locked eyes.

His drinks slipped from his hands, crashing onto the dark wood floor and shattering.

CHAPTER FOUR

"That answers my question. Those glasses are indeed breakable," Brent said, tapping on his glass as he sat back down with a new drink and raised it in a toast. The waitress had just given it to him after quickly handling the spill.

James laughed and clinked their glasses. "Good thing you tested it. I was so damn worried," he said, and Shannon faked a smile, still shaking in her skin. Blood pounded in her head, and the entire bar seemed to sway and bob, like a boat on the seas. She dug her fingernails into the leather of the armchair she'd claimed—a necessary stake in the ground because it gave her distance from that man. That man she wasn't supposed to see tonight. Who wasn't supposed to be there. Who had been just as surprised to see her. And who was doing a much better job at covering it up than she was, with his little jokes, and his self-deprecating humor.

Fucking bastard.

Everything was so easy for him.

The man was a master at ad-libbing, at covering up the hole in the routine.

She hated that he had the ability to patch a gaffe so quickly. But a small part of her was pleased that he'd been so shocked he'd dropped his glasses.

"In any case, now that my CEO has finished his quality control inspection of the Mandarin's glassware, I'd like to introduce everyone," James began, gesturing to Shannon and her brother. "This is Shay Sloan, the founder and head choreographer for Shay Productions. And her brother, Colin Sloan, a financier who advises Shay Productions. Shay and Colin, allow me to introduce Brent Nichols, who runs Edge."

Colin rose first. "Good to meet you. I've heard a lot about you," he said, and extended a hand to the man he'd met at Christmas the year Brent had proposed. But Colin knew how to cover up the past, and knew intuitively that she'd want him to.

"All good, I hope," Brent said, with a quirk to his lips, though he had to know it couldn't be good. Colin, Ryan and Michael knew exactly how Brent had dumped her.

"And this is—" James began, gesturing to her, but Brent jumped in.

"Shan—"

"Shay Sloan," she said quickly, correcting him before he said too much. "I wasn't expecting you to be here tonight."

"I wasn't expecting you to be here either," he said, and James shot Brent a strange look as if to say 'of course you were' but he said nothing aloud.

Brent shook her hand next, and instantly a million things zipped through her body. *Memories, feelings, promises.* He never once took his deep brown eyes off hers as their fingers laced together. She drew a breath and wished that she didn't feel a slight charge in her body from the way his gaze held hers. But she did. The fluttery sensation spread through her with every breath. For a second, maybe more, they were the only ones there. The handshake went on longer than it should have.

James tilted his head to the side and gestured from Shannon to Brent. "You two know each other?"

Worry gripped her instantly, breaking the moment. She had no clue if Brent felt tricked or hoodwinked that she was behind Shay Productions. She dropped his hand, gulped, and parted her lips to answer.

Brent jumped in. "We both went to school in Boston, I believe. Isn't that right, Shay?"

She squeaked out a yes, breathing easier. He seemed to be guiding the awkwardness out of the way so neither one had to admit how they had known each other, or how well.

"Yes. I went to the Boston Conservatory," she said, as she shrugged off her silvery wrap.

"And I was at Boston College. We had friends in common, didn't we, Shay?" he asked with a slight smile, keeping it casual, making it easy for her.

She nodded and wished she knew why he was knitting a fable, but she was glad he was. Their past was theirs. It didn't need to be part of their business partnership. Clearly, he was a pro at keeping entanglements off the table.

"We did. It's good to see you again," she said, plastering on her best seemingly natural smile.

His eyes never strayed from her, and he lowered his voice, speaking in the barest whisper, the words hardly audible, but his lips readable. "Is it?"

Her chest rose and fell, and she didn't know how to answer. Her skin was white hot all over. Seeing him again stirred up so many memories, not only of the cruel, callous way he'd ended their love, but also of the way she'd leaned on him so much, and how he'd been there for her every time she'd needed him. He'd been her rock.

Too bad he was as handsome as ever, and still stitched with the same mix of intensity and charm that he'd possessed more than ten years ago. She glanced down, adjusted her skirt, and reached for a glass of ice water, the cubes hitting her teeth as she knocked back half the liquid.

"Yes, it's great to see you again," she said, hardly knowing if she was speaking truth or lie.

"Let's get down to business then," James said, and for a while Colin and he did most of the talking while Brent leaned back in his chair, crossed his legs, and raked his eyes over her, as if he was undressing her again, as if he was drinking her in, cataloguing her hair and its new dark shade, considering her bare shoulders, roaming his eyes over her breasts, landing on her legs. She swallowed, her throat parched again, and took another drink. He'd always loved her legs.

A memory slammed into her of the way he would press his hands on her thighs, spread her open, then tell her to wrap her legs around his shoulders. She'd say yes and give herself to him. Let him take her there. Let him rain pleasure down on her.

A flash of heat tore through her body.

She had to collect herself. She stood up and grabbed her purse. "Excuse me, gentlemen. I need to powder my nose."

She walked past the hostess stand and around the corner, trying to calm her quickening pulse with steady, measured breaths. She grabbed the handle of the ladies room door, and a hand came down on her shoulder.

She whirled around, coming face to face in the darkened hallway with the man she'd once planned to marry.

"Shannon," he said. Her name sounded rough on his lips.

"Brent," she said, doing her best to stay cool in her tone. "How are you?"

After all those years, after all the pain, this was what they were? Two adults practicing benign civility outside the ladies room? She'd always imagined if she saw him again that she'd punch him. Or fuck him. Never had she thought they'd talk like this. Like they meant nothing to each other. The strained tone lit into her like a fuse.

"I'm fine," she answered, reminding herself it was better this way. Better to be able to stand near him and manage the basics. Even though the basics were stretching her thin.

"How have you been?"

"Good."

He stepped closer. She retreated against the wall. Her pulse pounded viciously.

"James told me he was talking to you. I've heard of your shows. But I never knew Shay Sloan was you. I guess that makes me a world-class idiot." He raised his arm, as if he were going to touch her. Muscle memory maybe. The past rearing its head. But he didn't. He kept his hands to himself, and she was both glad and angry. "But then, I think we both *know* I'm a world-class idiot."

She sighed, her heart heavy with his words. Was this his way of apologizing? They were long past apologies. The fact that he was apologizing in some way for not knowing who she was now felt... meaningless.

"Is this a problem? Is it better if we step aside so you can find another company to work with?" she asked, sidestepping his comment, staying focused on the issue at hand. Business, only business. The more she zeroed in on that, the better off she'd be. The less tempted her thoughts would be to stray to days gone by. Because lord knew, with him standing inches away, his strong body so dangerously near to her, she felt as if she were teetering on the edge of a cliff. His mere presence reminded her both of how much she'd loved him, and how goddamn hard she'd had to fight to get over him. "I'd understand if you don't want to work together given our..." She let her voice trail off.

He shook his head, his eyes still locked on hers. She wanted desperately to look away. Instead, she noticed every detail. The way he swallowed. The line of his jaw. The intensity in his gaze.

The tension that radiated from him.

Her nerves were frayed thin from the battle inside her, from the tug of war waged between heart and body. She was comprised of two opposing desires. Something soft and needy and desperate in her wanted to throw her arms around him and ask how he'd been and where the years had gone. Something hard and angry and bitter wanted to lift a knee and kick him right in the balls, then to slam her fists into his chest and tell him how everything hurt so goddamn much when he'd left her behind.

There was another side, too. A curious one. The one that still wondered what could have been.

Finally, he answered her question. "No, it's not a problem. I want the best for my business. James tells me you're the best."

My business.

Everything inside her snapped. That tight line of tension was severed. Like when a tightrope is chopped in half and the acrobat tumbles wildly to the ring, she let loose. "Guess comedy worked out really well for you," she said harshly, wanting to slice him with words. "It's a good thing you put your career first. Since you're not even doing what was so fucking important to you ten years ago."

She turned and pushed hard on the ladies room door. But she felt his hand around her wrist, and he yanked her back, spinning her in one quick move, so she was chest to chest with him. She felt his breath on her.

"It did work out well for me. I'm also not the same person I was ten years ago," he said, then did that thing again —that thing where he undressed her with his eyes, where he fucked her completely with his hot, dirty stare. "And you obviously have become a different person, too."

He tugged her, pulled her closer. His heart pounded against her breasts. His hand gripped her lower back.

He felt so good that she didn't resist because her stupid body was stuck in the past, was living ten years ago when he alone was the one who could help her, who could free her, who could erase all the pain in one touch. Then he took away the one pure, true thing in her life in his cruel exit. He took away himself.

She jammed a hand against the strong, firm chest that she knew intimately. The fucker. "I had reasons. *Real* reasons. Life and death reasons," she said in a low hiss.

He shut his eyes briefly, then somehow his arms were around her, and this time his touch wasn't sexual. It wasn't lustful. It was an embrace. From someone who knew nearly everything about her.

"Are you okay? Are you safe?" he asked in a whisper into her hair.

A tear had the audacity to slip out of her eye. To slide down her cheek, and fall onto his shoulder. It was a Pavlovian reaction. Too many tears had fallen on that shoulder.

"Yes," she said quietly, with a nod. "I am. It's fine. It's all fine."

He pulled back, tucked a hand under her chin, and lifted her face. She was so close to him she could trace the outline of his jaw, could run the pad of her finger over his stubble, his unbearably sexy eight-o-clock shadow. She could drag her fingernails through the soft, thick strands of his hair that belonged between her hands. She could look in his eyes as he moved in her, those deep, soulful eyes that understood her. Somehow, he was rough and gentle, he was charming and fierce, and he was funny and dirty. He was the man she'd wanted to spend the rest of her life with.

"Are you sure?" he asked, so much tenderness and worry in his tone.

She gathered herself, and willed that obstinate organ in her chest to stop beating in double time. She ordered her traitorous body to cease trembling just from being near him. "Yes. I'm sure."

He let her go, and tipped his forehead back to the bar. "I should get out there. They'll start wondering. See you in a few."

And he walked away. Like the last time she'd seen him, when he had so easily disconnected from her.

She pushed open the ladies room door, walked to the sink, dropped her hands onto the cool tile and let out the longest, hardest breath. She hoped to hell this was the only time she'd have to deal with Brent Nichols.

When she was near to him like that, she couldn't think straight. She could only feel. And that was far too dangerous for her heart.

Chapter Five

Brent couldn't let her leave.

Now that she'd reappeared in his life and was within the same fifty-foot radius, he had to secure time alone with her. Without James. Without Colin.

A few moments outside the restroom weren't enough.

On the return from the hallway encounter, he pressed his fingertips to his temple, weighing options.

Then he spotted a shimmer of silver on the floor under the table. A long shot, but it was his best opportunity so he grabbed the edge of the fabric as James and Colin were focused on business matters.

An hour later, the four of them held glasses and raised them high. The deal was done—all that was left was the signing of it.

"We'll draw up the papers this week, and get this show on the road," James said, then snapped his fingers. "Oh, and Shay, can I get your number, too?"

Brent reined in a grin. James didn't even know he'd just become his wingman and secured the ten digits Brent had most wanted in the world. As Shannon rattled off her number, James tapped it into his phone, and Brent repeated it in his head. Then James looked at his watch. "And on that note, I have a wife and a two-year-old who likes for his daddy to say goodnight to him. And I believe our friend Colin has a date."

Brent clapped his business partner on the back. "Get the hell out of here. I'll see you tomorrow. I'm going to catch up with Miles over at the bar. And Colin, hope the rest of your night goes well, too."

"Thank you," Colin said, as he stood up. Shannon did the same.

"It was great chatting with you. I look forward to the partnership with Shay Productions," Brent said, extending final handshakes to both.

"As do I," she said, flashing that same, professional smile she'd given him earlier.

As she reached for her purse, his shoulders tensed. He hoped that she wouldn't realize what she was missing. But she hadn't noticed all through the meeting, so perhaps she wouldn't notice now.

The three of them left.

Brent watched Shannon as she weaved her way through the tables to the exit. The black dress looked as if it had been painted onto her luscious body. Those red shoes, with the crazy, crisscross straps, were a beacon, guiding him home to where he wanted to be—between those absolutely, fucking perfect legs that he was dying to feel again. Her soft, smooth skin. Her toned muscles. Her curves. Most of all, the way she used to wrap her legs around him. His hips. His back. His shoulders. His face.

He scrubbed a hand across his jaw as his cock rose up.
Down boy.

Neither his dick nor his heart had forgotten Shannon Paige-Prince. They both worked overtime when she was near.

She turned the corner to the elevator banks. Out of sight. He leaned back in his chair, trying to catch one final look at her. No such luck.

He hated that he had to let her walk away, but if he was going to talk to her again—the way he wanted to—he had to play it smart. After three minutes, he figured she was down the elevator and walking across the lobby, but not yet gone. He texted her.

You left your scarf. Want me to bring it by your office to-morrow or do you want me to bring it down to you now?

He waited.

She might not respond. She might text him now or in the morning. She might simply send a messenger service to pick it up.

His phone buzzed. He slid open the message.

Hold onto it for me.

He stared at the screen for several seconds. What the hell was that? That answer was not in the multiple-choice rubric. He squinted as he reread it, as if that would trans-late her words into a clue what would happen next.

Ah hell. Maybe tonight wasn't the best time to talk to her.

He stood up, pushed away from the table, and grabbed the scarf from under his leg. If she wanted him to hold onto it, that was what he'd do. He'd figure out how to meet her alone and talk to her without her brothers being around. Hell, he could probably benefit from some time to plan what he wanted to say to her. She was the last person he'd expected to see tonight, so he hadn't scripted his lines.

How do you apologize for the kind of idiocy he'd perpetrated when he was twenty-one? He'd been young and selfish—he'd wanted everything that was in front of him.

He went to the bar to close out his tab and plot his next steps. He should sit down with his good friend Mindy and ask for her advice. Mindy was as solid and straightforward as they came, but she was diplomatic, too. She'd guide him through this unexpected reunion.

But when he tucked his credit card into his wallet and turned around, he came face to face with his own lack of planning. Time to improvise.

Shannon held out her hand. "My wrap please," she said, her tone even, her face unreadable. "It's my favorite."

"I didn't think I'd see you again tonight." He clutched the fabric, as if that would tether her to him for longer. It felt like a lifeline as his heart sped up just from being so close to her. The bar was filling up with patrons, the tables packed, the stools taken. But the hum of the busy Mandarin faded into the background with Shannon there again.

"I'd like the wrap," she said crisply, the meaning clear. She only wanted the scarf.

"Have a drink with me, please," he said, opting for honesty first. The last time he'd seen her, he'd played with words. He'd manipulated and twisted them. He'd lied, hoping the lie would win her for good. He'd lost her instead.

She sighed and shook her head. "Brent, I would like to go home. And I would like my scarf."

"One drink."

She licked her lips and exhaled but said nothing. In her silence, he sensed an opening. A chance to earn a laugh or two. With complete honesty.

He inched closer. They were less than a foot apart. He could smell her, and her scent was intoxicating—she smelled like honey and spice, completely different than how she'd smelled in college. This was more sultry than the jasmine lotion she wore then. It was heady. It made him high in seconds.

"Please." It was all he had. "I held onto the scarf to see you again. I saw it on the floor, took it, and hid it. I'm a thief, I'll admit it," he said, holding his arms out wide, one hand still gripping the silvery fabric. He wasn't letting go of the only thing he had that she wanted.

She furrowed her brow. "You took my wrap?"

He nodded. "Yes. You always left them behind when we were together," he said, stopping briefly when she winced at those words—*when we were together*. "When I spotted it on the floor, I grabbed it when the guys weren't looking, and I hid it. I sat on your scarf." He kept his eyes fixed on her, admitting the full truth even if it made him look like a complete ass.

Her lips quirked almost imperceptibly, but it was enough for him to think that he was gaining ground. He tried to build on it. "It's a nice scarf. Do you think I could pull it off for a meeting tomorrow with my real estate guys?" He tossed it around his neck and adopted a pouty stare.

She rolled her eyes, and he was ready to declare victory. "You're the worst," she said, laughing. "Stop it."

"You don't like the way it looks on me?" he continued, deadpan.

"It looks ridiculous on you, Brent," she said, but she couldn't stop smiling. "And by the way, it's a *wrap*. It's not a scarf."

"So…you really like this…*wrap*?" he said, as he removed it from his neck.

"I do. I like it so much I came back for it."

He raised an eyebrow. "Only for the wrap?"

"Only for the wrap," she said, enunciating each word, but the hard edge had evaporated. In its place was something … almost playful.

"What about a trade then? Wrap for a drink?" he asked, dangling it in the air, the metallic fabric shimmering under the lights in the bar. Vegas had coasted into nighttime, ushering in all the possibilities of the town, all its risks, all its opportunities. As he held the long scrap of material, his whole body felt poised on the edge of something. "You'll notice I used the proper name this time. *Wrap*."

He handed it over. Whatever she decided next had to come from her, not from him holding a piece of her wardrobe hostage.

Time slowed to a crawl as she held his gaze, her green eyes giving nothing away. The straight line of her lush red lips revealed no hints of her intent. Perhaps she was toying with him. Torturing him. He probably deserved it.

I definitely deserve it.

She raised a finger. "One drink."

He could breathe again. He'd been granted a reprieve.

"One drink," he echoed.

He guided her to a quiet table near the corner of the Mandarin, with the city spread out far below them. She sat first, and he was torn between trying not to stare, and watching every move she made. But he'd never been good at looking away from her, and now was not the time to learn new tricks. She crossed her legs, one bare-skinned calf sliding against the other. His breath hitched. *Those legs.* Those gorgeous, sexy legs. They were his downfall, his weakness, and his complete obsession. They were an altar he'd pray at. He'd spent countless hours caressing them, touching them, and tasting them. If he were an artist, he'd have drawn them over and over. He hadn't been able to keep his hands off them when they were together. He hardly knew how to keep his hands to himself now.

"So," he said, breaking the silence between them as he tore his gaze back to her eyes. "You've done well for yourself."

He hated that they were talking like any other man and woman without a history, but he sensed she was something of a wary animal around him, who needed to be coaxed out of the corner.

She nodded. "Thank you. It's been quite rewarding building the business."

"It's very impressive what you've done with your company." He had half a mind to kick himself as soon as he said it. What he wouldn't give to turn this conversation around to something that mattered. But he was going in cold, navigating without a road map and hoping he wouldn't crash.

"Can I get you something?"

The waitress had materialized at their side, giving him some breathing room. "We have some fantastic cocktails," she said, then waxed on about several concoctions. Shannon opted for the house martini and he ordered a whiskey. As the waitress walked away, Shannon folded her hands across her lap, shooting him another closed-mouth smile.

"And you're doing great, too. I'm so pleased that Edge is faring so well."

Shit. This was not how he'd wanted to spend time with her. It was so fucking formal. So immensely fake. So not them.

"It is," he said, but he didn't know how to steer the conversation out of this pothole.

"How did you decide to switch to a whole new business?" she asked, and she sounded curious, so naturally interested that he was about to give her the full truth. The answer was he hadn't wanted to wear out his welcome with comedy. He wanted to walk away when he was on top. So he had.

But he sensed that could be read wrong. Like, as a character assassination of how he'd left her since it might show he had a pattern of walking away. There was another reason too — it showed the work he gave her up for was no longer the center of his world.

"I was ready for a new challenge. I still moonlight, though. I do standup once or twice a month at some local clubs," he said.

"How interesting," she said, but she didn't sound enthused. "And does that satisfy your comedic thirst?"

"Yes. That's where I did the King Schmuck bit. I don't know if you saw that one online," he said, because it was better to get that out in the open.

"Hmm." She looked up at the ceiling as if she were trying to recall, then shook her head. "Doesn't ring a bell. I must have missed it. But I've been pretty busy, too, and I don't spend much time on the Internet."

Soon, the waitress returned with their drinks, and Shannon raised her glass in a toast. "To business."

"To reunions."

He knocked back half his drink, letting the burn fuel him.

Screw this small talk. He didn't want to be polite with her. He wanted to *know* her. To understand why she'd never picked up the phone when he called in those first few weeks, why she'd been so hard to find, and why she'd changed her name. He scooted closer. "Shan, what's going on? How is your family? How is your grandmother? Your grandfather? Are you really okay?"

She closed her eyes briefly, her fingers clutching her martini glass. When she opened them that hard veneer was gone, and she was the girl he'd spent his nights with in college, the one who'd relied on him for everything. "They're great. They've always been great," she whispered. She waved a hand in front of her face, as if it were a magic wand, erasing all her woes. "Enough about me. Tell me something happy. Your family was always the happy one. Mom and dad together, they actually liked each other, and still do, I presume. How's your brother?"

He caught her up to speed with Clay, who'd been married for a few years, and had a baby daughter now.

"I can't believe you're an uncle," Shannon said, shaking her head in wonder. It was crazy how she'd softened as soon as he addressed the issue of her family, the one thing she didn't like to discuss. Except, she always had talked about them with him. Maybe all this time she'd been looking for someone to talk to, and he'd filled that gap.

"My niece is adorable." He took out his phone, clicked open his galleries, and showed Shannon a photo of Carly Nichols, Clay and Julia's little girl.

Shannon moved even closer, and a wide smile spread across her face. "She's so cute."

"She really is. Here are the three of them."

"She's beautiful, your brother's wife."

"They're kind of insanely perfect for each other. They even have the world's coolest dog. Here's Ace." He flipped to another picture and pointed to the Border Collie mix they'd adopted a few years ago.

"My brother Ryan has a dog like that. Named him Johnny Cash. Because he's mostly black. The Man in Black and all."

"Great name."

"Ryan treats him like a king. I think he even cooks him steak on Sundays."

"Lucky dog," Brent said with a smile.

"Have you been back in Vegas for long?" she asked, as she ran her fingertip absently along the rim of her martini glass.

"A little over a year. I moved here for stand-up after *Late Night Antics*, then back to L.A. again for a few years when I got my own show, then I returned again last year to start the clubs," he said, tilting his head back and forth. His life post-college had swung like a pendulum between the two cities. "I live over near downtown. Want to see?" he asked, gesturing to the window.

"Yes."

He stood up and held out a hand. Not that he expected her to take it, and she didn't, but he placed his palm softly, ever so softly, against the small of her back. He barely touched her; there was a millimeter of space between them, but her breath caught, and she trembled slightly before straightening her spine.

They stood by the glass, him behind her. All of Vegas shimmered below, the lights of the city like fireflies, the skyscrapers rising up through the night, as neon streaked to the horizon. He pointed north, past the lights of the Stratosphere. "That's me over there."

"I love that neighborhood." She gestured beyond, and he was turned on simply by the way she raised her arm. Damn, he was easy. Anything she did, any move she made, bordered on sexual for him. She could have a baggy sweatshirt on and he'd still be ready to go. "And that's me," she said.

She was so damn near to him as they stood gazing out the window into the brightly lit night. His entire body buzzed like an exposed electrical line because of this woman—flesh and blood, curves and muscle, strength and beauty—mere inches from him.

"That's nice," he said, his voice raspy and hot, but there was nothing nice at all about this moment.

She turned to look at him, and neither one of them said a word. Her green eyes were dark and intense. Her lips were so close. The inches between them were swallowed whole by the connection that crackled between them. She seemed to sway closer, and he moved in, seizing the moment.

He lifted his hand to her hair, still sleek in its twist, different from the shade she'd had when he knew her, but beautiful just the same. A strand had fallen loose, chestnut brown and curled. He touched it, ran his finger across the single lock. Time melted away as he leaned into the familiar crook of her neck. The craving for her ran so damn deep it lived inside his bones.

He inhaled her, that honey scent, a new smell that in an instant marked her.

"*Shan*," he whispered, rough and gravelly, filled with so much want for her, which had built over the years, grown higher, spread further, formed roots. Inhabited him. He was desperate to have her in his arms again, to smother her in kisses that erased all the years.

"*Brent*," she whispered, his name sounding like sugar on her tongue.

He buried his face in her neck, layering kisses on her soft skin. "Where have you been?" he asked, though it was entirely rhetorical. She hadn't been with him. He hadn't been with her. That was the answer.

"Where were you?" she countered softly.

He lifted his face and looked her in the eyes as he brushed the back of his fingers along her cheek. "Thinking of you," he said.

He didn't know how he'd gone from breaking two glasses to finding her falling into his arms. But that was where they were. He cupped her cheeks in his hands. "You're so fucking beautiful," he rasped out, and then he crushed her mouth. He consumed her lips. He kissed her hard, and greedily, and the world around him turned black and small. It faded into a speck of nothingness because there was room for nothing else in his world but her. Nothing but the utter perfection of Shannon Paige-Prince wrapped around him where she belonged.

No time had passed.

No years had flown by.

No regrets had dug deep inside him.

They kissed like it was a first time, and a last time, and like it was all time. They kissed like two people who wanted to climb into each other's skin, to smash into the other person. There were no doubts. No questions. She *had* to feel everything he felt. She had to want a second chance, too.

This was not only a kiss. It was crashing back into orbit. It was gravity reinstated. In the press of her lips, in the slide of her tongue, in the gasps she made, they hurtled back in time. All mistakes were erased in this moment.

He dropped a hand to her lower back, yanking her close. Kissing was not enough. Lips would only get them so far. He had to feel her, touch her, taste her. She was his, and even though they were kissing in front of the entire city, he was all alone with her.

He couldn't get close enough to her. She pressed into him, a full body collision, grinding against him. He groaned as he reclaimed her mouth, his entire body consumed with a lust so powerful he didn't know how he'd make it out of the bar and back to his house, to a room, to her place, wherever, anywhere, without fucking her along the way.

As she rubbed her body against him, he could feel the heat between her legs. It fried his brain and short-circuited his skull. The desire to touch her enveloped him. He wanted to watch her undress, to stare at that to-die-for body that he'd missed so terribly, to roam his eyes over her curves as she lowered herself onto him and rode him the way she liked.

Hell, the way she fused her body against his told him all he needed to know. She wanted the same things.

He kissed a line along her jaw to her ear as she breathed hard. "Come home with me tonight," he said, skimming his hand along the outside of her thigh.

Her hand connected with his cheek, and his head snapped to the side.

His head rang. His skin burned from the sharpness—the unexpected sting from the slap that came out of nowhere.

"What the fuck is wrong with you?" she asked, pulling away.

"What the fuck is wrong with *me*?" he repeated, shock reverberating in his bones. He opened his mouth to say more, but no words came.

She leaned in close and whispered, "Let me give you a tip, Brent. When you haven't seen a woman in ten years, maybe say you're sorry for breaking her heart before you try to fuck her again."

Frustration seared his nervous system. "Fuck," he said in a low hiss. "I'm sorry, Shan."

She narrowed her eyes and shot him an icy stare. "That would have been a lot more believable if it didn't require a prompt."

Without skipping a beat, he gave it right back to her, firing off a retort. "How was I supposed to say it when your mouth was on mine? Tell me that, Shan. Tell me that," he said, jutting out his chin, waiting for her answer.

She grabbed her silver scarf from the chair and glared at him as she brandished it. "Next time you want to see me you'll need a better excuse than sitting on my scarf."

She stormed off, but when she was a few feet away, he called out, "It's called a wrap. Don't forget that. It's a wrap."

She stopped in her tracks. He swore red clouds billowed off her, and as she clenched her fists, he was willing to bet she was fighting every urge to give him the finger.

She resumed her pace.

As he watched her walk away, this time he was pissed off too. The woman wouldn't cut him a fucking break. She'd avoided his phone calls those first few days. She'd ignored every attempt he'd made to contact her. And now, she was kissing him back, then getting pissed at him for wanting her.

What the hell?

He used to think he understood her. He used to think he was the only one for her.

But she gave new meaning to the word whiplash.

CHAPTER SIX

She was one of two women in the gym, and the only one wearing heels.

"You can't behave that way."

The directive came from her brother Michael, who was in the middle of a workout.

He hoisted the barbell high above his chest with a measured exhale. A few feet over, a beefy guy in a muscle tank grunted as he raised his weights then dropped them in a loud clang on the floor. With pinpoint precision, Michael lowered the bar to his chest, inch by inch, then pushed up again. "You need to keep that temper of yours in check," he continued in a controlled breath.

"I know," Shannon said in a tiny voice, her head lowered, her hair falling in a curtain around her face. She'd unclipped her French twist on the drive home, gunning the gas and blasting pop music to drown out her thoughts as she sped along the highway, putting distance between Brent and herself.

But really, the space she needed was between her own untamed anger and the person she wanted to be. A person who should be in control of her emotions, of her feelings, and of her matchstick temper. She wasn't in control, so as soon as she'd pulled off the highway near her home, she'd spotted the sign for the gym where Michael went and turned in.

Ever disciplined, Michael was exactly where he usually was at ten-thirty at night—lifting weights, after having logged an hour on the cardio machine. Michael owned a security conglomerate and ran it with their brother Ryan. Michael arrived at the office at eight every morning after his five-mile run, worked a full day, then headed to the gym nearly every night for a second workout. Call him a workaholic. Call him an athlete. Call him a machine. He was all of that, and he was also the moral compass of their foursome.

The eldest of the siblings, he'd been their rock, and their leader.

He lowered the weight once more, then raised it for a final rep before placing it on the rack of the bench press. Sitting up, he draped a strong arm around her.

She crinkled her nose. "Eww," she said, pushing his sweaty arm away from her dress.

He grabbed her head and rubbed his knuckles against her skull, his light blue eyes twinkling. When he stopped laughing, he tugged her close. "So what are you going to do tomorrow?"

He was like a teacher, reinforcing the lesson.

"Apologize," she grumbled.

He punched her arm lightly. "C'mon. Say it with spirit."

She affixed a too-bright smile. "Apologize," she said with forced pep. "Even though he's the one who should be apologizing."

Michael nodded, his eyes darkening momentarily. He was no fan of Brent. "You'll get no disagreement from me on that point, but this isn't about him. It's about you." He pointed at her as he spoke in that gentle but authoritative tone he had. His *older brother* tone. "Who you want to be. How you want to behave."

"And who I don't want to become," she muttered.

He shot her a small smile. "I'm not worried about that in the least. But you can't give in to anger. Though, trust me, I'd like to with that fucker," he said. Michael had helped Brent with his proposal. He'd asked their grandmother for her wedding band to be used in the engagement ring.

"He's not that bad," she said, and that was the understatement of the night. Brent wasn't that bad. He was *that* good. Kissing him was like melting from head to toe, like being dipped in pleasure and coated in a fine dust of hot shivery tingles. He ignited her completely, lust and desire sweeping up and down her skin from his touch.

Not that she'd say any of that to her brother. Maybe to her girlfriend Ally, but Michael didn't need to know that Brent Nichols still turned her on like no man ever had. Besides, the purpose of the night's pit stop wasn't to conduct a post-mortem on being kissed unexpectedly above the Vegas skyline. It was because her brother always knew what to do and how to handle sticky situations, like her having hit a man.

She cringed remembering what she'd done.

But she reminded herself that she and her brothers had risen above their roots. They'd refashioned themselves into upstanding citizens, business owners—successful adults. As the Paige-Prince kids they'd grown up lower class and hadn't known anything beyond the outskirts of their dangerous Vegas neighborhood. Now they were better than that. They were the restrained, sophisticated, and successful Sloans.

"Call me tomorrow," he said, pinning her with wide blue eyes until she nodded.

"I will report back," she said with a crisp salute, then hugged him goodbye, feeling more centered and calm than when she'd pulled into the gym.

But as she drove the final blocks home, that feeling vanished and a deep shame washed over her. She couldn't believe she'd slapped Brent. What was wrong with her?

She parked and walked into her condo, then slammed the door hard behind her. The loud crash it made in the doorframe was mildly satisfying in the way that throwing a hairbrush or chucking a phone at the wall after a frustrating conversation could be. That was what she should have done instead of slapping him.

A picture frame on her kitchen counter had rattled and fallen over when she shut the door. She picked it up and repositioned it. An image of sunflowers. She brushed it lightly with her fingertips, then slumped into a chair at her kitchen table and untied the crisscross straps from her heels, heaving a sigh as she tossed one red suede shoe across the cool tiled floor, then the other. A heel smacked into the wall, thumping along the wood.

She muttered a curse. She didn't need to maul a good pair of shoes because she was pissed at herself. She rose, padded to the wall and picked it up, inspecting the heel to make sure no damage was done.

Safe and sound.

Unlike her heart.

Unlike her ego.

Unlike her stupid brain that was tricking her

She and Brent had gone from zero to sixty in mere seconds, it seemed. One minute he'd been holding her in the hallway asking if she was safe. The next she was grinding against him by the window. She was ready, so damn ready to have gone home with him, to have tossed out the past, ignored the hurt, and just let him take her. He was her good drug—when they were younger, one hit and he'd washed away all the anger and shame.

She'd been practically addicted to sex with him when they were together. Brent had been the only thing that had felt good after far too long spent feeling nothing but bad. Nothing but the black mark of her family that trailed behind her all through her teenage years. Nothing but being the Paige-Prince kids.

Before him, she'd only had dance and her brothers. Then he came into her life, and she had something pure and unsullied by the cold, cruel world. Brent was her sweet, sinful addiction, and she rationalized that it was much healthier to need him than the bottle or a needle. But it wasn't just the sex that had burned brightly between them. It was everything. He'd made her laugh, he'd made her smile, and he'd brought her so much happiness. She'd hadn't been close to anyone like him since. While she hadn't turned into a nun when they'd split, she hadn't been busy fornicating during the last ten years, either. Her list of lovers was remarkably short—no one had compared to him because no one *could* compare to him.

She'd spent the last decade mostly alone. She'd had dates here and there and a few longer-term relationships. But sex and love residing in the same person? That had happened to her once in her life, and it had been with the man she'd wanted to go home with tonight. That moment in his arms had reminded her of how much she'd needed him, relied on him, and *healed* because of him. And how she'd cratered when he took that away by leaving. Thinking of his departure was like punching a hole in her chest. It was turning off her gravity.

That was why she'd snapped in the lounge.

She hated wanting him so much.

Shoving a hand through her mussed-up hair, she spotted the mail she'd brought in earlier. On the top of the pile was a letter from her mother. Maybe because she felt like she deserved punishment tonight, she picked up the white envelope. It bore the same return address her mother had had since Shannon was fourteen.

Dora Prince. Inmate #347-921, The Stella McLaren Federal Women's Correctional Center, Hawthorne, Nevada.

Shannon took a deep, fueling breath, steeling herself for the latest round of unstable, needy, borderline insane words. With a hard stone residing in her gut, she pushed her finger under the flap and ripped it open. She took out the letter and unfolded the lined paper, girding herself for what lay on the page.

Baby,

How are you? How are your dance shows? Are your dancers as talented as you were? Sometimes at night, when it's quiet, and everyone's asleep, I close my eyes, and I swear I can see you on stage, with a smile so bright you light up the whole recital hall, like you did when you were my little girl in her candy pink tutu, up on the stage with your pirouettes.

I know it's different now, but in my mind you're still dancing. You'll always be dancing. Just like someday I'll be free. You'll get your knee fixed, and I'll get out of here, and life will be as it should again.

That's what I hold onto when it gets all dark and black in my head, because I swear, it gets darker every day. It's been more than seventeen years now, and the light is fading. I thought by now I'd be out of here. That they'd see I didn't do it. I didn't. I swear. I wish someone would find the people who did.

Can you come see me again and help me please? I'm not that far away. It's less than a five-hour drive. I had my visiting hours cut—I'll explain why when I see you in person —but they can't take away my rights. The law allows me four hours per month, and they're granting me two to see family on June 30th. You are my family, baby. See me. See me. See me. I'll write to you for a thousand years if I have to. I swear, baby girl, I swear.

Help me.

Your loving mommy.

Years of practice didn't ease the heavy knot in her gut. Letter after countless letter didn't make the words hurt less. Every note she read was a piece of her flesh being sliced.

You couldn't hide from that kind of hurt, she'd learned. You just had to let it bleed, and hope it didn't bleed out what was left of your heart.

Folding up the letter, she slid it back into the envelope, then tucked it away in a kitchen cupboard. She walked into her bathroom, washed her hands and face, brushed her teeth, then stripped off her clothes. As she removed the silvery wrap, she was tempted to bring it to her nose, to catch a final, trailing scent of that man who turned her on.

Instead, she resisted, letting it fall on top of a pile of black, shimmery fabric.

Sliding between the cool sheets of her bed, she reached for the photo album she kept in her beside drawer, then traced her thumb over the pictures from years ago. Some color, some black and white.

She turned the pages.

The ending was the same every time.

She shut off the light and flipped onto her belly, hating that she still ached between her legs. After everything in between touching Brent and falling into bed, she still wanted him. Even after she'd seen her brother. Even after she'd read the note from her mother. Even after she'd looked at the photos.

Still, she longed for him. Still, she felt the same damn pull.

Bodies were stupid things. Lord only knew, hers didn't work properly anymore. She was supposed to be dancing. Supposed to be doing so many things.

She'd remade herself though. She'd shrugged off who she used to be. She'd risen anew from the ashes of her family.

From her mother, who had killed her father in cold blood.

But some days, she wasn't so sure if she could ever outrun her history.

CHAPTER SEVEN

Mindy clutched her belly, the sound of early-morning slots soundtracking her laughter as they waited to be seated at breakfast.

Brent stared at her with narrowed eyes. "It's not funny," he grumbled.

"Oh, it's funny. It's completely hilarious," she said, poking him in the chest.

"I beg to differ. Other things are funny. Dry humor about politicians. Jokes about hipsters. Comedic bits about waxing gone wrong," he said, that familiar urge to start a riff taking over.

She shook her head. "No, this is funnier. The way you put your foot in your mouth is the height of comedy," she said, as the hostess at the Allegro's breakfast cafe walked up to them.

"Right this way," the hostess said. "We've got your regular table for you, Mindy."

"You're royalty here. That could be a good bit. The security chief who's treated like a queen," he whispered to his friend, who swatted him.

"Stop it," she said, but she was laughing.

The hostess led them to a green upholstered booth in the classy breakfast spot in the middle of the hotel on the Strip. Mindy ran security at the Allegro and had for several years now. One of his closest buddies, they had one of the rare male-female friendships where they truly were just friends, maybe because they'd known each other since high school. Maybe, too, because they'd had that obligatory moment that kyboshed the prospect of anything ever happening between them. At a high school graduation party, over beer and quarters, and truth and dare with their group of friends, someone had dared Brent to kiss her.

They'd kissed for a few seconds, and it was fine. Nothing more. Later that night, she'd brought it up. "That was like kissing my brother. Can we, you know, never do that again?"

He'd laughed, and clinked bottles with her. "Never is fine by me, sis."

It was a good thing, because he needed her on the friends side of his life. She seemed to need him, too. She was one of the smartest people he knew, but she had horrible taste in men lately. Understandable, since she'd given her heart to someone long ago. She'd spent time in the military, and had fallen for another soldier, and he'd fallen hard too. But he'd died in combat, and since then Mindy had kept relationships at a distance, preferring instead to date casually from time to time.

Usually assholes.

With disastrous results.

The hostess handed Mindy a menu, but she waved it off. "Don't you know I have it all memorized by now?" Mindy said, tapping the side of her head.

"Of course you do. I'll send the server over shortly to take your order," the hostess said with a smile, and handed Brent a menu.

"Like I said, royalty."

She narrowed her eyes at him. "And like I've said a million times—"

"I know, I know," he jumped in, cutting her off. He adopted a high-pitched tone, mimicking Mindy. "*You're an ass, Brent Nichols.*"

She cracked up once more, her light blue eyes twinkling with delight at Brent's impersonation. "I told you it was funny."

"Too bad I didn't record her slapping me so you could have it for cell phone posterity."

She snapped her fingers in an *aw shucks* gesture. "I would absolutely add that to my collection of stupid things Brent has done over the years. It's quite an extensive collection."

"I am well aware of that." Mindy was privy to the pranks he'd pulled in high school, the bar fight he'd gotten into a few years ago, and a bet he'd made at a bachelor party for a buddy last year. He'd come out unscathed on all accounts since he had some kind of magical lucky streak. But the Shannon situation was far more complex than going all in with his big mouth or the big ego that matched it. He needed help. He needed finesse. He needed Mindy.

Brent quickly scanned the menu, then shut it and stretched his arms across the back of the booth. "So, swami, tell me what to do."

"I'm not even going to say you need to apologize. Because you need to do more than apologize. You need to grovel. You need to beg her not to hate you."

He let out a long, deep, frustrated steam of air. "I can't do a damn thing right around her." He dropped his forehead into his palm, the sunburst black ink on his forearm staring back at him.

"You have an Achilles heel when it comes to Shannon."

Brent raised his face. "I know. Believe me, I know."

His confidante on all matters related to Shannon, Mindy had been briefed chapter and verse from the start. She knew the good, the bad and ugly. She'd helped him pick the diamond for the ring when he was getting ready to propose in college. She knew, too, that he'd fucked up that fateful day ten years ago. She'd encouraged him then to try to make it right. But Shannon hadn't taken his calls, so he'd been forced to move on. Now, she'd reappeared in his life, like a goddamn blazing neon sign, and he wasn't going to let her wriggle away again.

"So what do I do?"

Mindy was about to answer when the waitress popped by to take their order and serve them coffee. As she walked off, Mindy checked the time. She had to be at work soon, and she was already dressed for the gig, in her white button-down shirt and gray pants, designed to blend in as she surveyed the scene at the hotel. "Here's the deal," she said as she poured a pink packet into her mug. "You have two things you need to do. One, you need to remind her how good you were together. And, two, show her that you've grown up."

He wiped his hand across his brow. "That's all? That's a piece of cake." Then he turned serious. "Okay. Lay it on me. How do I show her I can be the man she needs?"

"Oh, sweetie. You're getting ahead of yourself. You don't even know if she wants you the same way as before."

He raised an eyebrow, a burst of confidence speeding through him as he remembered the way Shannon had shuddered in his arms last night. "I'm pretty sure she wants me in the same way as before," he said with a wide grin.

"Do you have any idea how big a rehabilitation project you are for me? I am starting at caveman level with you. You need to simply begin Project Win Shannon Back with an apology."

"How do I apologize for making the dumbest mistake of my life?" he asked, this time completely serious.

She pointed at him, her eyes lighting up. "That," she said excitedly. "What you just did. That would be a good start. But let her know it's not a joke and make it clear that you're aware you messed up. Let her know in a way that will show her you're being completely honest." She took a sip of her coffee. "Look, last night's little make-out fest aside, you have no idea if she wants to have anything to do with you. There's no way you could know that. You have to step back first before you go forward. You can't simply pick up where you left off. You need to get down on your hands and knees and do some groveling."

A minute later the food arrived, and Mindy flashed a bright smile. "And maybe get her a gift too, King Schmuck."

That was when it hit him.

* * *

After he finished his scrambled eggs and toast, and downed a hearty dose of coffee for fuel, he headed to his next meeting at the Luxe Hotel. Along the way, he made a quick detour into a boutique inside that hotel.

He scanned the shop quickly, spotting in seconds something that would be perfect for Shannon. She wasn't a flowers and chocolate kind of woman. And while he doubted that a material object would be enough for the mea culpa he needed to pull off, he had to start somewhere. He wasn't going to wait in his office and stare dreamy-eyed at his phone, wishing for a call. No, he was going to do everything he'd failed to do years ago.

There was no way on earth, no way in heaven or in hell, that he would let the woman he wanted slip away from him again. He knew precisely how to go after everything he'd ever wanted in life. Tenacious in pursuing his career, determined in climbing up the ladder, he'd achieved all he desired in the entertainment business, and now he was fortunate enough to build on that with his wildly successful clubs.

Only one thing had eluded him.

Her.

Now, he had the opportunity for a second chance. The game was on, and he was going balls to the wall to win his woman back.

* * *

As the meeting with their real estate team drew to a close, Brent rubbed the pads of his fingers across his cheek. Perhaps some part of him was trying to remember the burn from her slap. He wasn't a masochist. Not in the least. But it was *so* her. It was such a part of how they were together.

Fucking and fighting. Fighting and fucking.

As soon as this meeting ended, he'd call her. He'd pick up the phone and ask her to get together. If that didn't work, he'd head to her office and begin the grovel fest.

He'd make his first apology. He'd probably have ten thousand more to make, but if that was what it took, he'd do it. He was heading to New York in two days to deal with the hurdles Edge faced there, so he needed to move fast.

"So, that's the plan for the next six months, now that we've got Shay Productions on board for their dance shows. And that's what we need from you as we expand overseas," James said as he shut his leather folder and laid his pen on the conference room table with gusto.

"Love it," said Tate, the lead real estate attorney, who was tasked with handling their deals for new facilities. "I've got some properties in mind. Let me scope them out and we'll reconvene in two weeks."

As James and Brent left the meeting, James slowed his pace and lowered his voice. "You okay? You seemed a bit distracted there at the end."

Brent laughed, as if him drifting off to Shannon Land was nothing. It *was* nothing, because he could juggle. "Nope. I'm all good."

"Glad to hear," James said as they wove through the casino on their way to Edge. "By the way, what was the deal with you and Shay?"

Brent turned to James, and shot him a curious look. "What do you mean?"

James shrugged. "Just seemed like there was some vibe between you and Shay, who incidentally is smok—"

Brent's spine straightened and he sliced a hand through the air, cutting him off. "Don't say it."

James raised an eyebrow. "Don't say what?"

"What you were about to say."

"What was I about to say?"

Brent stopped walking in front of a roulette table and narrowed his eyes. "Look. I know what you were going to say, man. And it's not fucking appropriate. That's all," he said, as they resumed their pace past the blackjack games.

James held up his hands in surrender. "So you two were friends or something?"

Brent laughed. He wasn't going to get into it now. He didn't need to lay out his past. Shannon was a private woman. She clearly wanted her carefully constructed present identity kept secret. His first step in proving that he could be the man she needed would be to protect who she was.

"Like I said, I knew her in college," he said, giving nothing more away as they reached the front door to their flagship club on the property of the Luxe Hotel. Edge was quiet now in the late morning, since it didn't open until five. Much later, there would be a line snaking along the velvet rope by the brushed steel exterior wall. The purple sign bearing the club's name in crisp, clean letters would be bright and beckoning, calling out to the club-goers of Vegas who were eager to party, to lounge, to dance, to drink, to be treated to bottle service from gorgeous bartenders, and to move and sway. To celebrate pending marriages, weekends away, or just nights on the town.

"Maybe you'll get to know her better now," James said. "Because there she is."

As Brent turned the corner, Shannon was waiting by the front door of Edge.

CHAPTER EIGHT

The club had a different energy during the day. No music played. The lights were bright, shining in every corner. Shannon felt as if she was wandering backstage and peering at all the pulleys and levers, the sets and costumes that made a Broadway show go 'round. Because there were no smoke and mirrors now. Those would only come with an audience or a crowd in the evening.

Even with the lights switched on, Edge still possessed the sleek sensuality it was known for, with its silver bar, low divans, gauzy curtains, and its rich colors—colors of desire, like wine reds and deep purples.

Her footsteps echoed across the black tiled floor that would be lit up tonight, illuminated by rays of smoky light from the ceiling, by crescents of blue from the stage, by shimmery gold beams.

The click of her high heels punctuated the strained silence between the two of them as they walked through his quiet club. She wasn't sure what to say next. She'd simply asked Brent for a minute alone to chat, and James had scurried off. No one else was there, as far as she could tell, except the two of them.

"It's like seeing how a magician pulls off a card trick," she said as she turned to survey the scene, eager to break the quiet.

"Speaking of, I have a new one I can show you."

"You do card tricks now?" she asked, because she could picture it. It seemed like his style. He'd always loved cards and had played in poker games at school now and then. She could see him brandishing a deck with a 'now you see it, now you don't' sweep of his hands.

He laughed, and she sneaked a peek once more at the man by her side—so much taller, so much bigger than her small frame. Her eyes definitely hadn't been playing tricks on her last night. He was still devastatingly handsome, even more so with his casual look today—jeans and a navy blue button-down. It was untucked, and with the cuffs rolled up it revealed his strong forearms, and some of the ink he'd gotten in college. She'd gone with him for his first tattoo, the black sunburst just above his wrist. She'd joked that it fit his "sunny disposition" and he'd promptly scowled and glowered. But then he'd draped an arm around her and flashed her his winning smile.

"Nope. But I'll need to work on that next. Can I get you something? Water? Soda? I'm happy to serve you something stronger, but I don't imagine you've started drinking at eleven in the morning," he said as they reached the silver bar. A small red bag was on the counter, as well as the usual accouterments of napkins and cocktail straws.

She shook her head. "I have a meeting at noon at the Cosmopolitan. So, a Diet Coke could be great." Being near him, and needing to say the words Michael had told her to say, made her throat dry.

Brent offered her a stool at the bar, then walked behind the counter and poured a soda from the tap. He handed her the glass. "I'm not a bartender. I just play one on TV," he said, imitating the deep tones of a TV announcer. His attempt at humor made her smile.

She downed some of the soda. She'd never been so grateful for a sip of Diet Coke before. It quenched her thirst and gave her some newfound courage to own up to her actions last night. She held the glass in one hand and parted her lips to speak. But he was already talking.

"Shannon," he said, his voice intensely serious, his deep brown eyes focused on her. "You're right. You're completely right. I need to apologize for so many things. But first I need to apologize for pushing things too far last night."

She froze, her fingers gripping the glass. An unexpected bead of worry streaked through her. She didn't want to hear that he might not want her. Not when she couldn't extinguish her desire for him.

But she didn't show up at his club to satisfy the sweet ache in her body. She was there to right her own wrong. To soothe the shame in her soul. She held up a hand as a stop sign and shook her head. "You have nothing to apologize for. I came here to say I'm sorry. I shouldn't have slapped you last night." She put down her glass as she fidgeted with a silver bracelet on her wrist. She took a breath to center herself, then looked in his eyes. He was regarding her intently, as if she were an equation she didn't understand.

"I have no idea why you would apologize to me," he said, walking around the bar and joining her on her side.

"I shouldn't have behaved like that. Hitting you. That's not the kind of person I want to be."

He laughed deeply. "One, I deserved it. I was a dick. Two, I know what you're thinking. You're thinking it makes you like your mother. But you're not. That was completely different."

She shook her head, her voice rising as she disagreed with him. "You didn't deserve it. I shouldn't have done it."

He took a step back and narrowed his eyes. His voice was strong, overriding hers. "You are completely wrong. I'm the one who needs to apologize—"

"No, you're not!" she said, and now she was borderline shouting.

"Yes, I am," he said, his voice like a stake in the ground.

Then it hit her. The two of them were actually arguing over who had the right to be more wrong.

She reined in a laugh. "Do you realize what we're doing? We're fighting again. This time over who should apologize."

A small smile formed on his lips. "Yes, we are," he said. Then he turned serious as he dropped his hands on her shoulders, parking them there. She loved how he held her. His firm grip sent a flurry of sparks across her arms, bare in a silky black tank top. "But I'm winning this round," he added, a glint in his eyes. "Like I said, you have nothing to apologize for. You are nothing like your mother. And I deserved that slap because you were right. I haven't apologized to you and there's so much that I need to say, and I wanted to start by just giving you a little something."

He let go of her to reach for the bag on the counter. "I picked this up this morning. Dropped it off here," he said, handing her the shiny red shopping bag with slim handles.

Her heart beat faster. He had always given her little things when they were together. Pretty postcards of London, Paris, Vienna, and all the places where she wanted to go someday. A song she'd heard at a coffee shop and wanted to listen to on her computer. A mini lemon cupcake, because every now and then she permitted herself little treats.

She opened the bag, rustled around in the tissue paper and pulled out a thin, blush pink, silk scarf. She didn't even try to contain a smile. "This one's a scarf," she said.

"I know. And I bet it looks amazing on you. I also thought if you wanted to leave it behind, I can steal it again, so I can say I'm sorry another time. I'll say I'm sorry ten thousand times if I have to. And I know this scarf doesn't even begin to cover all of my crimes, so I hope you'll take it in the spirit I've given it. It's just a little something because I thought it was pretty and I thought it would look good on you. But then, everything looks good on you," he said, his hands clenched at his side.

She could tell he wasn't angry. Instead, he was holding himself back. He probably wanted to put the scarf on her. She probably would have let him in the past, but everything between them now was too raw, too new, too dangerous. So she tossed it around her neck, striking a pose. She was flirting, and surely she shouldn't be. But it was so *easy*, so familiar to play like this with him. And it felt so good, even for a sliver of a moment in time.

"Thank you. I love it," she said, stroking the fabric. His breath hitched as she touched it, and she let go quickly, reaching for the glass of soda and taking another sip. Her hands felt unsteady. She looked at him again. His hands were in his pockets now, and he was shifting back and forth on his heels.

"But Shan, that's not all I have to say. That just barely scratches the surface."

"Okay, what else is there?"

"Listen, I don't even know how to begin to say I'm sorry for breaking your heart, as you said last night," he said, holding her gaze. "What I can tell you is this. It is my biggest regret. And you know I never talked about the specifics of our relationship when I was doing standup in college," he said, his voice stripped bare, the way he'd always talked to her when he wanted her to know he was serious. She trusted that voice. She knew it cold, and she knew the promise he'd made to keep the details of their private life out of his comedy. So she'd never be *the girlfriend* that a comedian used as the butt of a joke in his routines. "That remains the case. But there was one bit that I did, and I suppose I was always hoping you would see it. I did it so you might see it. But you told me last night you never did, and I'd really like to show it to you because I think this says everything I want to start to say. Will you watch it?"

Shannon gulped, and nodded. She didn't push back as she had when Colin had started to show her the video. She didn't resist. Maybe that made her a fool, or maybe it just made her ready. Four million others had seen it, but she was the only one who'd watch it as the intended viewer.

"Show it to me," she said, her voice soft, nerves trickling through it. He dug into his pocket for his phone. She wasn't sure what to expect, but she was incapable of staying far away from Brent, not when he showed this sweet, tender, loving side. She'd come there only to apologize, never expecting he'd feel the need to do so, too. Not after his quick retort last night. Now that he'd begun saying his mea culpa, she wanted *all* of it.

She crossed her legs and leaned back against the bar, her spine digging into the metal as the clip began—the part she'd seen. He strolled across the stage talking about 'that guy' at a business meeting who gets caught with porn on his screen during a presentation. Then he talked about how he effectively became that guy when he was meeting with the head of a hotel chain.

There was something so surreal about this moment. She was with flesh-and-blood Brent, and she was watching Brent from a year ago, too.

"You're in two places at once," she teased, as she glanced at him then back to the screen. She stopped talking as the clip moved past the point where she'd hit stop the first time, when he'd said he Facebook stalked his ex.

The on-screen Brent tapped his chest, the look on his face one of utter disdain for his own antics. "Ever done that to your college girlfriend? Searched for her on Facebook? Looked up her pictures?" he asked, looking at the audience, as the camera swept out to capture several of them nodding.

"Yeah. Me too. I looked up my girl. Spent a *ton* of hours trying to figure out what she was up to. *Translation—is she still hot and gorgeous, and did she marry some other guy?*"

A rush of heat spread across Shannon's chest from those words. Meaningless words, but still the compliment thrilled her.

"And then I forgot to close the browser page before I went into a meeting. And that's what popped on screen as I was making my business pitch. Her Facebook page. So now all my new business partners know I'm the guy who pines away for his college girlfriend."

Her breath caught, and she turned to him. He was watching her, cataloguing her reaction to his bit. His eyes searched hers, but she returned her focus to the phone, more interested now in on-screen Brent. Because on-screen Brent wasn't talking about getting caught watching porn, as she'd once thought. He was talking about *her*.

"But in my defense, if you saw her, you'd pine too. She was..." He stopped walking, stopped talking, and for the briefest of moments, he was not on stage—he was lost in time, it seemed. The next word seemed to fall from his lips with regret and wistfulness, "...perfection."

She brought her hand to her mouth, covering her trembling lower lip. She sucked in her breath, holding in all that she felt, the overwhelming rush of emotions. It was just a comedy routine. He was great on stage, even when poking fun at himself. But even so, she was flooded with so much *possibility* from the way he talked about her.

"So not only was I busted for Facebook stalking my ex, but I'm also the complete asshole who let her get away. She was the one. The one who got away. Let this be your lesson, men of the world. Don't be me. Don't be King Schmuck."

The clip ended.

When she'd originally watched the first half of the video, she'd wanted to reach her hands through the screen and throttle him.

Now, she wanted to squeeze her own heart for the stupid way it dared to beat the tiniest bit faster when he'd said *perfection*.

Silence cloaked them both. She stared at the screen, not quite ready to meet his eyes, too afraid of what she'd see. She'd only come there to clear the air, and now she was spun back in time, feeling everything again.

Lust. Desire. Sadness. Anger, too.

Without looking up, she asked quietly, "What part?"

"What do you mean—what part?"

"What part did you want me to see?" she asked, keeping her voice steady so she wouldn't reveal the cascade of emotions waterfalling through her chest. "Because it's funny. But which part is for me?"

She kept her head down. If she looked in his eyes, she'd lose herself. She'd lose her center. She'd lose every ounce of strength she'd relied on during the last ten years.

His voice was a confession. "She was perfection... she was the one... and I was the complete asshole who let her walk away." Then his fingertips brushed against her wrist. She held in the hot shiver she felt from his touch. "I'm sorry I didn't go with you. I'm sorry I didn't talk to you. I'm sorry I gave you an ultimatum. I'm sorry I twisted words around because I was desperate to keep you."

His words now were a thread that pulled her up. She lifted her face and looked at him. In a second, she knew. He wasn't performing, he wasn't acting, and he wasn't faking a thing. His eyes were serious. She believed him. She wanted to believe her body, too, and her body knew what it wanted.

She'd always listened to her body, had always been deeply in tune with its wishes and wants. Since she was four years old she had wanted nothing more than to dance. She had danced every day, harder, faster, better, until she was at the top of her game, and then tore her ACL one day during a rehearsal. But still, she remained a physical woman. She liked to be one with her body. And just then, her body and her heart wanted the same damn thing.

For Brent to make her feel good again.

As only he could. As only he ever had.

When she and Brent had been together, he'd fucked all her troubles away. Every kiss, every touch, every taste was the antidote to every painful memory. Sex with him was exhilarating. It was the greatest rush, the sweetest high. It was ecstatic amnesia. When he fucked her, she was no longer one of the Paige-Prince kids. She was not the left behind, the whispered about, one of those kids whose mother murdered their father for money.

With Brent she was muscle and bone, and she was solid and strong. She was a woman wanted by a man.

She wanted that man too. With everything inside her. The desire burrowed into her blood. It called out insistently, like a beating drum, like a fire in her veins. She might regret this later. She might regret it in a few minutes. That moment she didn't feel regret. She felt hungry. She felt greedy.

She felt justified.

"Perfection?" she asked, tilting her head to the side, reeling him in with his own description of her. "I'm perfection?"

He inched closer, nearly inhabiting the same space. "Yes," he said in a low rumble that sent goosebumps over her skin, a promise of other things he'd say in that wickedly sexy voice. "You are perfection, and everything I said was and is true."

Her tank strap slid down the slope of her shoulder. "You pine for me?"

"You're the one who got away. And I can't stand the thought of that happening again. I will do whatever it takes to keep you," he said, and the words torched her heart. They started a goddamn bonfire in her belly.

And they scared the living hell out of her.

So she pushed back. "But you don't even have me."

"I am well aware of that. And I intend to change it."

She didn't know if she was ready to hear these things from him, not when she still had so much to say. She grabbed the collar of his shirt, tugged him between her legs, and practically snarled at him. "I don't know how to believe you."

"You don't have to believe me," he said, his voice matching hers, sounding furious, too. "Because I'm going to show you."

The heat in her core shot up. God, he turned her on when he was like this, even as she fumed. She gripped his shirt tighter. "I hated how you left," she said, airing her grievances like dirty laundry as she spread her hands across his shirt, his firm chest one layer away. "I hated that you picked your career over me. And I hated not seeing you every day."

His eyes narrowed. He wedged himself between her legs. His dick was hard against her thigh. Rock hard, and it excited her. "I hated not seeing you, too," he said, his voice rough and hungry. His entire body seemed to vibrate with restraint. She wanted to watch that restraint snap. She wanted to live in that moment when control spiraled away.

He grabbed her hips, his big hands wrapping around her bones, his thumbs digging into her sides. This was their dance. Their foreplay. They knew their steps. "Every day I wanted you," he said.

"I wish I didn't want you so much," she hissed, the words cutting her throat. He raised an eyebrow, his eyes blazing, his lips rising in the barest of a cocky grin—the one that had always melted her. The effect was as potent as ever. It seared her body.

"How much do you want me?" he asked.

"More than I should."

He pressed his forehead to hers. "*Want me*," he said, speaking the words like a command. But he didn't have to tell her that—she was already there. She wrapped her arms around his neck. She curled her legs around his hips. She crossed her ankles against his hard, firm ass.

"I do." She barely wanted to speak the words. But she didn't want to deny this desire. She pulled back and looked him in the eyes. "And I want you to say you're sorry the way you used to. The way you did when we fought before."

He froze. Then, his eyes floated shut briefly. When he opened them, he picked her up and lifted her onto the bar. "Stay right here," he growled.

She watched as he quickly stalked across the quiet, cavernous nightclub to the front door, making sure it was locked. He returned to her, placed his hands on her face, and said, "There's no one else here. Unzip your jeans."

She bit her lip, lust thrumming through her body. She opened the top button, slid down the zipper, and pushed her tight dark jeans to her thighs.

"*Fuck*," he groaned, as he stared between her legs. Her panties were pale pink and completely soaked through with her desire.

"Do you like what you see?" she asked, seductively.

He swallowed thickly, and breathed out hard. "You know I fucking love it."

"How much?"

He peeled her jeans down to her heels. She kicked off her shoes, then he pulled them off the rest of the way, tossing them on the floor. He groaned as he roamed his eyes over her legs. He brushed his lips across her left ankle and she shivered, then he licked a path up her calf. His mouth on her skin was divine. It was rightness returning to the universe.

But he stopped, standing up and grasping her chin in his hand. "Tell me what you want."

"You know what I want," she whispered.

"And you know I want you to say it. Say the words."

Her eyes met his. "Touch me. Taste me. Eat me."

"More," he said as he held her face. "Tell me exactly what you want."

"Brent," she moaned, writhing on the counter, the ache between her legs threatening to take over her mind, to devour her reason.

"You know it turns me on when you say it," he said, grabbing her hand with his free hand and guiding her to his crotch. She gasped as she palmed his erection. So thick and long.

"Fuck me with your tongue," she whispered, and he throbbed even through the denim. "Please, Brent. Fuck me with your tongue."

In a blur, he moved, his hands circling her ankles. Then her feet were up on the counter, her knees raised, and she was spread wide for him. His face was right there, his breath ghosting over her panties, his mouth so close to her slick heat.

"I'm sorry," he whispered.

"Say it again."

"I'm so incredibly sorry."

"Show me."

"I'll show you any time, babe," he said, using the term of endearment he'd used before, and it melted her. She burned hot when he flicked his finger against her clit. She cried out in pleasure. "Take these off for me. Take off your panties and show me how much you want me, too."

She slid off the underwear and threw them on the floor. His eyes glazed over as he stared hungrily between her legs. "You haven't stopped wanting me at all," he said, as he ran one finger through her center, and she lifted her hips, seeking out contact.

"I haven't," she murmured. "I still get off to you."

"You have no idea how much I think about you."

"Tell me," she said, her voice needy, her body seeking confirmation.

He stroked his index finger through her slippery wetness. "I jack off to this beautiful sight. I picture you dancing for me, stripping for me, and driving me crazy until you finally let me taste your sweetness," he said, as he kissed the inside of her thigh. "I bet you taste like heaven," he murmured.

"Find out."

He dived in and she moaned—a long, loud cry that carried through the club. Pleasure rippled through her instantly. He kissed, he licked, and he sucked. He adored her pussy with his sinful mouth. She threw her head back, gazing at the ceiling, as she took his forgiveness. She savored it, letting him worship her the way he always had.

"Do I taste as good as you remember?"

"Better," he said, breaking contact to answer her. "You are the best thing I've ever had. The only thing better is the way you taste when you come."

"Oh God," she said, words swallowed up by sensation as her body took over. He licked her mercilessly, his wicked tongue stroking her heat, sending her soaring, flying into a world of absolute bliss.

She trembled from head to toe. She burst with pleasure so intense it blotted out everything but his touch. She arched her back, lifted her hips, and rocked into him in a frenzy.

He'd always said that going down on her was like being fucked, too. That she'd get so into it, and it drove him wild. Her reactions, the way she moved her hips and grabbed his hair truly made it a face fucking, and he'd craved it just as much as she had. The evidence, the proof of how she loved his touch lay in the way she moved under his mouth.

"Shan, do that. Fucking go crazy," he told her, and she was right there with his command, thrusting wildly, writhing and wriggling as he groaned and consumed her pleasure with his mouth.

Stars circled her head. The earth fell out of orbit. The sky split open.

She grabbed his hair, screaming in pleasure, calling out his name, as she came on his tongue.

* * *

That had gone better than he'd expected.

Better than his fantasies. And while he'd had countless dreams about her sweet pussy, he'd never dreamed that today his face would get reacquainted with his favorite location in the entire universe.

He scooped her soft, warm body into his arms. She was practically glowing, and masculine pride burst in his chest. "I was right. You are perfection," he whispered in her ear.

She purred. At least, she made a sound that suggested utter contentment. He kissed her cheek. "Am I forgiven?"

She laughed, the sound so high it rang through his empty club.

"What?" he asked, furrowing his brow, as she pulled on jeans and shoes.

She took the scarf off her neck, wrapped it around him once, and held the ends. She looked him square in the eyes. "It's going to take a lot more than one orgasm for that to happen." She glanced at the scarf. "And that's why I'm leaving this behind. So you can find me again."

Then she walked out.

CHAPTER NINE

A patron sloshed beer on a table in the front row. Some dude snapped a photo with his cell phone camera from the back. A waitress circled through the tables carrying a tray, expertly dispensing beverages to meet the two-drink minimum.

Bob's Beer Haven and Comedy Club in Soho didn't change its rules when Brent stopped by. The dimly lit comedy club off Spring Street had a been-here-for-years vibe, a low stage, and merely adequate acoustics. The crowd didn't show up for the ambiance—they came there because the owner was known for his taste. Over the years, Bob had scouted and promoted some of the leading up-and-coming comedic talent, who went on to big careers. Damn shame that the landlord had just jacked up the rent astronomically—quadrupling it, so Bob was shutting down operations soon, and the location had been leased to a chain restaurant.

Brent and Bob had a long history; the guy had booked him for a few sets at a Los Angeles comedy club when Brent was working on *Late Night Antics*. Those club gigs had led to bigger ones that had helped Brent to grow his reputation in the entertainment business.

Whenever he'd visited New York for business or to see his brother, he'd tried to pop into the Soho club. He could easily draw a big crowd now, and fill out a fancier theater in midtown no problem, given the time he'd spent on screen hosting his own show on Comedy Nation before he shifted to the nightclub business. But he had no interest in that. He wasn't on stage tonight for the money. He was on stage for the fun of it, and for the farewell—bittersweet though it was, given the fate of this establishment.

But this wouldn't be the last time they worked together —Bob was a solid businessman, and Brent had promised him a job managing his club in New York, provided he got the approval from the city to open it. With two kids in college now, the man had needed to find a new gig quickly, and Brent was glad to potentially offer him something.

"So let's say that there's this guy," he began, pacing slowly across the creaky wooden stage. "I'm not going to name names or point fingers at who this guy might be."

He stopped to roll his eyes around, as if he were somehow looking at himself, and somewhere in the audience he could make out the silhouette of his brother pointing at him on stage. Brent held up his hands as if he was innocent. "Like I said, I'm not naming names. But, for the sake of argument, let's say this guy fucked up a situation with a woman. Because, let's face it, every now and then, from time to time, the man will be in the wrong, right?"

"Every now and then," a woman in the crowd called out sarcastically.

"Exactly," Brent said crisply. "It's rare, totally rare, that the guy is the one who messes up. Because men are usually on top of their shit in a relationship. They never forget birthdays, they always remember to bring gifts to their women, they never say stupid, dumbass, idiotic things," he continued in his deadpan tone. "Men, generally speaking, are really evolved creatures."

Several loud chuckles resonated from the audience.

"But sometimes a man makes a mistake. And he has to make it up to a woman. What is this guy supposed to do when the woman is just not one of those gals who likes flowers?"

He stopped to scratch his head as if he was thoroughly flummoxed by the situation, and truth be told he actually was. Perhaps he could work out what to do next with Shannon in this routine.

"You see, I thought about a few options." Brent stopped talking and quickly backpedaled, as if he hadn't meant to indict himself, when he clearly had. "I mean, *this guy*," he said in an exaggerated tone. "Not me, 'cause I'm not talking about me. Because this is clearly not about me at all. But this guy, who is obviously not me, he's trying to figure out how to do something really fucking awesome for his woman. Something that proves he's the man she needs. Something big," he said, emphasizing that last word as his eyes drifted downward to his crotch, so the audience got his meaning. "So I thought: what does she want? What does a woman really want? And the conclusion is..." He stopped, paused, took a breath, because comedy was all in the delivery, then finished, "*me.*"

A few more laughs.

"So I'm just going to dip myself in chocolate, head to toe, and give her me. Covered in chocolate. For her to lick off."

He held his breath as he tested out this new material for the first time. A ripple of laughter began, but there was still the punch line to deliver.

"But then I realized, that's not really a gift for her. That's a gift for me."

Laughter rang out across the club. There were few sounds better than this—better than the sweet laughter of a joke well told. It was the great exhalation—it was relief and buoyancy all at once.

But then, it wasn't a joke. He did need to prove himself to Shannon, and if she somehow happened to see this set, he was certain she'd know it was part of the big grovel, as Mindy had so aptly put it.

"So, yeah. Maybe not chocolate," he said, then continued on for another ten minutes, finishing up his set. When he was through, he joined his brother and his wife in the audience during a short break between acts. Julia clapped proudly as he walked over, then wrapped her arms around him in a big hug. "As always, you were magnificent," she said.

"I'm just sorry you didn't wind up with the funny brother," Brent said, adopting a frown.

"Shame she didn't get the *funny-looking* one, isn't it?" Clay said, deadpan.

Julia smiled and laughed. "You two are crazy. I know you were both lady-killers back in high school. All the Nichols men are fine-looking specimens," she said, then patted Clay's leg and wiggled her eyebrows at him.

Brent latched onto two words. He stared at her sharply. "High school? You think we stopped after high school?"

"Fine, fine. College, law school, and beyond," she added, then dropped her chin into her hands. "But seriously. What are we going to do about your little problem?"

He furrowed his brow. "What little problem?"

She gestured to the stage as an answer.

Clay chimed in. "Do you think you fooled us?"

Brent snapped his fingers. "Damn. You guessed it. I really am going to dip myself in chocolate. Should I do dark or milk chocolate, though? That's the million-dollar question."

Julia swatted him. "Brent! Seriously. Your lady problem."

"What lady problem?"

"You know you can't trick her, man. Might as well own up to it," Clay said, leaning back in his chair, parking his hands behind his head.

Brent laughed and held up his hands in surrender. "Fine, you got me. You saw straight through my routine."

"I know that, sweetie," Julia said, flashing a small smile. "But let me give you some advice. Whoever this woman is, she doesn't want you to solve the relationship problem by dipping yourself in chocolate, as cute as you may be."

Brent sighed, then laid out the story for his brother and his wife. "I've clearly got to big gesture the hell out of it. What do I do?"

Julia answered immediately. "The answer is simple. You need to focus on what matters to her. How can you show her how important she is to you? Where did you fail in the past in that regard?"

Brent scoffed. "That's gonna be a long list."

"Then take it item by item, step by step, and follow her cues."

Clay pointed his thumb at his wife. "She knows what she's talking about. Listen to the one and only Mrs. Nichols," he said, and those words dug into Brent's chest like a rusty shovel. He was thrilled that Julia and Clay were so happy together, but Shannon was supposed to have been the first Mrs. Nichols. She was supposed to have been his wife ten years ago. Now, she was simply a woman he'd had one dirty encounter with in his nightclub. He was at square one with her for all intents and purposes. Saying he was sorry yesterday was the barest beginning of trying to win her heart, and now he had to move past apologies and show her *why* she should want him.

After Clay and Julia went home, Brent made his way to the bar to catch up with Bob, who was pouring from the tap for another customer. "What does it take to get a beer around here?"

The man looked up and said dryly, "Evidently, it takes a chain restaurant."

"No shit. But hey, you'll be handling cosmos and top-shelf liquor in no time."

Bob gave him a quick salute, then handed out the drink. When he returned, he poured him a beer, then clinked an imaginary glass to Brent's. "Here's to the next phase—cosmos and fancy-ass drinks at your new club."

"And to landlords who aren't assholes," Brent said, raising his glass.

"Amen." Bob rapped his knuckles on the counter. "I'll miss this place."

"Yeah, me too."

Later, Brent hailed a cab and headed to his midtown hotel. As the cab ambled through traffic, he unlocked the screen on his phone, and opened up a new text message to

Shannon. Keep it simple—keep it direct. That was what he'd do.

I'm in New York... thinking of you... can I see you when I return this weekend?

In seconds she replied.

I don't know. Can you?

Oh, she was feisty tonight, toying with word choice. He responded with a:

May I?

As the cab rolled past the Port Authority and the neon lights and tourist traps on 42nd Street, her reply arrived.

What will you be wearing?

Okay, he was getting somewhere, if they were talking about clothes. Brent grinned to himself as the cab lurched to a stop at a red light. Maybe he wasn't entirely at square one. Because he *knew* this woman. Knew how she liked to flirt. How she liked to play. How she liked to keep him on his toes.

What do you want me to wear?

As the cab started up again, he clutched the phone and peered out the window, forcing himself not to simply stare at the screen and wait for a reply. As he scanned the billboards and neon signs, he spotted one up ahead with a body in motion. A dancer leaping through the air. He read the details on the sign, and something clicked. "Yes," he said triumphantly out loud, and he had the answer to the question Julia had posed to him—what matters most to Shannon. He was about to begin a quick Google search when she replied.

Honestly, you're pretty hot in nothing. But I don't think you should parade around naked at dinner, and I keep hearing the new restaurant in the Cromwell is fantastic. There's a four-month wait, though. And I know you hate waiting. But maybe you can get us in...

Like there was a chance in hell he wouldn't.

Consider it done.

The cab arrived at his hotel, and several phone calls later, he'd pulled it off. He knew enough people in Vegas, so he'd called in some favors and secured the reservation for the woman he wanted most in the world. He also had something else for her, thanks to a couple of extra minutes spent Googling and ordering, but he'd wait until dinner to give her that gift. As he got into bed, he wrote to her, letting her know he'd pick her up at seven-thirty on Saturday. Her response was swift.

Impressed. Also, no need to pick me up. I'll meet you at the restaurant.

Damn. She hadn't given up her address yet. But that was okay. He had a way to earn it when he saw her that weekend. He laughed to himself at the realization that he was thirty-one years old and excited as hell about a dinner date.

But then, the dinner date was with her.

* * *

Tanner Davies snapped his fingers to get the waitress's attention. The woman with the bouncy ponytail doubled back to their table. "Yes?"

"I said I wanted sweetened iced tea. Take it back," he barked, making a *get this out of my face* gesture with his fingers. "This is unsweetened."

"Right away, sir," she said, with a deferential nod.

Tanner, the landlord, turned to Brent, and shook his head. "Fucking waiters. Anyway. Like I was saying, the neighbors are worried about you, man. They think you won't address their concerns properly."

Brent nodded at the owner of the building he'd already leased space from in Tribeca. They were at McCoy's in midtown, rolling up their sleeves to discuss the latest two-steps-forward-three-steps-back routine that New York was pulling.

"With four clubs open in the first year, I think that shows how serious I am. We just opened Saint Bart's, and that follows our first club in Vegas, as well as our clubs in Miami and San Francisco," Brent said, carefully detailing the progress his business had made during the first twelve months.

Tanner shrugged dismissively. He might as well have just said *who gives a shit?* Brent wasn't so sure if Tanner was the enemy or just the gatekeeper of all the problems the city kept heaping on him. Permits were shooting up in cost. Hands needed to be greased. The zoning commissioner threw up roadblocks. But New York was a linchpin in Brent's plans for Edge. It was vital to the growing success of his operation, and Brent needed Tanner to help him win this city over, even though just then he wasn't sure if Tanner was even on his side.

"So what's the real concern?" Brent said, opting for directness. "And what can I do to help ease them?"

Tanner scratched his jaw, and cleared his throat. "Look. I'm just the messenger here, so don't shoot me. But the neighbors don't trust you. They think you're a flash in the pan. Impulsive even. They see you as the bad boy of comedy who hosted a foul-mouthed TV show. And they worry you're just some former TV celebrity who's going to bring a lot of noise and crowds into their neighborhood at night," Tanner said, and Brent reined in the flash of anger he felt over that word—*impulsive*. "And they want to know why they should allow another club in their neighborhood, especially one run by someone with a high profile."

"The location is zoned for a nightclub," Brent said, pointing out the obvious, because that was the reality of the property. Rather than deal with intangibles, Brent wanted to try to focus on the facts. "You had one in the building before mine and it went out of business."

"That's what I've been saying to them," he said.

"And how do they take it?"

Tanner sighed, a frustrated stream of breath that seemed to peter out of him. "Not well."

Irritation knotted in his muscles. He didn't even know who was friend or foe. He might not ever know though, so he shifted gears. "So I need to prove to them why it should be my club?"

"Yeah. Why you and not some other nightclub."

Brent launched into his pitch about Edge. He wanted to make sure the landlord would go to bat for him. "Because we don't attract the raunchy crowd that the previous club drew. You won't find twenty-one-year-olds puking outside the loft apartments at three in the morning. We don't cater to the whole deejay culture that attracts the crazy fans. My clubs are upscale and classy. They have a certain mystique, a lush sensuality, but it never crosses over into trashy. Edge is seductive, it's sexy, but it's never raunchy."

The waitress returned with a fresh iced tea. "Here you go, sir. Sweetened, as you requested."

Tanner grunted, then spoke to Brent. "That's what we need the neighborhood association to see." Tanner lowered his voice to a whisper. "And it wouldn't hurt if you threw in a few thousand to have some of the Tribeca parks re-done. There are a couple in need of a makeover, and that could make the residents happy."

"Easy enough. I'll be glad to do that. Anything else?"

"Yeah, how about you peel off a little extra for me? The ex is trying to take me to court about alimony payments." Brent didn't answer because he didn't like the sound of the request, but Tanner quickly waved a hand and flashed his yellowed smile. "I'm just kidding. I won't let the bitch have a dime of my money. And I'll help you with all this. I want your club in my building."

"Great. And I want Edge there too. So let me know if there's anything else you need from me."

"That's all for now. But I'm sure there will be something else soon. That's how it goes in New York. You gotta do whatever it takes."

That seemed to be the new mantra in his life, whether with women or with business.

CHAPTER TEN

Shannon extended her arms high above her head, her palms flat together, her fingers pointing towards the sky. Perfect warrior pose. Just like her grandmother beside her.

At age seventy-three, Victoria Paige showed no sign of slowing down. She was fit, trim, muscular, and determined to keep up with anyone and everyone.

"Even the dog is getting jealous of my yoga skills," Victoria said with a wink as she and Shannon shifted poses on the sun porch of her ranch home in one of the nicer areas in the Vegas suburbs, a house that her four grandkids had bought for her. Her Boxer mix raised his snout at the two women, then returned to lounging in the sun.

"As well he should be, Nana. Your downward dog is the best," Shannon said as they both planted their hands on their mats. Shannon had taken up yoga in college when she tore her ACL, hoping it would help rehab her and send her back to the stage. No such luck. ACL injuries were pretty much impossible to come back from. But the practice had helped her to recover, and she'd kept it up since it was one more way to stay active. Her grandmother had taken to yoga quickly too, and now it was something they did to-gether whenever Shannon visited her, which was at least once a week.

Her brothers were in the backyard. Michael, the handi-est of the crew, was fixing a fencepost with their grandfa-ther, while Ryan and Colin drank beers and tended to the grill. The homey scene was almost enough to make anyone forget *why* the six of them were so close.

"I hear from Colin that you're doing business with your old flame," Victoria said, as they finished their final stretch. There was no judgment in her tone. No haughty raise of the eyebrow. Victoria was never like that, not now, and not when she'd taken them in when they were teens. She'd done her best to finish the job her son had started, seeing the four of them through the end of their high school years after their mother went to prison for conspiracy to commit murder, sentenced in a swift and speedy trial mere months after the killing of their father.

Shannon's stomach clenched, as it often did just think-ing of the last moments of her father's life. Thomas Paige was shot four times in the driveway of their own home, a run-down, ramshackle house in North Las Vegas, the worst section of the city, riddled with crime. He'd been found with fatal gunshot wounds and an emptied wallet, as if a robbery had simply gone wrong. A robbery was plausible enough in that neighborhood.

Shannon and her brothers didn't come from means. They came from desperation. They were bred from broken dreams, from a mother who'd wanted to be a Vegas star but never had the talent, so instead eked out a meager living as a seamstress, and from a father stuck driving cabs in the nightshift. But his situation started to change, and he'd thought he'd finally caught his lucky break when he began driving limos. He started making more money, and after a couple of years at his new gig, the future looked bright.

But there was no lucky break the June night he was shot after eight hours of chauffeuring rich kids from the swank suburbs to their after-prom parties.

Social services sent the pack of unruly Paige-Prince kids to live with their paternal grandparents once their mom was arrested for murder. Shannon hadn't even started high school then, and at the time she'd never fully comprehended how horrible her grandparents must have felt. Their son was dead, his life taken at the hands of his wife, the very same woman who'd carried these four messed-up, fucked-up, troubled kids who had been dropped on their doorstep as teens—orphaned through death and then through prison bars.

As she grew older, Shannon came to understand the terrible balancing act that her father's parents had had to pull off to raise them with love and kindness during those last few critical years. Shannon and her three brothers were grafted by murder into their grandparent's home, united by the death of the flesh and blood that linked the two generations.

Some days, she missed her father fiercely. Today, she felt that empty longing envelop her in a split second as she stepped out of the pose, finishing their yoga session, and looked at a sun-faded photo of her father in his young twenties that hung above the end table on the sun porch. Sepia now in tone, the image showed his hands wrapped around Michael's waist as he hoisted the toddler onto a slide. She could remember him taking her to the park, too, sometimes with his parents. He'd loved the outdoors, and loved to soak up the sun with his kids.

Her grandparents were the reason she returned to Vegas after a few years working in London, Miami, and Santa Fe for various dance companies and touring shows. Despite all that had happened, Las Vegas was the epicenter of her fractured family, her grandparents the heartbeat. Together with her brothers, they'd moved their grandparents into a new house in a safe and affluent section of Vegas. They'd made a pact as teens to live differently than their parents, to pull themselves out of the shit circumstances they'd grown up in, and to make sure they'd never be like their mother, who'd do anything for money.

Who'd done the worst for money.

Shannon looked at the picture again, pressed her fingers to her lips, and then touched her dad's photo in the frame. Victoria did the same, and murmured, "Rest in peace." Shannon's throat hitched. Even now, even eighteen years later, she still felt so much emotion welling up inside her.

Better to focus on the conversation about Brent than to drift off into photos of days gone by.

"You hear correctly," Shannon said, answering Victoria's question about working with her old flame. "He hired my company to arrange for some dancers and choreography at his night clubs."

They walked across the cool tiled floor to the kitchen. Victoria turned on the tap and poured some water, and handed a glass to Shannon, who downed half of it quickly. "He's a sweet boy," Victoria said in a whisper, first checking to see if any of Shannon's brothers were in earshot.

"*Boy*," Shannon said with a laugh. Brent was hardly a boy. He was all man, and the memory of how he'd touched her on his bar the other morning crashed back into her, like a comet of lust.

"He came back to bring me my ring, you know," Victoria said, leaning her hip against the counter as she pushed a hand through her silvery hair.

Shannon furrowed her brow. "You never told me before."

"I did try to tell you at the time, sweetheart. But you didn't want to hear a word of it. You weren't interested in any news about Brent, so I let it go. The ring doesn't fit me anymore, but he came by and dropped it off himself shortly after you split."

A strange sense of shock raced through her system as she flashed back in time. She remembered tossing the ring at Brent the day she'd walked out. She recalled too the red-hot rage, coupled with the soul-ripping sadness that her one true love had chosen something other than her. The days after the break-up were an agonizing blur of tears and investments in boxes of tissues, of anger and impromptu sessions using her couch pillows as punching bags. The weeks that followed were worse, the missing intensifying, the emptiness deepening, and they'd made her wish she had answered his calls earlier because his calls had stopped.

Shannon vacuumed up those memories. She knew her grandmother had the wedding band again, but she'd never stopped to find out how it came back to her. She'd always figured it had arrived by mail, never by personal courier in the form of Brent Nichols.

"He called me in advance. Made sure I was here. Said he wanted to return it to its rightful owner," Victoria continued, as she poured herself a glass of water.

"He came to see you at your house?" she asked, processing this news for the first time.

"He did. Pulled up on his bike and came inside. I offered him some tea, and sat with him for a few minutes. Russ was at work, so it was just your boy and me. He said he didn't want to risk putting the ring in the mail, or FedEx, or any of those services," she said, and this little detail somehow worked its way into Shannon's heart, chipping away at the tiniest piece of ice that had coated that organ to protect her from Brent.

"That's actually really thoughtful," she said softly.

"He asked about you. He wanted to know if you were okay. How you were doing."

Her heart beat faster. She wanted to grab it and tell it to settle down. "He did?"

"I knew you'd split up, and you were busy working on *West Side Story*, but I think he was just trying to find out how you were," her grandmother said, stopping to take a drink of water.

That lump in Shannon's throat resurfaced, and tears threatened her eyes. She blinked, holding them in. What was wrong with her today? She needed to get a grip. That was ten years past, and this was now, and she was seeing the man tonight. She hadn't told a soul about her plans for the evening.

"I'm seeing Brent tonight," she blurted out, desperate to tell someone she could trust.

"You are? About the business deal? Or maybe about more," her grandma said in a sly tone.

Shannon went with it, turning the moment playful. "Maybe more. We'll see."

"Some things are worth second chances." Then her voice turned cold, as she held up a finger. "Other things—one must never grant a second chance."

"I know, Nana. I know."

Then the softness returned. "For what it's worth, I always liked him," her grandmother said.

"Liked who, Nana?" asked one of her brothers.

Shannon straightened her spine. Shit. Michael had just sauntered into the room with the toolbox, heading to the garage.

"Liked you, my love," she said patting her eldest grandson on the cheek. "I've always liked you."

Michael narrowed his eyes. "Hmmm. Doubtful," he said skeptically, but continued into the garage.

Once he was out of sight, her grandma hugged her. "Some secrets are just between us girls."

"Girl power," she whispered, as her grandmother winked in response, then headed to her room to change out of her yoga clothes. Shannon turned the other direction to hang with her brothers in the backyard, passing Colin and her grandfather on their way into the house.

"Just going to make some more marinade," Colin said. "My marinade rocks."

"It's not better than mine. We might need to have a taste test contest," her grandfather chimed in, and Shannon smiled at their competitive ways, then joined Ryan by the grill. He pressed a spatula on top of a burger.

"Are you going to bring one home to Johnny Cash?" she said, asking about his dog.

"Of course. Nothing but the best for man's best friend," he said.

Like all her brothers, Ryan towered over her, but she was used to being surrounded by those sturdy men. Ryan's brown hair looked lighter in the noonday sun, as if several strands were streaked with gold.

He flipped a burger. "You gonna eat today, Shannon bean?"

"Maybe. Maybe not. Don't give me a hard time just because I don't eat like a grown man or a teenage boy," she said, nudging him with her elbow. They'd always teased her because she'd never been a big eater. With a petite frame and a dream to dance, she'd never been a big foodie. Though, truth be told, she was saving her appetite for dinner. She wanted to enjoy that restaurant, especially since she didn't usually splurge on meals.

She'd asked for the reservation partly because she knew Brent would be able to pull it off. He loved challenges, so she'd given him the kind he craved. The consummate man about town, he was known for greasing wheels and opening doors. Shannon knew her way around Vegas, but unlike Brent, she operated out of the limelight personally. Her dancers and her shows were the star. Not her. She prided herself on being able to walk around town, up and down the Strip, in and out of hotels and casinos without anyone recognizing her.

Ryan glanced carefully at the house. "Hey," he said in a low voice. "Did you hear from Mom?"

She nodded. "Yeah. It's the same old, same old."

"But is it?" Ryan asked, holding up the barbecue tongs as if punctuating a point. "What if she's right?"

Shannon sighed and placed a hand on his shoulder. "Ry, we can't do this every single time she writes to us."

"But what if she's right that there were others involved?"

"Well, there *were* others involved. The other guy is also in prison because his fingerprints were all over the gun," Shannon said. The details had been splashed across papers and the news at the time, and the specifics of how the local detectives had followed the trail of evidence to their mother was in black and white for anyone to find. She and Ryan had hashed this out a million times, and probably would a million more. It was an endless cycle with no answer, because the answer was this—the twenty-two-year-old Jerry Stefano, card-carrying member of the local gang the Royal Sinners, had pulled the trigger. Jerry Stefano had been in touch with Dora Prince many times, and was instructed to make the crime look like a robbery that had gone too far.

But the murder was never about the money in Thomas Paige's wallet. Thomas Paige had a $500,000 life-insurance policy. Dora Prince was the beneficiary. And Jerry Stefano had been promised ten percent of that if he could get away with it.

It was murder for hire.

Ryan shook his head. "I know, but what if, Shan?" He dropped his voice to the barest whisper. "Listen, a buddy of mine in the DA's office said one of the attorneys visited Jerry in prison recently. Hasn't been there in years, but wanted to ask him some questions. See if he knew about some other crimes."

Shannon groaned. "He was a fucking Royal Sinners gunman. Of course he knows about other crimes. He was probably involved in them."

Ryan was undeterred. "We should at least visit her again."

"She'll do her usual routine. Like she did at Christmas. She'll try to manipulate us."

She didn't share Ryan's sympathies. Not one bit. She harbored guilt though. Too much guilt over her mother, and all those years when she and her mother were as close as a mom and daughter could be. Her mom had been there for her, for every dance, every recital, every performance, every moment. Maybe that was why Shannon had such a hard time severing ties with the woman in orange. Or maybe it was because she believed that her mother, in some bizarre way, loved her and her brothers.

Deeply.

Ryan seemed to sense an opening because he pressed. "Look, if you didn't want to see her, why'd you give her your new address when you moved back to town a few years ago? So she can write to you. Michael and Colin never did. They cut her out completely. They never see her," he said, then leaned in closer, and clasped her shoulder. "But you did, and I did. I'm not saying she's innocent, Shan. I just think she's our goddamn mother. The least we can do is see her again in jail."

She gritted her teeth. Visits with her mother were exhausting. They wore her thin. But as that kernel of guilt pulsed through her veins, she threw him a bone. "I honestly don't know if I'm up for it again so soon. But let me know when you go, okay?"

"I will."

As she headed into the house, she glanced at the time, grateful that the clock was ticking closer to her date. She wanted to speed up the next several hours, run through them in fast forward, because she needed something that felt good. Something that was the complete opposite of her fucked up family story.

* * *

After she tied the slim strap of her charcoal gray top at her neck, she smoothed her hand across her black skirt, which hit just above her knees. The material was soft to the touch. As Shannon ran her palm across it, she closed her eyes, and imagined the feel of Brent's hand. He had strong, solid, masculine hands that knew her. That had mapped every inch of her body. That had traveled across the terrain of her skin. Images and sensations whipped through her, and an unexpected moan escaped her lips. The sound coming from her own throat snapped her eyes open.

Was she truly so easy with him that the sliver of a memory ignited her? But the answer seemed self-evident in the way the goosebumps rose on her flesh, and heat bloomed between her legs. And, really, that was all she wanted from him anyway. That was why she'd agreed to dinner that night.

Wasn't it?

Because he was her magic pill, her sip of champagne, her bite of smooth, dark chocolate. He was an endorphin, the most powerful, potent one she'd ever had. That was why she'd agreed to see him. For a quick hit of a feel-good drug.

She walked into her closet, perused the racks of shoes, then selected a pair of plum-colored pumps with four-inch heels, which would still leave her half a foot shorter than her date tonight. Next, she rooted around in her jewelry box and found a favorite necklace of hers. She fastened the slim silver chain, letting the ruby red pendant fall to her breasts. She laughed out loud—poor Brent. He wouldn't know where to look first.

Boobs or legs.

Good. She didn't mind the possibility of torturing him. Not only because she enjoyed it from a purely physical standpoint, but also because it gave her the upper hand. She wasn't into mind games, or control, but she thought of what her friend Ally often said about relationships when she'd recap her dates. "*The French have a saying: 'In every relationship there is always one who kisses and one who offers the cheek.' Be the one who offers the cheek.*"

Shannon ran her hands through her brown hair one last time, fluffing it out before she turned around and left the bedroom. She shut the door, too, as if that would somehow remind her of the promise she'd made to keep parts of her life from Brent. Her home was her private zone, full of letters, full of pictures, full of mementos. It was safer for her to meet him elsewhere.

Her phone buzzed on her kitchen counter. She grabbed it from its spot next to her sunflower picture frame. There was a text from her driver saying he was one minute away. Driving and parking in Vegas on the Strip was a bitch on a Saturday night, so she'd opted for Uber. She shut and locked the front door, then nearly smacked into Ally, who lived two flights up. The gorgeous brunette wore workout pants, a sports bra, and a form-fitting tank. She was laughing with her head bent over her phone as she walked up the steps to her condo.

"What's so funny?"

Ally looked up, the broad smile still on her face. She pushed her big round sunglasses high up on her head. "This video is killing me. You have to see it. I know you'll never look on your own, Miss Anti-Internet, so let's start it over for you." Evidently, Shannon needed to spend more time online hunting out videos. That was where all the action was, but she'd never put much stock in hanging out in the web world.

"Show me," she said, because Ally had a good sense of humor, and Shannon was curious.

Ally scrolled through her news feed, then tapped a video. "Check it out. Here's this chick eating outside at this barbecue restaurant, and her boyfriend starts..." Ally paused, lowered her voice, and whispered the rest of it.

Shannon's jaw dropped, and her eyes widened. "Let me see," she said eagerly, and then the two of them proceeded to crack up on the steps as they watched the clip of a woman riding her boyfriend's hand on a picnic table bench, clearly thinking they were being sly, when instead they were so obvious they'd been captured surreptitiously by someone's cell phone camera. Shannon shook her head in amusement. "Just another reminder that all the world's a stage and you better behave in public."

Ally nodded and laughed. "You never know who might be watching you," she said, then she raised an eyebrow and looked Shannon up and down. "You look gorgeous. Date tonight?"

"As a matter of fact, yes. And thank you. I better get going. My ride is here."

"Is your date hot? Is he good in bed?"

Shannon mimed zipping her lips, even though in her head she was answering *yes*.

"Shay!"

Shannon glanced back up the step.

"I have to go out of town in a couple weeks. I keep meaning to ask if you can feed my cat."

"Of course. Just let me know the days. Nick is so cute. I love that tomcat."

"He's a total ladies man," Ally said with a wink.

When Shannon slid into the air-conditioned white Nissan, she gave the Uber driver the location of the Cromwell near the Bellagio. As they drove, she decided to do a little online hunting herself. Brent had mentioned he'd had a gig in New York earlier that week—maybe a clip had surfaced somewhere. When she found a short snippet from his act at Bob's Beer Haven and Comedy Club, she laughed, his routine cracking her up as he mocked himself so wonderfully. His clever self-deprecating style at times had always made her laugh. She leaned forward and asked to driver to drop her off at the candy shop near the Bellagio instead.

She had a purchase to make. She'd show Brent how she liked her sweets.

CHAPTER ELEVEN

Temptation got the better of him as he walked to the hostess stand at Giada in the Cromwell, a trendy, boutique hotel on the Strip. Shannon was waiting in the entryway, her back to him, looking far too sexy for him to keep his hands to himself.

Because... that ass.

Small, but firm and round.

And absolutely delicious.

He knew precisely how fantastic it felt to grab that flesh while he sank deep into her. He shook his head, like a dog shaking off water, but it didn't deter the dirty thoughts that invaded his brain. Hell, they launched a full-scale attack, completely taking over his sense of propriety as he strode up to her. No one but him should be allowed to see her in a skirt that hugged her ass like that. But then, she couldn't hide that perfect body in a burlap sack if she tried, and he couldn't hide his rampant desire for her either.

The hustle and bustle of a Saturday evening surrounded him as he crossed the final distance to the restaurant entrance. Music floated through the air, and heels clicked on the floor, and from somewhere he swore he could hear the sound of money even if there were no slots jingling nearby. The thirst for payoffs was never far away in this town.

Three more steps. Two more steps. One more step.

His hands reached out. He couldn't help himself. Well, he *could*. He chose not to.

He cupped her ass, and she flinched for a second, but then he brushed his lips against her neck, and whispered, "You are so unbelievably beautiful, that I hope you'll forgive me for not being able to keep my hands off you."

She trembled against him, shifting the slightest bit closer, leaning into him. "You aren't winning any medals for self-restraint tonight."

"I'm not competing in that event."

"You never could keep your hands to yourself in public," she said, but she wasn't swatting his mitts away, so he ran his hands along the sweet curves of her ass.

"Or in private either. But can you blame me? Have you looked at yourself lately?"

She turned around, breaking contact. Her lips curved in a small grin. "Yes. Why?"

"If I were you, I'd never be able to resist touching myself either."

She rolled her pretty green eyes. "Amazingly, I can find the will to resist incessant self-touching," she said, but she wasn't smacking him, she wasn't yelling at him, and she wasn't walking away. Progress. They were making progress from the last few encounters. It was almost as if they'd slipped back in time, forgotten the way they'd split, and had returned to the way they were—*good together.*

He whistled low in admiration. "Impressive. But then, you don't always resist. You told me the other day."

She arched an eyebrow, then trailed her fingertips down the front of her shirt. Oh, hell. She was already playing dirty. Everything she did turned him on, and she knew, she *fucking knew* he was done for when she touched herself. When she'd strip for him, or tease him with a dance and run her hands along her legs, or through her hair, he was an oven turned past broiling. What he wouldn't give to toss her on his shoulder, carry her out of there, and take her someplace right that second. Screw her against the wall. Bent over a bed. In a cab. He didn't care.

"Do you have a reservation?"

The sweet, cheery voice of the hostess broke the trance Shannon was working on him. He was like a man hypnotized who'd just snapped out of it. He turned to the pony-tailed, fresh-faced young lady in a black dress and said, "Nichols."

His name came out all gravelly. His voice was hoarse with wanting Shannon.

The hostess scanned the computerized list, and then tapped the screen. "There you are. I see Mario has requested one of the best tables for you," she said, dropping the name of the restaurant manager he'd called in the favor from. "You'll love this table."

Shannon turned to look at him, her lips forming a puckered O. *You're fancy*, she mouthed.

"Thank you so much. I really appreciate him doing that," Brent said to the hostess.

"Right this way then, Mr. Nichols."

The restaurant had a soft glow, its lighting showcasing an open kitchen and a wide, expansive floor plan. Too bad there wasn't much privacy. There were no quiet corner tables, or little nooks. There weren't even any tablecloths.

Damn. Tablecloths were a man's best friend when dining out with a woman he wanted to touch. The hostess guided them to a table on the terrace, with a view of the fountains at the Bellagio.

"Your table," the hostess said, then walked away.

Brent pulled out a chair for Shannon, and she smiled at him once more. "This is lovely. Even though there are no tablecloths."

A rumble worked its way up his chest, and he looped a hand around her waist, tugging her close. She didn't resist. She moved with him, aligning her body with his. "I was thinking the same thing," he said, low in her ear, then kissed her there, nibbling on her earlobe.

"Or we could just get a room," she said sexily, letting her voice trail off.

He wrenched back, looked her in the eyes, and grabbed her hand. "Let's go. Now."

"I was only teasing. I'm terribly hungry," she said as she shook her head and dropped his hand, then settled into her seat. "Besides, I've been waiting for a long time to come here."

"Oh, you'll be coming at some point tonight, Shannon. You'll definitely be coming."

* * *

Over appetizers and a bottle of wine, he learned about the productions she'd choreographed, her career path, and how she'd started Shay Productions. He asked her questions, eager to hear what she'd been up to since college. It was as if he had a black hole in his knowledge of Shannon for the last decade, and it was starting to get colored in. Like a paint-by-numbers drawing, he was beginning to see all that he had missed. She'd worked on *West Side Story*, *Anything Goes*, and *Chicago*, had logged a gig as a behind-the-scenes choreographer on a reality dance show in Los Angeles, then spent some time with a Cirque du Soleil production, before returning to Vegas and working on a dance revue at Planet Hollywood. That show was the launch pad for her company and the production she staged for the Wynn.

"The show at the Wynn really put me on the map," she said, as she took another drink of the wine.

"That's a great venue and a great opportunity."

"It's funny because I've never really thought of myself as a lucky person," she said, looking philosophical as she stared off in the distance for a moment. "But I've had a few lucky breaks in my career—meeting the right people, getting the right introductions—and it's made all the difference. Like the reality show I worked on. I might do some more work for them. I've got a meeting in L.A. with the producers in a few weeks, about staging a one-night reunion show with some of the former winners, so there's another bit of luck," she said, rapping her knuckles on the table. "Knock on wood."

"Hey. You deserve some luck," he said.

She shrugged and waved a hand dismissively. "I don't really subscribe to the notion that someone deserves good things in life. Things just happen. Some people are lucky and some aren't."

"And some people are immensely talented and recognized for their talent. And that's you," he said, keeping his gaze firmly on her. He wanted her to know how much he admired her work, especially since he'd done a poor job showing respect for her career before.

"Thank you. I love what I do, and I wasn't sure I would. I didn't think I'd be able to survive without being the one dancing, as you know. You were there when I was injured. It was devastating, and at the time it felt like one of the worse things in the world. But then I moved on, and I've really come to love choreography."

"Tell me what you love about it," he said, resting his elbows on the table as he listened to her share her passion.

She tilted her head to the side, as if she were briefly considering his question. But she didn't need to think about it for long. "I love being able to have a vision. To imagine what something beautiful will look like," she said, talking animatedly with her hands. "And then to make that vision become a reality on stage. I love what my dancers are capable of doing, and being able to take the kernel of an idea and translate it into this moving, fluid entity in front of an audience." She stopped, took a beat, then added, "And soon that audience will be your club-goers."

He shot her a small grin. "Can't wait to see that."

"The show we have planned for Edge is amazing," she said, enthusiasm latching onto her words. "It's going to be so sensual and lush. We're rolling it out in San Francisco first, I believe?"

"Yes, at our club there. I have no doubt it will be great. Thanks to you," he said, then he reached across the table for her hand, lacing his fingers through hers. He tensed for a nanosecond, hoping she wouldn't pull her hand away. But instead, she squeezed back. "You've accomplished so much," he said, and it occurred to him that she might never have found her way down this career path if she'd followed him to L.A. "I'm really proud of you."

"And you have, too."

"Shan," he said softly. "I'm not saying this makes up for how things ended, or what I said then, and if I could go back in time I would completely do the whole thing over and find a way to be with you. But I'm glad for *you* that you didn't put aside your career. I was desperate to have you with me, but I'm glad that you've been able to accomplish all that you have."

She didn't speak at first, and he wasn't sure if he'd said the wrong thing yet again. Tension flickered through his bloodstream as he waited for her to pull her hand away or shoot him a harsh stare. Instead, she cast her eyes down at the table, folding and unfolding her cloth napkin. When she raised her face, she swallowed. "You're probably right." Then she continued, "My grandma told me you went to her house. To return the ring in person."

He went with her segue, nodding and acknowledging that moment from years ago. "I did."

She pressed her teeth against her bottom lip briefly, then breathed out hard. "I really appreciate that. You making the effort to get it back to her. To be certain it was with her."

"It was the least I could do. Shan, I really did try to find you at first. As best I could. You weren't easy to track down."

She shot him a rueful smile. "I was too hurt. I missed you too much."

"I missed you, too," he said, running the pad of his thumb along the outside of her hand, not wanting to let go of her, not wanting to stop touching her.

"Can I ask you something?" she asked.

"Of course."

She took a deep breath. "What did you do with the diamond?" Then she snapped her hand away, and held both in the air, shaking her head. "Wait. Don't answer that. It's nosy. You probably used it for living expenses and that's what I would expect."

He leaned back in his chair, and ran his hand roughly through his hair, wishing he didn't feel so... *cheesy* admitting this. But he had to tell her the truth, now that she'd asked. "I didn't use it for expenses," he said in a low voice, as if he had to protect himself from anyone else who might hear.

"You don't have to tell me. Really. You don't," she said, insistently.

"I'm going to tell you. Just don't take away my man card."

"Did you turn it into a necklace that you're secretly wearing or something?"

"No. I sold it," he blurted out.

"That's what I expected, but why would that forfeit your man card?" she asked, crossing her arms over her chest.

"I'm not done. I sold it in L.A. to a diamond merchant. And I gave the money to the scholarship fund at Boston Conservatory. The one that put you through school," he said, feeling like a complete pussy-whipped cheeseball. Somehow he'd managed to avoid ever telling anyone what he'd done with the diamond. Not his brother, not Mindy. It just made him sound like a forlorn guy, stuck on a girl.

Even though that was what he'd been back then. And what he still was.

He looked up.

Her mouth fell open. She froze in place. Shit. She must be thinking the same thing. That he was a sad, pathetic guy. He couldn't believe he'd said the wrong thing again. But then he stopped thinking when she rose, stretched across the table, cupped his cheeks in her hands, and pinned his gaze with her sweet green eyes. "That means so much to me."

She kissed him, softly at first, her tongue darting out as she ran the tip of it across his lips, then more roughly, as she gripped his stubbled jaw harder. She kissed feverishly, crushing her lips against his, and he groaned as she led, sweeping her tongue over his mouth, diving deeper, consuming him. A shudder wracked through him from her sheer possessiveness. From the feel of her hands on his skin. She didn't hold back, not one bit. She did everything with passion, everything to the fullest, as she fused her mouth to his. He was reduced to nothing but desire for her as she took a chance—reaching across the table with a basket of bread below her arms, with wine glasses perched precariously on the table, with hundreds of patrons nearby. She didn't care. Nor did he. He was damn near ready to shove everything across the table and forget they were in public.

He heard a throat being cleared.

The waiter arrived with their dishes.

She detached from him, adjusted her top, and smirked just for him. As if they had a secret. Even though it was a very publicly known fact that the two people seated here at this restaurant on the terrace on a June night with the fountains behind them wanted each other badly.

* * *

After the waiter served his fritto misto and her tortellini, Brent broached a subject that had once been a source of friction between them, but then had brought them closer.

"Is your mom still writing to you?" he asked gently, picking up his fork. He watched her, careful not to push too far.

She closed her eyes briefly, her fingers clutching her wine glass. When she opened them, she was the girl he'd known in college, the one who'd relied on him for everything.

She nodded. "Yes. Every few months. She still says she didn't do it."

"She probably always will say that," he said, softly, wanting so badly to erase all her sadness. He'd always wanted to, ever since she'd finally let him in. They'd nearly broken up once in college over this. She'd been so closed off at first about her family, so secretive, and it had driven him mad. He'd wanted to be let in, to talk to her, to help her through her troubles, but she hadn't even told him what it was that tore her apart. He only knew someone kept sending her letters.

That had been one of their worst fights ever. He'd been frustrated beyond words over the way she'd kept him out. She'd been terrified to let him know the full truth about her family. But before the two of them blasted apart into smithereens, she'd confided in him, telling him all the things that weren't in the press, that weren't known simply from growing up in Vegas when it happened. He'd known her as the girl whose mom had killed her dad, but he hadn't been privy to the backstory, the details that didn't make it into the local news.

The full story had shocked him to the core.

His family was so... *normal*. His parents were still married. They were both retired now and played golf together a few days a week in a swank suburb on the outskirts of the city. He tried to see them once or twice a month, and always visited on holidays. He even baked a pumpkin pie every year for the Nichols family Thanksgiving. There was no drama, no dysfunction, and certainly no murder for hire.

Maybe that was why he'd been able to comfort her when they were younger. Maybe that was why they'd been drawn together on some subconscious level. He'd grown up unequivocally happy, and he had extra doses of it. He had a whole storage closet full of additional happiness, and he tried to bring that to her. *Lean on me*, he'd told her. He could handle it. He handled all her tears and sadness. He'd do it again if she needed him to. "And have you seen her recently?"

"I went at Christmas with Ryan. She asked if anyone had found the people who did it. Same thing she always says, even though she knows Stefano is behind bars." Then she lowered her voice to a feathery whisper, her tone confessional. "I still check his inmate number every few months. To make sure he's still in prison. It's silly, I know, since he's in for life. But I just like to know he's where he belongs."

Brent shook his head, reassuring her. "It's not silly in the least to find some kind of comfort in knowing he's locked up."

"It's not like it makes me happy," she said, sadness washing over her eyes. "It just makes me feel as much peace as I guess I can feel."

"You don't have to be happy. You can just... be," he said, and that was what he'd told her in college, too.

She met his eyes, a sliver of a smile forming on her beautiful lips. "I'm happy right now," she said.

And hell if that didn't add an extra gallon to all those stores he had.

Chapter Twelve

After the plates were cleared, Shannon declared the meal a feast. "I knew I asked the right man to get me into this delicious restaurant. It was amazing, and everything I hoped it would be," she said, then launched into a new topic. "I watched a funny video before I met you for dinner."

He raised an eyebrow in question. "I thought you weren't into Internet videos?"

"I'm not. I only watch videos of my dance rehearsals, and I shoot most of those myself. But my friend Ally showed me a video she saw on Facebook. It's this clip of a girl who grinds on her boyfriend in public while his hand is under her skirt, and they don't even try to hide that he's fingering her and getting her off."

"I like getting you off," he said with a naughty glint in his brown eyes.

"You cannot resist segueing back to dirty talk when I'm telling you a story."

"I'm so sorry," he said, placing his palms together. "The story was about a guy making a girl come. Forgive me for thinking about making you come. It's only my favorite thing in the entire world to do."

She shot him a *tell me more* look.

"It's a hobby I once practiced a few times a day," he added. "One I'm very interested in taking up again."

A ribbon of warmth spread through her chest, both from the suggestion of one of her favorite activities, too, but also from the way he was so quick on his toes, so fast with a joke. The man had always made her laugh. He was handsome as sin and funny as hell, and that combo had been all she'd ever needed. He had filled all the sad places inside her. He'd burrowed into her with his laughter and his wit, replacing her darkness with his light. Tonight, he was firing on all cylinders—his caring, tender side in full force, along with his clever one, not to mention that handsome side. In his jeans and long-sleeved Henley stretched tight across his chest, he was a sight to behold.

"Anyway, back to the video. So the funny part is they had no clue they'd been caught on camera, even though they were totally obvious. They thought they were being quiet and sneaky when he was trying to make her come."

"I could make you come quietly," he said with an easy shrug of his shoulder. "I can make you come loudly, too. I can make you come in pretty much any way."

She scoffed. Not because it was untrue, but because he was so damn sure of himself. "Confident much?"

"Yeah, I am. I have the track record to prove it. You're pretty much the only class I aced in college."

She laughed, looking down at her lap. He was too much sometimes. "Straight As, Brent?"

"Hell no. Higher. I earned A-pluses across the board in your pleasure."

She rolled her eyes. "You're relentless."

He leaned forward across the table, flashing her that cocky grin she'd loved so much. "When it comes to delivering multiple orgasms for you, yes. Relentless is precisely what I am."

She held up her hands. "Fine, fine. You win. You win for being the King of Distraction again. Because I was trying to tell you that watching this video made me think to go looking for videos of you."

He straightened his spine and furrowed his brow. Excellent. She'd regained the thread of the conversation. "You looked for videos of me?"

"I did. I did a little Googling of Brent Nichols."

For a second, he seemed unsure, nervous even. Then he returned to his cool, confident demeanor, leaning back in his chair. "Really? What else did you see?"

She dipped her hand into her purse, and took out the item she'd purchased at the candy store. A lollipop. She unwrapped it, taking her time peeling off the plastic as he watched her. His eyes darkened as she brought it to her lips, gently kissing the sucker.

His breath hissed. His eyes turned feral. This was what she wanted—him turned on and in the palm of her hand, and it had taken mere seconds. She flicked her tongue across the red candy, licking it once as he shifted in his chair. She pictured his cock standing at attention, straining against his jeans. She wondered if he still wore black boxer briefs like he'd worn in college. If he still looked hot in them as he did then, the outline of his dick so alluring when he'd take off his clothes for her. Her mouth watered as she pictured him unzipping his jeans, pushing down his briefs, his cock springing free.

Ready for her. Always ready for her

"But I need to correct you," she said.

"About what?" His voice was husky.

"I'm not opposed to licking sweets off you."

He sat up straight "You saw my bit?"

She nodded, then licked the red lollipop, swirling her tongue across the candy. She watched him as he swallowed, his Adam's apple bobbing up and down. Giving him away. But then he wasn't trying to hide a single thing right now. She leaned across the table, lowered her voice to a whisper, and asked, "If I put my hand on you right now how hard would your dick be?"

"Rock fucking hard," he said in a growl, the rough and sexy rumble of his admission sending a rush of heat between her legs.

She returned the sucker to her mouth, moving it back and forth between her lips. As she licked and kissed the candy, giving him a hell of a show, he stared at her with hungry eyes. In them, she saw the reel of his desires. All his dirty thoughts, all his dirty dreams—everything he wanted from her.

The waiter rushed by, dishes balanced on his arm.

"Check please," Brent called out, and the man nodded, then continued on his way.

"Actually, allow me to clarify my feelings about sweets," she said as she drew the lollipop all the way into her mouth, then let it pop out. "I'm not really a chocolate person. I'm more into the red, sugary candy. Like this sucker. I love how it tastes." She paused, her eyes on him, then asked, "Do you wonder what my mouth tastes like right now?"

"Spectacular. I bet it tastes spectacular," he answered, his voice strained, and full of heat. "Kiss me now," he said, giving her a clear order. He leaned across the table and claimed her mouth, marked his territory with a passionate, crushing kiss that made her dizzy.

When he broke the kiss, the haze cleared and she returned to starring in her show. She kicked back in the chair, striking a casual, seductive pose as she sucked the candy deeply, reminding him of her talents.

He gripped the edge of the table. He inhaled through his nostrils. He looked as if he wanted to rip the table in two.

"You see, I'd be much more inclined to lick something like this off you."

"A lollipop?"

"Candy, lollipop, anything sweet. By the way, how's it going down there? A little tight in the jeans?"

"Unbelievably tight, but I don't mind. Because my hard-on is within a few feet of my favorite place in the entire universe.

"My mouth?"

"*Anywhere* on you," he corrected. "Your mouth. Your pussy. Your beautiful fucking ass," he said, reminding Shannon that he'd explored her thoroughly. He was the only man she'd let take her any way he wanted, because she'd loved everything with him. She had given him all of her body, and he'd worshipped every inch of her.

"Mmm," she moaned, licking her tongue across the sugary surface. She rolled her eyes in pleasure, then held the candy in the air. "I'm thinking of how much I miss the taste of you coming in my mouth."

"I can gladly reacquaint you with that taste."

"I like the way you feel hitting the back of my throat," she said, dirty talking him as she swirled her tongue against the sucker, revving herself up as much as him, she was sure.

The waiter brought the check, and in a flash, Brent reached into his wallet, threw some bills on the table and gripped her elbow, leading her out of the restaurant. His fast pace and his firm hold told her that he wanted more, more than she was willing to give right now. She placed her hands on his chest, dropping the games for a moment. "I know what you're thinking, but we can't get a room. I'm not ready."

A sliver of disappointment crossed his eyes, but was then replaced by that confident look she knew well. "Did I say I wanted a room?" he said, tossing the question at her like a dare. He shook his head, supplying the answer. "Nope. I'm just taking you to the fountains to watch their show. I thought that would be a nice end to this date."

"Oh," she said, frowning. She thought he'd take her to a bathroom, or find some quiet little nook where they could get frisky. But she couldn't argue with the view either, once they'd stepped outside and walked across the palazzo to the fountains at the Bellagio. "I love the fountains," she said softly.

"I know you do," he said, his voice matching hers.

The warm June air caressed the bare skin of her shoulders. She leaned against the stone railing that edged the gorgeous water display. He stood next to her, wrapped an arm around her, and tugged her close. His erection pressed against her thigh. "I did all that to you," she said in a naughty voice. "Just from talking about blowing you."

"You know I love your blow jobs."

"I wish I could give you one right now," she whispered, as she pushed her rear against his hard-on. He groaned.

"Yeah, it's hard to give a blow job in public without being like that couple in the video. But this is doable," he said, then he shifted her so her back was aligned with his chest. He crowded her in, standing behind her. The stone wall blocked any view of her from the front, and he was shielding her back.

"*Brent.*"

He pushed against her once more, the outline of his erection nudging her back. The feel of his hard length thrilled her, even as he got closer than she was used to in public. A low moan escaped her lips, and instantly his mouth was on her ear. "You be quiet now," he whispered harshly. He slipped a hand under the soft material of her top, pressing gently against her belly. "If you're loud, someone might record you, and you'd hate that."

Before she could protest, he slid his hand from her belly to inside the front of her skirt.

She nearly gasped out loud before clamping her lips shut and swallowing the murmur of pleasure. His fingers danced across the outline of her underwear. "I would hate it," she whispered, giving in to him, to his touch. He caged her in, his big, strong body shielding her. Her belly was flush against the hard stone railing, and as the gorgeous fountains began their nighttime ballet, he dragged his fingers across the lacy fabric of her panties.

She ached for him. He neared her throbbing clit, and the desperation inside her intensified. All that sucking, licking, and teasing she'd done with the candy had turned her on fiercely. Tempting him had heated her up, and she was operating at high levels of lust already.

He kissed her earlobe softly. "Don't make a sound. Don't say a word. Don't let anyone know but me."

She nodded her agreement. He lined his body firmly against her. God, how she wanted to feel him slide into her. To fill her completely. She was ready for him, so slick and liquid.

His hand made its way inside the waistband of her panties, then lower and lower still, and... oh dear God... his fingers were on a fast track for her hot, wet center. When he glided them across her, she nearly screamed.

"Was it all that sucking that got you this hot?" he whispered as he stroked.

"The sucking and the talking and now the touching," she answered quietly as she shuddered in his arms.

He stopped his movements. "Hold still, babe."

"I will."

"Promise me you can stay still or I'll have to stop."

The prospect of him stopping was horrible. She was dying for his touch, for him to get her off as only he could. "Promise."

"Good. Because all this wetness is fucking perfect for my fingers to slide through," he said in her ear, so low only she could hear as he stroked her. "All this fucking beautiful wetness. I want to feel you grabbing my dick with this sweet wet pussy."

"Me, too," she whispered, and started to rock her hips into his hand.

He tsked her in her ear. "Don't do that. You don't want to be the girl on the video."

"I don't," she said softly, her voice trance-like, her body overcome with silver sparks of desire as he rubbed his fingers across her heat. She drew a breath, as if that would give her the ability to stay still. She stood rigid and tense against the stone, even though she wanted to let go, to give in. She held in all the anticipation as he stroked faster, more expertly.

She bit her lip, driving her teeth sharply into her own flesh to hold back all the sounds eager to fly from her lips. She wanted to close her eyes, to rub against him, to moan and groan and sing out his name. But she refrained because she wanted one thing even more.

To come.

* * *

She was hotter than she'd ever been. Slippery wetness coated his fingers. Her slick heat was all over him. Her panties were useless. He was dying to rip them off her, hoist her up on this railing, spread her wide and properly worship her perfect pussy. But this was a high, too—her, ramrod straight, hiding her pleasure, fighting back her screams. It was such a thrill. Her need to come was intoxicating. Her ability to stay quiet was so impressive, when he knew how much she wanted to move. He slid his fingers across those delicious pussy lips, wet and warm and inviting. She trembled against him as he stroked up and down, then focused on her swollen clit, so needy, so hungry for his touch. He rubbed his finger against her, and he could feel the way tension tightened in her body as she neared the edge.

"Don't move, Shan," he commanded. "I know you want to. I know you want to ride my hand so badly right now, don't you?"

She nodded the back of her head against his chest.

"You want to fuck my hand like the wild woman you are."

Another nod.

"And it'll be even harder for you to hold back when I slide my fingers into you," he said. Her shoulders rose up in a sharp line of tension. Her beautiful body was strung tight, stretched to the limits of her own desire, her own sexuality. He loved knowing how to play her, how to touch her, how to send her into a land of bliss.

So he did as promised as the sprays of water soared higher, and the music grew louder. Crowds surrounded them, but he didn't care. No one could tell his hand was in his favorite place, and no one knew the gorgeous brunette in his arms was seconds away from nirvana. He slid two fingers deep into her. She gripped him and started to move her hips.

He brushed his mouth against her ear, and spoke sharply. "You move, I stop. You want me to stop?"

"No," she said, breathy, so desperate.

"You want to come?" he growled.

"Yes," she whispered.

"I'm not going to cover your mouth," he said, in a warning. "And I'm not going to let you bite down on my arm. You're just going to be quiet. Got it?"

She murmured something that sounded close to a yes. He thrust deeper, his thumb rubbing her gorgeous clit, and her body tightened. "Yeah, babe. Come on my fingers. Let me feel you come all over my hand," he said, and she clenched tightly around him, her body shuddering in his arms.

He watched her face, her gorgeous, beautiful face, as she squeezed her eyes shut, and nearly sealed her lips together to zip up her cries as she came on his fingers.

As she trembled, he uncurled her fist from around the lollipop she'd been gripping tightly in her hand. He brought the candy to his mouth and licked it once, smacking his lips.

"Mmm. You're right. That is delicious."

* * *

Later, as he walked her to her ride, he didn't press. He didn't ask again if he was forgiven. Instead, he kept moving forward, because that was what they were doing.

"When I was in New York, I saw a sign for the Alvin Ailey dance company on tour," he said.

Her eyes lit up. "I love Alvin Ailey. It was my dream to win a spot in Alvin Ailey."

"I know. And I remember in college you wanted me to go with you. But I had a gig so I cancelled on you."

Her smile erased itself. The memory of another one of his dick moves must have just returned to her. He kept talking, eager to right that wrong from years ago. "So I bought tickets to see them here next week. I'd really like to take you. And I will keep my promise to take you."

She looped her arms around his neck. "Yes. I would love to go with you."

He wanted to pump his fist in the air, to shout a victorious *yes*. Then he wanted to close his eyes and groan in pleasure, because she was running her fingers through his hair. He loved the feel of her hands in his hair.

"You really know how to treat a woman you used to go out with, don't you?"

"Speaking of that," he said, pulling back and cupping his hands on her shoulders. Tonight had gone so well, and he wanted to build on it. To keep up the momentum. To do that, they'd need to let go of the old wounds. "Shan, how would you feel if we agreed to move on from the past?"

"To put it behind us?"

He nodded. "Yes."

"Are you asking if you're forgiven?"

"Kind of," he admitted with a small grin, hoping it might help his cause.

She looked him square in the eyes. The corners of her lips curved up, as if she was considering his request. He held his breath, waiting for her answer. Then it came, as she nodded. "I think we could both use a fresh start, so let's focus on the here and now, not the way things were."

He smiled broadly. "Good. So we're dating then," he said as they reached the front of the Bellagio where her ride was pulling up. He'd parked his Indian Dark Horse there, too.

"I think it's best if we don't label what's happening between us."

He could live with not labeling. But he couldn't live with the possibility that someone else might try to date her. He had to lay down one ground rule. "I'm fine with not labeling, as long as the not-label includes not dating other men."

She arched an eyebrow. "Or other women."

"Yes. That, too. I don't want you dating men or women. Good point," he said, in mock seriousness.

She wagged a finger at him. "You know exactly what I meant."

As he said goodnight, he couldn't help but hold tight to those words—*what's happening between us.*

Labels or not, something was definitely happening. As he straddled his bike, and tugged on his helmet to ride home, he was determined to make sure nothing stood in the way of him loving this woman again.

CHAPTER THIRTEEN

Not labeling what was happening was pointless.

They were clearly dating again. Shannon couldn't even try to pretend it was anything but real, honest-to-goodness dating. As if they had just met, and were so taken with each other they had to see each other every day. *That* kind of dating.

It was scary and amazingly fun at the same time.

On Monday, she visited Edge in the morning with her assistant choreographer, Christine, to make notes on the space, since the layout was similar to the club in San Francisco. James showed them around, but Brent popped out of his office to say hello.

"Hey, Shay. Good to see you," he said, as he walked to the other end of the club. While she wasn't worried for her safety per se, or that clients would pull contracts if they learned her real name, she simply preferred the new one in business matters. The fact that Brent moved fluidly between the two warmed her heart. After they reviewed the plans for the show, Christine said she needed to return to the studio to rehearse the dancers, and James had other meetings to attend.

As Shannon walked to the exit, Brent caught up with her. "Can I interest you in lunch?"

"You can definitely interest me in lunch."

Saying yes was easy. Saying yes felt right.

After they finished pho and chicken dumplings at an upscale Vietnamese restaurant on the Luxe's property, he told her he had a gift for her.

"You really don't have to give me anything," she said as the waiter cleared their plates, even though inside she was delighted. She adored his zest for giving her sweet little things.

"I know, but truth be told, it's not something I can control. My desire to give you gifts, that is." He reached into the pocket of his jeans. "I come from a long line of gift-giving men. It's in my blood and it can't be bred out of me."

He handed her a small, champagne-colored drawstring pouch. She'd never had much growing up, and she'd learned to live with that. But perhaps that was why Brent's generosity had thrilled her so much—it was all so new and fresh and fun.

It still was. With quick, eager fingers, she untied the bag and plucked out a pretty rose-gold bracelet. She gasped. It matched the silver one that she wore every day. It wasn't too gangly or too busy. Simple and stylish, it was just right for her, and for how she chose to dress these days.

"I noticed you started wearing bracelets," he said as he stretched his arm across the back of the booth, looking so casual and confident, but also hopeful. He clearly wanted her to like his gift. "You never did before, but you do now, so I picked this out for you."

"I love it," she said softly, her gaze on him. "So much."

His brown eyes seemed to sparkle at her response, and warmth rushed through her from knowing this simple give and take, this little back and forth, seemed to matter. It was *only* lunch, but it was suddenly more.

She held out her wrist, letting him clasp the jewelry on her. Instantly, the moment shot her back in time to another night when he gave her jewelry. A ring.

The night he'd proposed he'd taken her ice-skating. It was a sport she could still do well enough in spite of her injury. She'd shown off for him, gliding and spinning across the rink while he'd skated…well, the way most men who weren't hockey players or professional skaters skate. *Clumsily.*

It hadn't bothered him, though. He'd laughed at his own clunkiness. He was never one to embarrass easily, if at all. On a long circle around the rink, he stumbled like a cartoon character whose feet spun wildly beneath him, then he fell. It had been an awkward, flat-on-his ass tumble, and she laughed even harder as she glided over to him.

"Pull me up," he said, still cracking up. She offered her hand, and tugged him. He made it to only one knee. All laughter had stopped and the moment had turned both serious and breathtakingly romantic at the same time when he said, "I meant to do that. And I mean to do this, too. I am so madly in love with you and I want us to be together now, and next year, and always. I want a life with you, and I've never been more certain of anything."

She fell to her knees, tears streaking down her cheeks, and kissed his face. "*Yes. Yes. Yes.*"

Amazing how, in spite of what she saw happen to her parents, she'd never had a single doubt about Brent. She had wanted to be his wife as much as she had wanted to dance—a pure, perfect, passionate love. She'd loved him more than she'd thought possible.

As she gazed at the new bracelet on her wrist, she blinked away the memory, and the tear that was threatening to slip from her eye. The past was behind her. She couldn't linger on what they might have had before. She knew the ending to that story. Besides, past love was no indication of future choices. Her mother had loved her father. All her parents' friends and family had been shocked when her mother was arrested, because they could recall so many happy days between Dora and Thomas.

When had Dora crossed the line from loving mother to killer wife? Was there a switch that had flipped in her, or had the possibility always been there, latent through the years? Her mother hadn't been a murderer when she'd walked down the aisle, or when she'd given birth, or when she'd attended Shannon's early recitals. Shannon could still remember so many moments during her younger years, back when her parents cared for each other, before their marriage turned bitter, before her mother started cheating on her husband with a well-liked local piano teacher.

The past was meaningless. The present was the only thing that mattered.

But, even so, the hardened part of her fragile heart took some comfort in the fact that she was different from her mother. She loved this bracelet because it was from *this* man, not because of what it might have cost.

This present—*her* present—was something she could embrace right now. So she moved to the other side of the table, ran her hand through his hair and whispered, "I always loved your gifts, and I still do. Because they're from you."

* * *

On Wednesday, Brent invited Shannon to the Thai restaurant at the Luxe. There was something so freeing, in a way, about the pattern they seemed to fall into with lunch. He hadn't intended it, but these brief moments in the middle of the workday, with a clear beginning and a clear end, were perfect for getting to know her again. That was what Shannon seemed to need to let him into her heart again.

Or to get to know him anew.

Because she turned the questions on him.

"Why did you leave comedy?" she asked as she rested her chin in her hands at the table and looked at him, a curious expression in those green eyes. There was no judgment in her tone—no caustic retort like the first night he'd seen her again. Just a simple question, and one he'd been asked by many others when he'd announced he was leaving his show.

But still.

His fork froze in midair over the chicken pumpkin curry. "Why?" he repeated, stalling for time.

She nodded. "You were so successful, so popular. It's odd why you'd leave when you were the toast of the town. Inquiring minds want to know," she said with a bat of her eyes.

His muscles tensed, a visceral response to the one topic he didn't want to get into with her. There wasn't some awful secret he was sequestering away. He wasn't kicked off the network for banging an intern. He wasn't given the boot for sniffing coke on his desk before his monologue. And he wasn't found skimming off the top of the ad revenue his show raked in.

Nope.

But he feared the truth would make him look bad.

Unreliable. Disloyal. The kind of guy you can't lean on. The kind of guy he was fighting to show her that he *wasn't*.

He looked away, staring at the golden Thai dragon on the wall, at the red embroidered jacket behind the hostess stand, then at the sea of busy tables and booths full of tourists, high-rollers, and Vegas businessman and women doing deals at the Luxe.

Brent pulled his eyes away from the crowd and back to Shannon. Her long brown hair fell loosely around her face, so different from the short, fresh-faced style she'd had in college. She was different too. Tougher than she'd been back then, but softer as well. More vulnerable, too, at times.

He briefly considered his answer. He could easily spin a quick tale about loving the nightclub business, and while that was true, he'd lost her once before by being less than honest. He wanted to show her that he'd changed—by giving her the full truth, warts and all.

He inhaled deeply, and steeled himself. "Look, I could make up a nice story, Shan. I could tell you something about how I've always craved the challenge of running a club, and some of that is true. Because I do love Edge, and building it has been exciting and I've enjoyed it. But the truth is, I left comedy because I didn't want to wear out my welcome."

She tilted her head to the side. "How so?"

He launched into the backstory of his show. "My show had record ratings. It was the biggest show on cable. It was beating broadcast some nights. It was the kind of gig most entertainers would've held onto forever. For years. It was the type of job you'd ordinarily have to pull someone away from kicking and screaming." An image of the Hollywood trade articles on his departure popped into his head. The entertainment industry and the viewers had been shocked that he left after only three years. "But I wanted to go out on top. I didn't want anyone to cringe when I did my monologue. I didn't want anyone to say, his jokes are stale, or, he's phoning it in."

She nodded a few times, as if she was processing his decision. "I get it. You wanted to leave on your own terms. But why would it bother me?"

Okay, he was just going to have to spell it out, no matter how bad it made him look. "Because I was worried you'd think it proves I don't stick around. That when the going gets tough, I pack up and get out of Dodge. That I leave before things can turn difficult," he said, the words tasting bitter. His own indictment of himself.

She didn't speak at first. In her silence he wanted to kick himself for having spoken so honestly. Maybe he should have given her his canned line—*I was ready for a new challenge.*

"Does it mean that?" she asked, but her tone wasn't cutting. It was earnest. "That you don't stick around when things get tough?"

He shook his head several times for emphasis. "I don't think so. I don't regret leaving the show, but I think—at least I hope—that I've learned that what might be a good philosophy in business isn't necessarily a good way to approach relationships."

She flashed him a sliver of a smile, and in it he felt exonerated. Not from the choice to step down, but from the prospect that she was only going to see him as a certain type of guy. He felt like he'd shed some of the bad reputation that might prevent her from trusting him again.

"I'm glad you're being honest with me now, and that you're changing," she said. "We all are, aren't we? Changing? I know I am. I'm trying not to see people for the things they *might* do. I'm trying to believe in second chances, as my grandma would say, and to focus my energies on that."

"She's the smartest woman I know. I agree with everything she says," he said, slicing a hand through the air as if making a declaration, and Shannon laughed.

"But I noticed one thing about you hasn't changed..." she said, letting her voice trail off.

"Besides my stunning good looks, strapping build, and huge cock?"

She rolled her eyes and burst out laughing. "I have no idea if your dick is still huge."

"You could find out."

"Sure, whip it out right now, Brent," she said, leaning back in her chair, crossing her arms over her chest. Daring him. God, he loved this about her. She went toe to toe with him.

He lowered his hands to his crotch, and pretended he was getting ready to unzip his jeans.

"Kidding! I'm kidding," she said, and he stopped. "Anyway, what I was getting at is this." She pushed up his shirt-sleeve, her fingers tracing the sunburst on his forearm. His skin sizzled under her touch, and matters south of the border grew harder as she stroked the ink on his skin. She trailed her fingertips across the tribal bands. "You have the same ink you had in college. You never got any more?"

He shook his head. This question was easy. "I got it all with you. You came with me for the first one, and then my others, so it seemed wrong for me to get more without you."

"Did you want to get more? Was there something you had in mind?"

He'd had about as much seriousness as he could take for one lunch. As many admissions as he was up for making. So he returned to familiar ground, fixing a studious look on his face. "A zebra." He held out his arm, showing her the canvas he'd use. His right bicep was free of ink. "Right here."

"That sounds perfect. You could even have the stripes go all the way around," she said, tracing a pattern on his arm. Ah, this was good. He hadn't expected his joke would get her hands on him, but he'd keep it up to keep her touching him.

"The other option is a badass, flying Pegasus. Breathing fire and all. You see, Shan, now that you're back, all I want to do is just cover myself in ink. Coat myself in it."

"You let me know when you're ready to go under the needle. I'll be there," she said, as she danced her fingertips up his arm, hitting the cuff of his shirt from where she'd pushed up his sleeve. She wrapped her arm around his bicep and squeezed, then let go of her grip.

That was his cue to move on. "I got you something else," he said, handing her the bag he'd brought with him today. It had been next to him in the booth, since this one didn't fit in his pocket.

A smile spread across her face—that was reward alone. She dug into the shopping bag, and took out a box, then opened the top. He catalogued her reaction. Her eyes seemed to twinkle with happiness, then she brought a hand to her chest, then she took out the pair of red leather shoes with a strap over the arch of the foot.

"You're still a size six, I presume?"

She nodded as she slipped off her black heels, and tried on the new ones. "I can't believe you got me shoes."

He leaned across the table and lowered his voice. "The shoes looked hot, and you're hot, and I always liked to fuck you in shoes, because you used to leave them on and that was insanely hot. Which pretty much describes you. Hot."

"So let me get this straight. You think I'm hot?" She raised an eyebrow.

"Yeah. Your understanding is right on," he said, deadpan.

"And is this your way of trying to fuck me again, Brent? By buying me shoes and making me laugh?"

"Yes," he said with a nod. "Does it turn you on?"

"You know it does." She stretched out her leg across his, and modeled the new shoe, then spoke in a smoky whisper. "Does this turn you on?"

He nearly groaned as he answered, "You know it does."

"Do you want me to wear them on Saturday night? When you take me to Alvin Ailey?"

"Yes."

All he could think about now was her in those shoes on Saturday, and what might happen later that night. Images flashed wildly before his eyes. Her legs on his shoulders.

Her legs in a *V.* Those heels digging into his back. His tongue all over her naked body, spread out before him. Her spine curving in an arch as he took her once again, and sent her over the edge.

Damn, he liked the reel his mind was playing. Far too much.

"I'll even let you pick me up if you want," she said, and he nodded vigorously, thrilled that she was giving him her address finally. She reached for her phone. "I'll text it to you right now, and then I'll be wearing these shoes when you come get me," she said in a come-hither voice that made him want to come hither that instant.

He wasn't going to be able to get up for a long time because he was so fucking hard. Good thing his phone rang, and Tanner's named flashed across the screen. Perfect boner killer when he needed it.

"Let me grab this for one minute," he said to Shannon, then answered the phone. "Hey, Tanner. What's up?"

The man wasted no time with hellos. "Here's the deal. You need to meet the leader of the neighborhood association. Let him know Mr. Late Night Funny Guy can be a real businessman. Can you get to New York this weekend? I set up a meeting Sunday night."

He cursed silently. Saturday night was his big date with Shannon. No way was he backing out. Not after the time he'd missed taking her to Alvin Ailey in college, and not when he was trying to do everything right now. But he could catch an early Sunday morning flight. "I'll be there in time for a seven p.m. dinner."

"Fine. I'll send you details," Tanner said in a gruff tone.

"Hey, I put in a few calls to the parks department in the city. I made a donation to have some of the parks there re-vitalized, like you suggested."

"Good. Keep that shit up. You got a long row to hoe."

After Brent hung up, he gestured to the phone. "The neighborhood association in New York is being difficult about my plans to open a club there," he said, then caught her up to speed on the situation as he paid for lunch.

"Hmm," Shannon said, tap dancing her fingers on her chin as they walked out of the restaurant.

"Hmm, what? You coming up with a perfect plan for me or something?" he joked.

"Actually, I was thinking. Even though your meeting is Sunday, I could record a rehearsal in San Francisco next week when I'm there with the dancers. You can show it to them after so they can see it's more Cirque du Soleil than Scores."

He stopped in his tracks, and raked his eyes up and down over the woman at his side. This time, though, he was admiring her business savvy. "That's brilliant."

As they left, he vowed to do whatever he had to in order to keep her in his life. Work had won his heart ten years ago. He had to show her that she was more important than work.

CHAPTER FOURTEEN

A pink and purple illustration of an animal stared at her.

"I don't even want to ask why you're buying *that*," her grandmother said with a laugh, pointing to Shannon's purchase as the cashier at the party store rang them up.

"It's a surprise for someone," Shannon answered with a wink and snatched the little gift and tucked it into her purse.

"That'll be fifty-seven twenty-one," the cashier said, bagging up the balloons, streamers, cups and party favors that Victoria had picked up for the birthday party she was throwing for her great-granddaughter's third birthday—the grand-daughter of Shannon's aunt.

Before her grandma could stop her, Shannon slid her credit card through the machine to pay.

"You didn't have to do that," the older woman said.

Shannon flashed her a smile as she tucked her card into her purse. "I know I didn't have to. I wanted to." She scooped up the bag and headed to her car. They'd attended a sunrise yoga class, then stopped at the store on the way home, and now Shannon needed to return to the studio for a few hours before her lunch date.

It was definitely a date.

"Might that someone you're surprising be your old beau?"

"*Beau. Boy.* You're so old-fashioned, Nana," Shannon said as she backed out of the lot and turned onto the main drag.

"Well?" she asked pointedly. "Is he?"

Shannon shrugged, but her lips curved into a grin. "Maybe."

Victoria patted her knee as they slowed to a stop at a red light a few blocks from her home. "Excellent. So what are we going to do about your brothers then?"

"What about them? The fact that all three are total pains in the ass?" Shannon teased.

"Not that. The fact that they're all single. Maybe we need to set up a matchmaking service for those boys."

"Good luck getting the three cavemen married off," Shannon joked as the light changed, and she turned left onto Victoria's street.

Her grandmother gestured grandly, as if she were putting their names in lights. "Matchmakers for the Paige Men."

Shannon startled for a moment at hearing that name. They were all so used to being Sloans now.

"I meant the Sloan men," her grandmother quickly corrected.

Just like that, Shannon's mind latched onto another Paige man. The one who was long gone. Try as she might, the past was never far away. Little things slammed her back in time. Like her old name. Like driving, of all things.

Her father's final moments had been in a car, driving home from work late one night, pulling into the driveway of his home. The one place where he should always have been safe from harm.

She pressed her teeth into her bottom lip, holding her emotions in as she turned into her grandmother's driveway.

It was *only* a driveway. A mundane, ordinary slick of concrete. Her grandmother didn't even live anywhere near the home where her dad had been shot. But as she cut the engine and looked at her father's mother, she knew, without a shadow of a doubt, that Victoria was thinking the same thing. That she, too, had been jolted out of a festive moment of party planning and pretend matchmaking and hurtled back in time to eighteen years ago. She saw it in her grandma's eyes—the same sadness she felt was reflected back at her.

"Sometimes it's hard just turning in the driveway," Shannon said softly. "Makes me think of my dad."

Her grandmother clasped her hand. "I know. Every day, I think about him."

Shannon looked down at their hands. "I miss him."

"I do too, sweetie."

After she walked her grandmother inside and said goodbye, she returned to her car. She scanned the surrounding area, as always, alert for anything amiss. Listening for that footstep crunching on the grass. Seeking the shadow of someone who wasn't supposed to be there.

The hair on her neck stood on end, and for a second, she wished she carried her gun with her. But that weapon was locked away at her home.

Shannon's eyes roamed the sidewalk, the house, and the garage before she unlocked the car door. This hyper-alertness fried her nerves. No one was there. It was morning. She was safe, and Victoria was fine, and she had to refuse to live in fear. She had to kick the damn specter of hidden guns, and gangs, and shooters, and plots for murder far out of her daily agenda.

She took a deep breath, letting it spread through her body, coaxing it to ease away the stranglehold of the past. Good thing she was seeing Brent that afternoon. He was her antidote. He'd wash away the cruel memories.

But by the time lunch rolled around, she no longer wanted to rely on her old habits with Brent. He'd always been her magic bullet to extradite the pain. Maybe to truly change, she needed to *give* instead of to take.

Over salad and pasta at an Italian restaurant inside Caesars Shops, she asked him more about work, peppering him with questions about his clubs, the expansion, his vision for Edge, reminding herself the whole time not to be jealous. She listened intently, because she didn't want to feel an ounce of resentment for his choices, including the one to ditch the very industry that had once been so important to him.

"And Edge will keep on growing," she said.

"That's the goal," he said with a wide smile. He truly seemed happy with his new path. That was his special talent. He knew how to find the happiness in everything. Someone like him never seemed to need much, while she often felt she required far too much. That was exactly why she'd picked up the gift at the party store. He loved the little things in life.

"Close your eyes," she said, after the waiter cleared their plates and she joined him on his side of the table.

"You gonna blindfold me? I'm game," he joked as he followed her order.

She reached into her purse, rolled up his shirtsleeve, and dipped a cloth napkin in a water glass.

"Go ahead. Undress me here. I don't mind," he continued.

"I know you don't, you dirty man."

"You wouldn't have me any other way."

"You're right," she whispered as she positioned the square of paper on his arm, then pressed the wet napkin on top of it and counted to thirty. When she peeled the backing paper off, she told him to open his eyes.

"Tada!" She showed him the mark she'd left on his arm, and his big, deep laugh rumbled across the restaurant.

He nodded approvingly at the pink and purple temporary tattoo of a little horse she'd fixed to his bicep. "A pony. You got me a pony. It's everything I've ever wanted."

"It's not quite a badass flying Pegasus, but if you're a good boy, I'll get you a winged one next," she said.

"Or a unicorn maybe?"

"That could be arranged."

After they left the restaurant, they wandered past the designer shops of Caesars, with luxuries from the likes of Gucci and Louboutin. She peered in the windows of her favorites, admiring a pair of black shoes and a dove gray bag.

"Thank you for taking time out of your day for me," she said as they continued their stroll.

"Nothing I'd rather do."

"Will you have to work late to make up for playing hooky?"

"Maybe, but it's worth it."

A flash of color caught her eye. In the midst of all the black and silver high-end items, she spotted an old-fashioned photo booth down a quiet hallway that led to the restrooms. Painted bright red and white, the booth boasted a sign advertising FOUR PHOTOS FOR $1.

"That's a bargain," she said, then grabbed his hand and tugged him to the booth. "Let's get a picture to go with your cool new ink. Show it to your brother. Let him know how wild and crazy you can be."

"We can even put on disguises and shoot cool selfies," he said, rubbing his hands together. "Please let there be a fake mustache. Please, pretty please." He held up his hand and crossed his fingers.

She swatted him and grinned. In the past, contact with him had blotted out the bad. But this was better. This was about laughter, and talking, and her giving something to him. Something silly, but then, she knew he liked those gifts best of all.

Strange as it sounded, she knew he would cherish a ridiculous photo of the two of them. She pulled him inside and yanked the curtain closed.

"Damn," she said, snapping her fingers when she saw the BROKEN sign slung across the viewfinder. "No wonder no one was down this hallway."

"We can make our own photo booth picture. You must have something in your purse."

"Right. Of course. Let me just get out my purple wig. And the fake nose I keep in there," she said, deadpan.

"Now you're talking."

Instead, she grabbed her sunglasses, and slid them to the bridge of her nose, puckering her lips. He bared his teeth in an exaggerated grin and flexed his bicep, showing off his new pink and purple pony ink. She snapped a picture on her phone and showed it to him.

"We are so hot together," he said, with over-the-top admiration. He patted his thighs. "Climb up. Take another picture."

"You're just trying to get me to sit on your lap."

"Yes. I am."

She straddled him, the soft cotton of her black dress flaring across his jeans, then held out the phone. "Smile," she instructed.

But instead of smiling, he wrapped his arms around her, planting a soft, wisp of a kiss on her neck.

Her eyes floated closed as her thumb slid aimlessly across the screen, capturing them. She didn't stop to look this time, because he was brushing his lips along her neck, buzzing a path to her ear. She let the phone fall to the bench along with her sunglasses, and turned to meet his lips. The goofiness vanished. The silliness evaporated as the moment folded and unfolded into something else, shifting from temporary tattoos and selfies to a hot, wet, deep kiss that swamped her body with desire.

She moaned his name as if he were all she wanted, and he was. "*Brent.*"

"You can't resist me," he said, breaking the kiss for a moment. He ran his hand up her back, against the fabric of her dress, and she arched into him, moving in time with his touch.

"You're such a cocky bastard," she tossed back.

"Just admit it," he said, as he gently tugged her bottom lip through his teeth, making her moan. He flicked his tongue across her top lip in such a slow, sexy, seductive fashion that she thought she might reach the peak of a climax if he kept it up. "Admit you can't resist me."

She sighed and gave in. No point denying the truth they both knew. "Not when you kiss me like that. Not when you touch me the way you do."

"I better do both again, then," he said as he worked his way up her neck, kissing her throat, her jaw, her cheek, then her earlobe. Her body practically vibrated from the tender and delicious way he traveled across her skin. The kiss was driving him wild too, judging by the bulge in his jeans and the pressure from his fingers as he dug them into her hips with each each lick, each sweep of his tongue.

She could subsist on this moment. She could use it as the balm to her overactive brain, to all the harsh moments that rattled into her life from out of nowhere. Keep taking more from him—more kisses, more touching, more contact.

But she wanted to give, too. To give to him as he'd done for her.

"My turn," she said, as she returned the favor. She worked her way up his neck, kissing his jaw, then his earlobe. He grasped her harder as she mapped his skin, loving his clean scent, his rough stubble, and his hard body.

"You're quite good at taking your turn," he murmured.

She nibbled on his earlobe, and he pumped his pelvis up into her on a muffled groan. A blast of heat tore through her, and taking and giving smashed together.

"Ride me," he said in a rough, husky voice. They were wanting all the same things. Wanting the give and the take as well. "Ride me hard. Like I know you want to."

His words ignited her. She followed them to the letter, as they collided in a mad frenzy in the photo booth. Through their clothes, she was grinding against him in seconds, her white panties and his jeans the only barriers. They became a tangle of teeth and heat and madness, as she kissed him ruthlessly and slammed against him. He kissed back the same way, wild and untamed, his hands knotting through her hair, pulling hard. Grabbing. Biting. Tugging. Hands and fingers clawing everywhere. Their breaths turned loud. If anyone walked by on the way to the restroom, surely they'd hear her moans of desire.

She didn't care.

Not with the way his lips consumed her, taking over this bruising, needy, dangerous kiss that felt like tipping over. Like she was losing what little control she had of her emotions for him. She was poised, teetering on the edge of something. This week had been so sweet, so delicious, so like a perfect courtship that it made her remember how deeply she'd been in love with him before. The way he'd treated her stirred up all those feelings she'd forced out of her mind and shoved into a box for the last ten years. They were resurfacing, breaking free of the past, and fighting their way up her body. Terrible, dangerous feelings that threatened to take over her mind.

She moved faster, harder, kissed more deeply, her desire climbing higher.

But then he placed his hands on her shoulders, and gently, but firmly, pushed her away. Forcing her to look at him.

"Shan, why don't we get a room?" he asked, his eyes hazy with lust. "You know I want you so much. You're driving me wild, and we're practically fucking with our clothes on in a photo booth. C'mon," he said, tipping his forehead to the curtain as if to say *Let's go.*

And then, like the motherfucker it was, the past grabbed her throat. Like a slingshot, it snapped her back to everything that had broken between them.

She clenched her jaw, grabbed his collar. "I can't just go have sex with you, Brent."

"Why not? Isn't that pretty close to what we're doing now?"

She swallowed hard, and let it out in a harsh, broken whisper. "Because it was never just sex with you."

But she didn't stop moving on him. She only slowed the pace, because she couldn't break the connection. This electric thread was part of them, part of who they were, part of who they were becoming again. She downshifted from the madness to a slow grind. He followed her lead, adjusting his rhythm too, shifting his touch to a softer one, as he ran his hands along the bare skin of her arms. Gently, he kissed her shoulder, making her shiver. "What was it with me?"

She cupped his cheeks, and looked him in the eyes. Spoke the truth. "It was everything," she said, as she moved against him, the friction sending another powerful wave of desire through her. "All of it. This. You. Us. You were *everything* to me."

He laced a hand through her hair. "Do you have any idea how much I want to be everything to you again?"

She shook her head. She was still stuck in time. The freshness of the hurt felt so new again. "Do you have any idea how devastating it was when you broke up with me?"

He groaned, sounding annoyed. Defeated. "I thought we weren't going to talk about the past," he whispered as he kissed her neck. His lips were barely there, just the flutter of a hummingbird's wings. Even so, the kiss turned her liquid. How the hell could they kiss and argue? But then, that was what they'd always done. Even while they fought, they could never stop touching.

"I can't hide from the past. I can't move on unless we talk about it."

"Then tell me," he said roughly. "Tell me what you want to talk about so we can start over."

"How do I know it will be different?" she asked, as she leaned her head back and succumbed to the strange combination of kissing and confessing. Or touching and talking. "Because of the shoes, because of the bracelet, because of scarves and lunches and the dinner and the tickets this weekend to Alvin Ailey?"

"No. Those are just things. It's what's behind those things that matters, and that's how I feel for you. Because I would do anything to have you back," he said, holding her face and forcing her to look him in the eyes.

And as she did, something inside her cracked open. The ice that she'd packed around her heart that he'd been chipping away at day by day, thawed completely.

"It's harder for me to just start over than it is for you," she blurted out, even though it was selfish, what she was saying. She knew that. But she couldn't escape the painful truth of who she was. She stared fiercely at him, keenly aware of both the intensity of this conversation and the pressure from his erection between her legs pressing hard against her damp panties.

"Why? Why is it harder for you?"

"Because you broke my heart—don't you get it? Mine had already splintered into a million pieces one night in a driveway, and I can only sustain so many breaks before it's shattered."

She stopped moving on him, and let the tears slide down her cheeks, as they'd done so many times with him. He gathered her close in his arms, and stroked her hair.

"Let me be the one for you. I won't break your heart again. I promise."

She wanted to believe him. She wanted to believe herself, too. But there were things she had to tell him. Things that might tear him apart. "I don't want to break your heart either."

He smiled that crazy, gorgeous, cocky lopsided grin. He rapped his knuckles against his chest. "I'm tough. I can handle anything you throw at me."

She wasn't so sure, but even so, she loved this side of him.

Heels clicked against the floor. Someone was walking past them. The sound of the footsteps sped up. She covered her mouth and widened her eyes, and he laughed silently.

Then, maybe because of his admission, or maybe even more so because of hers, she brushed her lips against his, and kissed him softly, picking up the pace once more. She felt a freedom from the weight of memories. Maybe simply voicing them was what she had truly needed to move on. Oh, how she wanted to move on.

In every way with him.

Every. Single. Way.

"Soon," she whispered in his ear. "Soon. I want to be with you again. I want you in every way. I swear."

The talking of the past stopped, as it needed to. She'd said all she truly needed to say, and now all she wanted was to feel. Because she felt so much for him. More than she'd wanted to when she'd first agreed to dinner. More than she'd ever expected when he'd walked back into her life.

Damn him, damn the heart, damn the body.

"*Babe*," he said in a soft but firm voice. "Rock your body against me."

"How is it we can talk like this and I'm still hot for you?" she murmured in his ear.

"Because I turn you on and because you're crazy about me, too," he said, low and sexy, and just for her. She shivered against him, saying nothing, refusing to give voice to the *yes* that formed on her tongue as she began moving again, her small body riding his big, strong frame.

"Just like that. Keep it up," he told her, urging her on. "I can feel you getting close."

"I'm so close," she said on a quiet gasp.

"Let go. Let go for me," he said as he thrust his hips up against her, and yanked her down harder on him.

She let the past fall behind her once more as she returned to what they'd been doing before. Coming together. She moved on him, harder, faster. There were no more words, no confessions, and no questions. Just movement. Their need for each other had never been quenched. She didn't know if it ever would be, even as her belly tightened and she felt the start of that intense rush of pleasure. She pushed onto him, hitting that point where she lost control, and came apart for him, grabbing his back, biting down on his shoulder, falling apart in his arms.

In a broken photo booth in the back of a casino.

Of all the damn places in the world. Yet it felt so right.

But even through the haze of her orgasm, she knew she couldn't escape the past. She couldn't hide from it in all this contact with him.

Soon, very soon, she was going to have to tell him that he'd been the father of her child.

CHAPTER FIFTEEN

The ace of diamonds winked at him, a mate to the ace of clubs that the dealer revealed next on the green felt of the blackjack table at the Luxe.

"I'll split," he said to the goateed dealer.

Together, Brent's two aces were a bust. Torn apart, they gave him a second chance in the game.

"I've got a very important question for you," Mindy said, as the dealer laid a three on top of her eight and Matchbox Twenty played overhead. The band was in concert at the Luxe in two weeks, after the Alvin Ailey troupe departed from its brief stay at the hotel's new theater.

"Hit me," Brent said to his friend, and she rolled her eyes at his pun. "What's the question?"

Mindy adopted a girly, love-struck tone. "Have you thought about what you're going to wear tonight to Alvin Ailey?" She batted her eyes and squeezed his arm. "It's such a big decision."

"Bow tie. Seersucker suit," Brent said with a straight face, as the dealer slapped two new cards face up for Brent. Only the two of them and a lone bald guy nursing a tropical drink played at that table on a Saturday afternoon. The goateed man dealt Mindy another card, too. A six, giving her seventeen.

"And a panama hat. That'd be a nice touch," Mindy added, nudging Brent with her elbow as he stared happily at his new cards. Eight and a nine. Didn't get much better than that.

"Absolutely," he said. "Or, call me crazy, I could just go with jeans and a nice button-down shirt."

"I'll stay," Mindy said to the dealer, then to Brent, "Fine. Be that way."

The bald man busted on his turn, then the dealer drew until he reached 17 and had to stand. It was house rules, and Brent beat him with his 18 and 19.

"You lucky bastard," Mindy said in a low whistle.

Brent simply shrugged, an admission that he'd always had some kind of Midas touch at the tables. But he also had another more important skill, and while it was one he'd told Shannon he was not applying in relationships, it was a rule to live by if he wanted to survive in the casinos with a wallet intact.

Scooping up the chips, he tipped an imaginary hat to Mindy. "And on that note, I'd better quit while I'm ahead."

"Thanks a lot. You killed me there, taking all the good cards," she muttered.

"Play another round. I'm out."

The bald man with the piña colada took off, too.

"Stay with me. Be my lucky charm," she said, and Brent relaxed in the chair as Mindy went up against the house again, trying to win back some of her losses. "By the way, have I ever told you that Michael Sloan is insanely hot?"

Brent groaned. "Can we not talk about how hot you think her brother is?"

"Oh, they're all lookers. All three of them," she said, with a breathy sigh. "All three. I'd take any of them, honestly. Ryan, Colin, Michael." She counted off on her fingers.

"Okay, you really need to stop now."

"Hey," she said, lowering her voice, a sign that she was downshifting to a more serious moment. "Speaking of tonight, does she ever talk about what happened with her family?"

Brent nodded. Mindy had lived in Vegas her whole life. She knew the Paige-Prince saga, since it had been in the local news when they were both in high school.

"It's weird, don't you think?" she continued. "The Royal Sinners."

"What do you mean?"

"Just the whole idea of them. Like the Latin Kings, or the Crips and the Bloods. I hate them," she said, her voice a harsh seethe as the dealer slapped her cards on the green felt and "Overjoyed" sounded through the casino.

"They're street gangs. Of course you hate them. That's like hating cancer."

"They went kind of quiet for a while there. A few years ago. Did you know that?"

He shook his head. He honestly hadn't tracked the goings on of the gang culture. But Mindy knew the underbelly of the city of sin better than anyone. "Five or six years ago, it seemed like they'd all kind of fallen apart. But I hear they're trying to be active again. Recruiting new members. Hitting the streets again with drugs, tagging, fights over territory."

He clenched his fists. His blood went cold. "Should I be worried? For her? For her family now?"

Mindy shook her head and squeezed his shoulder. "I wasn't saying that at all. When you started seeing her again, I did a little digging into Stefano with some of the guys I know on the force. A couple of them were active when it all went down. They say Stefano was on the outs when he killed Thomas Paige. He was doing his own thing. Kind of separating from the Sinners."

Brent's jaw tightened. A fresh wave of hate surged through him. He hated that Shannon had gone through that, that this kind of canyon of awful had not just touched her life, but had marked it. Had been the line in it. The before and the after. "So, he was, what? The odd man out in the local gang?" he asked, as the dealer tipped his forehead to Mindy, his way of asking her next move.

"Hit me," she said to him, then dialed down the volume. "Supposedly. They said his girlfriend disappeared, too, around then. They'd wanted to question her to see what she knew, but couldn't find her. Anyway, those were just the things I heard. That's all."

That's all. That's all. That's all. The words reverberated in his head, mingling with the anthemic chorus of the pop song about a love so powerful it consumes you with joy.

Joy. Hate. Love. Death. They were inextricably linked.

"Hey! Look! I got twenty-one!" Mindy clapped in glee.

"Then it's time to cash out," he said.

She shook her head. Her eyes lit up with a fresh wave of excitement. "No way. My lucky streak is just starting. It's my day off. I'm staying."

"I'll catch you later then, lucky lady," he said, and headed to his office, needing work, needing business, needing the relentless focus on contracts, and deals, and plans to erase the cold metallic taste of hate that the discussion of gangs had left in his mouth. No fault of Mindy's, and all things being equal, he'd rather know the details than not know them. But he was ready for that part of Shannon's past to stay firmly in the ground, and never fuck with her future.

Focus on the present. Focus on today. Focus on tonight.

The trouble was, the conversation gnawed at him. He opened a browser window and searched Google for news on "Royal Sinners." He read a few articles—drug busts and convictions here and there. That was it. Like she'd said, the gang seemed to have petered out for a bit. All in all, this had to be a good thing—that the gunman her mother had hired hailed from a gang that had dwindled in power and was now focused on drugs. Shannon's father's murder had never been about drugs; it was a cut and dried murder-for-money crime.

Brent shut the browser, parked his boots on his desk, and rang his buddy who ran the Luxe hotel chain—Nate Harper, who lived in New York with his wife. After they caught up briefly on work and business, Brent made his request. "Hey man, you know anyone at this hotel who can score me a nice suite last minute on a Saturday night in Vegas? Happy to pay top dollar."

Maybe it was wishful thinking. Maybe it was just some mad hope. Or perhaps he simply wanted to be prepared for any and all possible outcomes tonight. Hit, stand, or double down.

Nate laughed loudly. "You hoping to get lucky at my property this evening?"

"I'm always hoping to get lucky," he said.

"I'll take care of you. Stop by ops on the way out. Alfonso will get you a key," he said, referring to the property manager on site. Brent knew the guy well.

"I owe you," he said.

"I owe you. Your club is driving business like crazy. It's like a goddamn slot machine that pays off every time," Nate said, and Brent grinned. That was what he liked hearing. Edge was indeed the golden goose. He zeroed in on that for another hour, then checked the time. He needed to head home and get ready to pick up his date. No motorcycle tonight. He'd reserved a town car.

On the way out through the casino, Tanner's name flashed across his phone screen. He nearly crossed his fingers, praying the man wouldn't say something to ruin his Saturday.

"Hey Tanner. What's up?"

"Meeting was moved up. Gotta do lunch instead of dinner," Tanner barked.

Brent's shoulders tensed. "Tomorrow? What's the deal?"

"The neighborhood association president, Alan Hughes, has to drive his daughter to summer camp on Sunday night, so dinner won't work tomorrow. Only lunch. But listen, I think I've got him fluffed nicely for you."

Fluffed. The man actually used a porn term. "So he's leaning our way?"

"It's looking like that. See? I told you I'd be good for you. I bet you want to pay me extra each month on the lease, don't you?" Tanner said with a raspy laugh.

Brent shook his head in exasperation. Tanner was a piece of work. "Glad to hear that about Alan," he said, avoiding the other comment. He flashed briefly to his conversation with Bob from the comedy club, who'd been getting fleeced by his landlord, too. Fingers crossed that this meeting tomorrow would send them all down the right path. Brent could continue the expansion of Edge, and Bob would have the new job he needed to pay the bills.

"So be here by noon, got it? Same location. McCoy's."

"See you tomorrow."

Brent sighed heavily in frustration as he hung up. Win some, lose some. He called his assistant and asked her to change his flight from the morning to the midnight red-eye to New York. That gave him two hours with Shannon after the show ended. Crap. Make that one hour, since he'd need that hour to get to the airport and through security. Even so, he picked up a key from Alfonso.

Wishful thinking for sure at this point. But sometimes you had to roll the dice.

Chapter Sixteen

"Not too long now," Michael said. "A few more edits."

Shannon drummed her fingernails against her kitchen table as she peered at the computer screen with Michael. "Colin's such a loud mouth," she said with a laugh.

"I know," he said, taking a break from tapping away on her keyboard to pat her on the back. Michael had stopped by to help her finish editing a video she'd shot of rehearsals for the Edge show at her studio. The dance was almost perfect, but there was a section she wanted to review with her assistant choreographer. The problem was that Colin had stopped by during the rehearsal and had started talking her ear off about a new investment his firm was making.

"Ding dong," she'd told him. "Now I'm going to have to edit out the audio."

"Oh shit," he'd said, covering his mouth.

"I'm assuming you don't want to take a chance on anyone but me hearing about the new data storage company that has a ten times valuation of blah blah blah," she'd said quietly, parroting him back as she held her phone to record the dancers.

"That'd be a no," Colin had whispered, then mouthed a *thank you* as he zipped his lips shut and let Shannon finish shooting the video.

Michael was a whiz at editing video, so he'd stopped by to help her remove Colin's audio. Which also meant now was as good a time as any to tell him what she was up to tonight. She hadn't said a word to him last weekend at her grandmother's house, but she didn't know then that she'd actually be dating—seriously dating—her ex-fiancé. Now she was, and she didn't like cloaking her life in lies around her brothers, especially Michael. They were as tight-knit as a clan could be, and that was because they'd protected each other and trusted each other through thick and thin.

She steeled herself for his reaction. Of all her brothers, Michael had been the biggest fan of Brent, and then turned the other way when Brent left her.

Best to rip off the Band-Aid.

Michael zoomed in on the software, pushing a flop of dark hair off his forehead as he worked. She cleared her throat. "I'm going out with Brent tonight," she said before she could back out of her confession.

His fingers stopped moving. She didn't see his eyes, just his forehead as he furrowed his brow. He raised his face, and rubbed his knuckle against his ear. "Pretty sure I just heard you wrong," he said slowly. "Say that again."

"I'm seeing Brent," she said, straightening her spine, keeping her chin up.

"You're dating him?" he said, as if she were speaking in tongues.

She nodded.

"I thought you were just doing business with his clubs," he said, taking time with each word, as if he could restitch them into a pattern that made sense.

"I thought so, too. But then it turned into something more."

"How? How did it turn into something more?" he asked, cocking his head to the side.

"We started spending time together again," she said, keeping it PG.

"Why would you do that? You were pretty damn clear ten years ago you never wanted to see him again. You told all of us—me, Ryan, Colin. You made it abundantly clear he was persona non grata."

"I didn't want to see him then. But that was ten years ago, Michael. Things changed."

"What changed?" he asked through gritted teeth. "I can't imagine what could have changed in the last week or two that would erase what you went through."

She bit her tongue. She didn't want to serve up all her feelings for everyone to judge. It was hard enough to say them to Brent, let alone to her big brother. She didn't feel she needed to defend her heart. Some things were personal. Some things were private. Like the fact that she was falling again for someone who was tender and kind, rough and fiery, funny and sexy, and who only had eyes for her.

Someone who was putting her first.

"He's different. I am, too. That's what has changed," she said in a crisp voice.

Michael closed his eyes, gripped the side of the table, and breathed out hard. "I have no idea why you would want to do this. After everything that happened," he said, opening his eyes and staring at her.

"Nothing that happened was his fault."

Michael's eyes widened. "If it wasn't his fault, whose fucking fault was it?"

"Both of ours," she said, holding her ground, even as something darkened inside her.

"Shan," he said in a heated whisper, as if that was the only thing keeping him from shouting, and Michael Sloan never shouted. Michael Sloan never raised his voice. Michael Sloan stayed in control of his emotions at all times.

Except when it came to his sister. "I was with you in London. You were devastated," he said, his eyes black and hard.

"Of course I was."

"You were torn in pieces," he said between gritted teeth.

She slammed a hand on the table. "I know! I fucking know. I was there. It was my body. Goddammit, Michael. I'm sorry you don't like him, but I'm seeing him again and I care about him. And I'm not asking for your approval. I'm simply telling you because I don't like to keep secrets from you. So if you could just chill out, that would be great." She pushed back from the table, the legs of the chair scraping against her wood floor in a shrill shriek. The sound jolted her brother.

"Shan," he said gently.

She held up a hand. *Don't come closer. Not now.* "I need to get changed," she said, and tipped her forehead to her bathroom. She wasn't ready for him to say he was sorry for getting mad.

"I'll be done soon," he said, in a gentler tone.

She shut the door to her bedroom, headed to her bathroom, and stripped off her clothes as she turned on the shower. As she stepped under the hot stream, the water pelting her, she closed her eyes, returning to ten years ago.

* * *

Brent had been gone for a few weeks, and she was six days late. She'd hoped and prayed and bargained and bartered with the universe that she was simply that—*late*. Women all over the world were late, and it didn't mean they'd been stupid. It didn't mean the pill hadn't worked. It only meant they were late, but that red was coming.

Right?

Right, she told her freaked-out brain.

While they'd stopped using condoms a long time ago, she was on the pill. She'd switched prescriptions, though, since the one she was on had been giving her headaches. They'd used condoms during that time, but something must have gone wrong. Hell if she knew when the little bastard sperm had breached her body.

She pressed a hand to her belly, alone in her tiny Brooklyn bathroom in a room she rented for one month from an older couple, fingers crossed behind her back, trying to remember if a condom had broken during those times they'd relied on them. But when the two pink lines appeared, churning her stomach and stabbing holes in her future, it didn't really matter if she could recall the moment when the protection failed.

Her body had spoken, changing her life yet again.

Twenty-one, pregnant, and alone in her first job out of college. With the father of the baby on the other side of the country and out of the picture. Without a clue what to do, how to feel, what to think.

She sank down onto the toilet seat, dropped her head in her hands, and asked the universe for a redo. She waited for the tears to roll from her eyes, to saturate her cheeks. But, strangely, they didn't come. Maybe she'd used up her lifetime supply when her daddy had died. Maybe whatever droplets were left had been reserved for the re-opening of that wound with her mom's letters.

She did what shocked women around the world have done for years when confronted with two pink lines: re-traced her steps to the drug store, glanced furtively around in case she saw anyone she knew, and grabbed another test from the shelf. She bought it, ran home, then peed on the stick again.

Another pair of pink lines punished her with their clarity.

You're knocked up, bitch, the twin lines seemed to say with a cruel sneer.

She sank to the floor of the cramped bathroom, parking her rear on the cold teal tiles. Options flickered before her eyes. But really, the choices were very few. Terminating a pregnancy wasn't on the table. That wasn't anything she'd ever do.

So it came down to this—keep the baby or give up the baby.

Keep. Give up. Keep. Give up.

Over the next month, Shannon swung back and forth by the day, by the hour. Depending on what she ate, or what she didn't eat. What she wore. How hunched over the toilet she was at *West Side Story* rehearsals. How well she hid her morning sickness from her boss.

If there was one thing Shannon Paige-Prince knew how to do it was keep her own damn secrets.

She hid it so well that no one knew why she kept popping into the ladies room to yack up her morning toast. Mercifully, the morning sickness didn't last long.

As she packed up her bags for London, ready to move with the cast and crew to open the show on the West End, she picked up her cell phone. She flipped it open, ran her thumb across the screen, and started to dial the most familiar string of numbers in the world to her. The ones she'd called during college, every night, every day. Her man's number.

She didn't know what to say. Or what to do. Maybe it was better that way. A call for help. Let him listen. Let him talk. Let her not have to make this decision alone.

She ran a hand over her belly, still terribly flat. She threw caution out the window and dialed his number. She didn't wait long to hear a voice.

"This cell service has been disconnected," a recording said, tinny in her ear.

She tossed the dumb thing on the floor, and it clunked dully on her rug as she cursed her own stubbornness—she should have taken his calls those first few days. He was truly gone now. Off in Los Angeles, living his new life, with his new Los Angeles phone number that she didn't know.

Or perhaps this was the sign that she wasn't ready to talk to him yet, so she flew to London, no one the wiser that she was stowing away an extra passenger in her belly. She saw a doctor twice. An ultrasound told her the baby was growing perfectly.

That made her sway closer to the *keep* side.

So damn close.

But then there was work, and her future, and those things seemed to tug her back to the *give up* side.

Work consumed her in London as the production began. Indecision swamped her nights and gripped her dreams. She and Brent had both wanted kids. They'd talked about having a family, but as a someday-down-the-road possibility. Knowing he'd wanted to though, eventually, was a heavy weight on her. Telling him would kill two birds with one stone—she'd have him back, and she'd have a decision. She could track down his number, call him, and tell him she was pregnant. If she did that she knew that they'd be together again.

He was too good, too upstanding, and too family-centric to ignore his duties.

He'd leave *Late Night Antics* in the blink of an eye, fly to London, and be by her side. As she rehearsed the cast through *Officer Krupke* on the new stage, her fingers itched to track him down again. She could drop this bomb on him, and he'd come running back to her. She desperately wanted him in her life again.

But as the dancers finished, she rewound to the day he'd shattered her heart. She clutched that memory in her hands, like a lifeline to her brain. Somehow, she had to connect her heart to her head. To find the wires, and reattach them properly, so her brain would receive the right message.

Keep the baby. Give up the baby.

One or the other.

She crossed the weeks off on her calendar, but she was no closer to a decision. Week sixteen. Week seventeen. Week eighteen. Week nineteen.

They came and they went. No one knew. She was barely showing. Even so, she snapped a photo of herself in the mirror, as if the reflection could confirm the small curve in her belly.

Michael had an assignment in Europe for a few weeks, and she vowed to decide when he arrived in London to visit her for a couple days. She'd lay it all out for him. Ask for his help. He'd always been her rock. Her guidepost.

They went to dinner at a pub after the theater, and she told him everything, then asked him what to do.

His answer was swift and immediate. He pulled his phone from his pocket and locked eyes with Shannon. "Call the motherfucking bastard. Tell him he knocked you up. And tell him to get his fucking head out of his ass and take care of the mother of his baby and his child. Done," Michael said crisply.

"Oh, that's all?"

"Do it, Shan. Do it," he urged.

"I don't have his number. His cell service is disconnected."

"He works on that late-night show, right?"

She nodded.

"I'll get it for you," he said, and a few phone calls later Michael was writing Brent's new phone number on a cocktail napkin. "Here you go."

She put the napkin in her purse. A weight eased off her. It slid to the dirty, hardwood floor of the pub as Michael knocked back a beer, and she nursed a soda. The decision had been made.

"Tomorrow," she said with a nod, resolute. "I'll call him tomorrow."

It was the first decent night's sleep she'd had since those two pink lines had the audacity to fuck with her life. All she'd wanted was a path. A roadmap. A decision. She had it now.

She woke up early the next morning needing to pee.

The bed was already wet.

Embarrassment washed over her, even though she was alone in her tiny studio apartment. She hadn't wet her bed since she was a child. But when she stood up, it wasn't her bladder that was gushing. It was the water in the baby's sac. A rush of utter helplessness slammed into her, then she rang Michael at his hotel and asked him for help. He called a taxi for her, and told her they'd meet at the nearest hospital. He gave her the name of where to go.

Fear seized her as she buckled the seatbelt, as if that safety measure would somehow protect them both— mother and child. As the cabbie drove her to the foreign hospital—it didn't matter that the doctors there spoke the same language, everything felt foreign—she did what she'd already intended to do that day.

Called Brent.

Her cell phone service routed her to a switchboard, and then sent the call through to Los Angeles. International calls were hard to make directly. Usually only the country codes appeared on the screens. She hoped the London code would tip him off to pick up the call. But he didn't answer. It was the middle of the night in Los Angeles. Then she remembered—it wasn't even after midnight. It was the night before, and his show was on. He was working. Always working. The thing he'd loved more than her. His job.

She hung up.

The tears she'd held back the last few months were unleashed, like a lashing of the windows during a hurricane, like the punishing of a cold storm. Wild and ravaging streams of tears, matching the way her body was once again letting her down. She hated the way she'd lost the ability to dance because of a fluke injury in rehearsal. Hated the way she'd become pregnant when trying not to. And hated the way her body was expelling a baby she didn't know she'd wanted, but would now do anything to keep safe inside her.

She reached the hospital a wet mess.

"Your water's broken, love. There's nothing we can do," the nurse said, her warm British accent almost fooling Shannon into thinking everything was going to be all right. But nothing was all right. Not as she went into labor—did they even call it labor at twenty weeks? It was fast and furious, and it barely hurt her physically. But it tore apart her already-shattered heart an hour later as she delivered a baby boy. Less than one pound. His heart no longer beating. The nurse wrapped her son in a white hospital blanket and handed him to the mother who was no longer a mother.

Her.

That was her.

She was there, but somehow seeing it all through a lens, as if that lens was supposed to protect her from the pain. It didn't. It couldn't. Not even as she watched the scene play out. Not as she sobbed into the blanket, and cried over a life she hadn't even been sure if she was keeping for her own. A life that had stopped sometime in the early morning when she woke up. Or on the cab ride to the hospital. Or on the hospital bed. The nurses and doctor didn't know when the baby had slipped from the living, but it didn't matter. Her water had broken prematurely for unknown reasons. The baby would never have survived. It didn't matter when his tiny heart stopped working.

The only thing that mattered was that the decision had been taken out of her hands.

Michael walked into the room and sat with her as she said goodbye to the son she would never name and never know.

Chapter Seventeen

As soon as she was dressed, Shannon returned to the kitchen. Michael rose, and hugged her.

"I'm sorry, Shannon bean. I didn't mean to get mad at you."

She rested her cheek against his chest. "It's okay. I just want you to respect my choices."

"I know," he said softly.

"Even if you don't agree with them," she added.

He chuckled. "You know me too well."

"I do."

She pulled apart. "I need to put on my makeup and dry my hair. Is the video done?"

He nodded. "It's just compressing. I'll be out of here in a few minutes."

"Thanks for doing that."

"You know I'd do anything for you," he said, tucking a finger under her chin so she looked him in the eyes.

"Duh," she said, playfully. "Tell me something I don't know."

A faint trace of a smile appeared on his lips. Rare for Michael. He was usually so intense, so serious. But the smile was a rueful one. He looked her up and down. "Could you wear a sack instead of that dress? Maybe a paper bag?"

She scoffed. "No such luck."

He sighed heavily. "What time should I pick you up? You only need an hour with him, right? Tell me where to come get you."

"Ha. Ha. Ha. Nice try, buddy."

He parked his hands on her shoulders. "Be careful. I don't want anyone hurting you."

"I know," she said softly. She didn't want that either. Not one bit. Seeing Brent again was like tearing off the protective coating she'd worn for the last decade. Like peeling it off, leaving it in a heap on the floor, and whispering *please don't hurt me.*

"Are you going to tell him? About what happened in London?"

"How do I even say it?" she asked, sinking down to a kitchen chair. "I haven't talked to anyone but you and grandma about it in years."

He took her hands in his, and his touch was comforting, as it always had been. "You just say it. You say *there's something I need to tell you.* And then you get the words out."

Her shoulders rose and fell as she took a big breath. Michael always made things sound so... doable. Surely this was one of those things. She swallowed and parted her lips to speak. *Brent, you were going to be a dad.*

That was as far as she made it in her head before the tears welled up. Michael wrapped his arms around her and comforted her. "It's too hard," she said.

"It is hard. But it's important."

She nodded into his chest. She'd have to find a way. She hadn't expected she'd be at this point so quickly. She hadn't entertained the idea that she'd be facing this hurdle so soon. A dinner here, a few lunches there, and she'd already reached this crossroad, this terrible truth that she had to serve up. But she needed to spend more time with the words. With the right order to say them in. Maybe tonight she could manage it.

She returned to the bathroom, drying her hair as she practiced.

I was pregnant with your baby.

I wanted to tell you. I tried to find you. I didn't know what to do.

Then my body failed me again.

The words were awful, like jagged glass in her mouth. They hurt so much. Too much. The reminders of her failures were overwhelming—her body failed her as a dancer, her body failed her as a mother.

She wanted a night that didn't fucking hurt.

Tomorrow. She'd deal with it tomorrow. Truths like this were best delivered in the morning, right? She could have this evening with him, spend the night together, and then in the morning she'd discover the right words.

In the morning she'd be ready.

As she applied blush and mascara, she focused on locking up the memories so they wouldn't ruin her present for the next few hours. Memories had a way of sneaking up on you, and knocking you down. They could grab you by the throat and throttle you. Images of her father's blood in the driveway, of her mother's screams that night and then again when the detectives came to arrest her, of her own arms wrapped around a tiny person who wouldn't live. Memories could be cruel in their ambushes.

Heartless things.

Reaching for her phone, she opened her picture gallery and found the shot from yesterday. Brent kissing her in the photo booth. Blurry, yet so clear. He was the pain, and he was the protection from it.

* * *

After Michael left, she closed her eyes and practiced one of her yoga techniques. As she raised her arms high above her head in the mountain pose, she imagined clearing her mind of all that hurt, freeing her body from the harshness of all that had gone wrong with it, and returning to the woman she had been before. The woman she used to be with Brent, and still could be. Physical, sexual, connected with him in that way. She felt connected to him in so many ways already, and maybe it was selfish, or maybe it was necessary, but tonight she wanted to be one with her body, not warring with it. Because her heart, mind and body wanted that man again.

As she opened her eyes, she spotted the framed photo of the sunflowers on the kitchen counter. Her way to remember what she'd lost in London. She brushed her fingertips to her lips, then pressed them against the image.

A kiss for the boy who wouldn't be.

* * *

Cool white lobby. Etched glass on the double doors. Sleek blond wood floors and stairs that matched. The kind of stairs that were see-through, that almost seemed to be floating because you could look down and see the floor below. He drank it all in. Her building. Her home. She'd buzzed him in, and he still couldn't believe he was *there*. It was as if he'd gained entry to a secret castle, to the tower at the top of it. Follow this path, take the fork in the road, and climb all the way up. At the top, there she will be.

The woman he wanted.

The *only* woman for him.

The soles of his shoes echoed on the steps as he walked up the three flights to her home, staring left then looking right, inhaling everything. For so long, he'd searched for her. He'd tried to picture her, to imagine her life, her home, and her place in the world.

Right here. He was in it now. Mere feet away from where Shannon Paige-Prince had lived for the last few years. Only a handful of miles away from his home. So damn close, and so incredibly far away. He turned the corner on the next landing, and lifted his foot on the step, then he froze.

He didn't move. He was stuck in a sliver of stalled time.

Michael walked down the stairs. His eyes were razors. His jaw twitched. The sound of the other man's shoes clanged loudly in Brent's ears, snapping him back to attention.

He unfroze.

"Hey, Michael," he said, doing his very best to keep it casual, keep it chill. "Good to see you again."

Brent hadn't spoken to the guy since Michael had helped him get the ring. He hadn't seen Michael since Christmas that same year, when he'd met him, along with Ryan, Colin, and Shannon's grandparents. Brent and Shannon had flown back to Vegas together for the holiday break.

He'd met her family and she'd met his. A few months later, he'd proposed. Her brothers had all liked him.

Didn't need to be a rocket scientist to know the opposite was true now.

Michael's dark eyes raged as he stared at Brent. He raised his left hand, clapped it on Brent's arm. But it wasn't a friendly pat. It didn't speak of years missed. It didn't say *good to see you too, man*. His hand sent another message. *Do not fuck with my family.*

Michael spoke, low, but powerful. Like a hiss. "My sister is one of the most important people in the world to me. I swear," he said, letting his voice trail off like the smoke from a fired gun. Brent parted his lips to say something, anything, but Michael left him no room. This was not a conversation. It was a speech. "If it were up to me, you'd never get close enough to hurt her again. You have no idea what you did to her. You fucking broke her heart—"

He held up a hand. "I know, man. And I am sorry. And I have told her that—"

Michael didn't even acknowledge the words. "And if you do it again, you will know a new kind of hell." Michael's hand moved to Brent's collar. He smoothed it out. Brent's collar didn't need smoothing. "I will not hurt you with fists, because I am not that kind of a man, but I will make sure you are *fucked* in this town. Is that clear?"

Brent shrugged off Michael's hand. As much as he understood where Michael was coming from, he wasn't going to let himself be manhandled.

He raised his chin. "Message is loud and clear, Michael. But I want you to know I'm not the same guy I was ten years ago, and I will do whatever I have to do to prove that to your sister," he said, then paused, because as much as he didn't intend to get pushed around, he also knew he had to show some respect to a man who looked out for his own. "And to you."

Michael didn't answer. He simply stared at him and breathed out hard. He lifted his chin slightly, a nearly imperceptible nod.

"You better," Michael said, then resumed his pace, walking down the stairs, the confrontation over. Each man had said his piece.

Brent cleared the moment from his head and made his way to Shannon's door, knocking twice. When she answered, there was no real estate in his brain for anything but her. He forgot about everything else in the world—schedules, plans, flights? Gone.

"Wow."

He'd never been short of words. Never.

But as he repeated himself, he wasn't sure he'd ever be able to speak again. She knocked the breath from his lungs and stole the words from his tongue. "Wow."

Her eyes sparkled, and she jutted out her hip. The dress she wore had been painted on. The color of champagne, and with some kind of shimmer to the fabric, it hugged her hips, her thighs, her flat belly, and her beautiful breasts. He wished he had been there to watch her slip it on and zip it up. More than that, he hoped he'd be taking it off tonight. Feeling everything underneath. Tasting every inch of her skin. Watching her arch beneath him.

"You like?"

He shook his head. "I love."

He loved everything about her. The dress that was caressing her body. The bare legs boldly on display. The red leather shoes that he'd bought for her.

Most of all, what she'd said about those shoes the other day. *And is this your way of trying to fuck me again?*

Yes. Yes. Yes.

Right now.

Skip the show. Spin her around. Fuck her against the wall.

Wait. No. Spread her on the table. Get those legs of hers where he wanted—up on his shoulders.

She stepped closer to him, ran her hands down the front of his dark blue button-down shirt. Her touch was electric. It torched his blood. It was a bolt of lust slammed through his body. She trailed her fingernails down the buttons on his shirt, and he was sure she was reading his mind, seeing straight through him.

"You look so handsome tonight," she said, and there was softness in her voice, an affection that surprised him, maybe because his mind was so damn focused on the rest of her. On having her body.

But this side, this sweet side...it worked its way through him like a good drug. He wanted this side of her, too. All of her.

"Thank you," he said, once again robbed of quips and wit.

She raised a hand and cupped his cheek. "So damn handsome," she repeated, and that tenderness turned him speechless. There was vulnerability in her voice tonight and he wanted to handle her with care. To shove all this lust and desire aside and give her whatever she wanted, whatever she needed.

He threaded his hands up the back of her hair, letting the soft strands spill all over his fingers. She closed her eyes and sighed contentedly. Oh hell, he stood no chance. He didn't *want* to stand a chance of fighting anything he was feeling for her.

Because he felt everything.

He whispered her name.

She whispered something better. "Kiss me."

He ran the pad of his thumb over her bottom lip. She murmured and melted into his arms. She fit him so perfectly, sliding against him, their bodies like magnets, seeking their opposite, finding their way home.

He kissed her, soft and tender, and he could have gone on all night. Could have kissed her forever. But he wanted to take her to the theater, too. To prove he'd changed. That he could put her first. Ahead of himself.

When he pulled away, he spotted a picture on her kitchen counter, a close-up of sunflowers, lit from the sun with a bright, golden glow around the petals.

He tipped his chin to the image. "Did you take that?"

"I did," she answered without looking at him, as she gathered her purse from the table.

"Didn't know you were into photography."

"I'm not," she said.

In the corner of the photo, he could barely make out the edge of a stone. He was about to ask where she'd taken the picture, but when he turned around she was on the other side of the door, ready and eager to go.

He clasped her hand and walked her down the stairs, leaving her home far behind them.

* * *

It worked. It always worked with Brent. His touch erased the bad. His mere presence made her start to feel good again. To feel happy. To feel hope. She loved who she could be with him. And she wanted to be that woman tonight. Not the woman who'd lost so many pieces of her family, young and old, leaving her with just memories in frames.

Memories she'd have to share soon enough.

For now though, for this second in time, as she slid into the town car with him, she was the woman she wanted to be.

There would be time to say all those things.

Chapter Eighteen

Her mind was officially blown.

She'd seen countless ballets and watched thousands of modern dances, but Alvin Ailey had been her favorite since she was a girl, and also her fantasy. While other dancers dreamed of becoming a prima ballerina, Shannon had pictured herself in a starring role in the Alvin Ailey American Dance Theater. The company's modern ballet style and athleticism had always spoken to her. As a young kid on the outskirts of town, growing up in a broken-down neighborhood, she'd been determined to dance her way out of her circumstances, and to win a spot in a prestigious company.

That had never happened, and while she'd moved on, picked herself up, and carved out a career that she loved, a small piece of her heart still longed to be the one on stage, still wished to captivate an audience as she herself had just been captivated.

As they neared the end of the show, the dancers moved with such passion, such exuberance that her heart was full, overcome with their joy in movement. She squeezed

Brent's hand in the darkened theater. He'd been such a trooper. She knew he wasn't innately a dance fan. Most men weren't. Hell, her own brothers didn't go to the theater with her. And while she doubted Brent had personally delighted in the production, the mere fact that he'd taken her, watched with her, and focused on the stage meant the world to her.

He had stepped up from the second she'd shown up at his club last week to apologize. He hadn't been kidding when he'd said he'd do whatever it took to win her back. He'd been honest, and open, and giving, and everything she'd known him to be. All the more reason for her to lay her cards on the table tonight. Well, tomorrow. Because she was pretty damn sure tonight was going to turn into an all-nighter with him. She had no desire for this date to end. She wanted it to unfurl through the darkness, and roll on into the sunrise.

After the euphoric finale on stage, she was the first to her feet, clapping and calling out *bravo*. Then she threw her arms around Brent's neck, and planted a quick kiss on his lips.

"Thank you. I loved every second of it," she said, standing on tiptoes. "I feel like I'm floating on cloud nine."

A dancer's high.

"I'm so happy to hear that," he said, his expression earnest. There was no teasing, no joking. He really had wanted her to be happy, and hell if that didn't make her heart beat in overdrive for him.

They clapped once more during the final curtain call. She picked up the thread of the conversation as the audience started to shuffle out, the bright lights flickering on in the Luxe Theater. "Even if it did make me feel the tiniest pang of regret right here," she said, tapping her chest.

"I hope it wasn't too hard for you."

She shook her head. "Nope. Just makes me a little sad every now and then that I can't do that anymore. But that's all," she said, as she ran her fingers along his arm. She squeezed his hand as they exited the row, replaying her words—*can't do that anymore.* While she might not be able to dance like those performers on stage had—leaping, stretching, soaring beyond the atmosphere—there were other ways to dance. Oh yes, there were many other ways to move.

She tugged him close to her against the edge of the aisle seat. The crowds filtered by as she leaned in, whispering in his ear. "But I can dance for you. The way you like."

Noise filled the theater. The chatter and hum of the crowd. The music that ushered the patrons out the door. The sound of shoes on carpets, of seats folding up, of phones buzzing. But beneath all that, she heard the sexiest groan escape his lips, a low rumble that came from deep within his chest. It touched down in her nervous system, and sent the desire that had been on a simmer all evening to a flashpoint.

Her pulse doubled. Her belly flipped. Want engulfed her.

"Now," he said, his voice a husk.

"Do you want to come back to my—" she began, but he cut her off.

He produced a gleaming white key card from his back pocket. "I was hopeful," he said, raising an eyebrow.

She adored that hope in him. She adored it for so many reasons. Because he had so much of it, because he could call on it whenever he needed to, and because he'd always freely shared it with her. His brightness, his happiness, his luck.

"Your hope will be rewarded, you handsome man."

She'd take some of his luck tonight and make it theirs.

* * *

The elevator doors whooshed shut.

He was a coil, tightly wound. He grasped her face and kissed her hard as he backed her into the corner, in clear view of the camera that was surely watching anyone in the lift.

He didn't fucking care.

They were alone.

She sighed, she gasped, she moaned as the elevator chugged higher into the sky. Somewhere it slowed and stopped. He glanced briefly at the number pad. Twelve. Not their floor. He returned to her lips, red and full and eager. The doors opened while he fused his mouth to hers, dropping his hand to her ass, gripping her soft flesh, with the kind of hunger that came from knowing there'd be no stopping tonight.

"Um, we'll catch the next one," someone behind him said, and the doors shut again.

"When did you get the room?" she whispered, her voice all breathy and sexy.

"Earlier today," he said, rewinding briefly to his call with Nate. And then, holy shit. *Fuck me with a chainsaw.* The call with Tanner. He heaved a sigh. He'd packed a bag, and tossed it in the trunk of the town car on the way to pick her up, but had promptly forgotten about his flight the second he'd laid eyes on Shannon.

"What's wrong?"

"I have to catch a flight to New York at midnight," he said, frustration laced through every word, stringing them together.

She stepped away, her jaw falling open. "Seriously? It's a quarter after ten right now."

"The call I got earlier in the week when we were at lunch? About the New York club? They had to move the meeting to lunch tomorrow instead of dinner tomorrow, so I have to catch a red-eye tonight instead of a morning flight."

She inhaled sharply. "Brent. We were on a date."

"I thought we could fit everything in."

Her eyes bugged out, and she stared bullets at him as the elevator landed on the twentieth floor. "You thought you could fit it all in? Fit what in? Taking me out? Fucking me? And then flying to New York at midnight? Is that before or after the fucking?"

The doors slid open. She dug her heels in, but he hadn't come this far to have her pissed at him again. "Shan, let's get out of the elevator," he said firmly.

She shook her head. She was like a dog grabbing grass and refusing to walk. Tension twisted in his chest, squeezing his lungs. The last thing he wanted was to fight with her, not when she'd been melting in his arms moments ago. He pressed his finger against the open button, holding it. "C'mon. We can talk in the room."

"We can talk here," she countered, pointing at the floor of the elevator, then at him. "Because I'd really like to know when you were planning on telling me you were cutting our date short."

"It's not like we even made official plans for a sleepover," he said, firing right back at her, his matchstick temper getting the best of him, too.

She narrowed her eyes, turned them into slits. "Oh, excuse me. I didn't realize I had to book you to spend the night with me," she said, puffing out her chest and practically spitting the words at him.

He held out his hands wide. "It's not as if you've been giving me any signs that you wanted to."

She gestured grandly to those red shoes that looked like sex on her. "I guess wearing the goddamn shoes you said you wanted to fuck me in wasn't a big enough sign? Or maybe letting you finger me in front of the fountains last weekend? That wasn't clear enough for you?"

"Those nights all ended," he said, pointing out the flaw in her logic. He pushed hard against the silver button, fighting both with Shannon and the elevator that was starting to beep loudly.

"Looks like this night is about to go the same way then, doesn't it?"

There was no fucking way he was letting her walk away tonight. The blaring grew louder, sounding like a siren. Shannon crossed her arms over her chest, pushing up her breasts, revealing the swell of her curves.

Curves he intended on having his hands on tonight.

His desire fueled him. Instinct led him on, a caveman drive. In a lightning blur, he grabbed her waist, lifted her onto his shoulder easily and carried her out of the elevator just as the doors whisked shut with a final ping.

"Put me down," she shouted, pounding her fists against his back. Marching down the hall, he carried her away from the lift as she banged on him. "I mean it, Brent Nichols."

"I will, woman. I will," he said with a huff, setting her down carefully on her four-inch heels. She didn't even wobble. She was born to wear stilettos. Pressing his palms against the wall above her shoulders, he caged her in. "Look, I forgot to say anything about the change in my flight. It happened this afternoon at four o' fucking clock. This guy is running me around, working me over, and it's not like I *want* to go to New York at midnight."

She shot him a look that said she doubted him. "It's always about work with you."

"I am doing my best to manage it all. I want to spend every damn day with you," he said, his voice hard and firm. "How is it not clear where I want to be right now?"

"Then why are you telling me now?" She sounded like a cross-examiner, punching holes in his argument. "Maybe when you picked me up tonight would have been a better time, not ten seconds before you try to bring me to a hotel room for one frigging hour, Brent. *One hour* before you have to jet out of town. You know how that makes me feel?"

"How does it make you feel?" he asked, dreading the answer.

Mercifully, she didn't say *whore*. "Cheap," she hissed.

"You are not cheap. You are classy, and gorgeous, and beautiful, and why can you not see that I would much rather spend the night worshipping your perfect body, and showing you how much I fucking adore you?" he said, his voice rising again. A door opened down the hall, and a man exited his room. Brent didn't care if anyone heard him saying out loud how crazy he was for this woman. He dropped his hand to her shoulder, trailing the pad of his finger along her skin and down her bare arm. She didn't swat him away, or bite him. That was good. "I meant to tell you that he'd called, and I was all set to say something about the change, but then I showed up at your place, and you looked like this," he said, gesturing to her stunning figure in front of him.

Her lips quirked up. There, in that small crack in her anger, he had his chance. The door was ajar. He'd slink inside.

"Looked like what?" she asked, her tone segueing away from pissed, and towards that teasing seductress he loved.

"Like the only woman I have ever wanted this much," he said, resuming his path along her arm, leaving a trail of goosebumps in his wake. He moved his hand to her waist, tracing circles with his thumb against her hipbone.

"How much?"

"So fucking much it consumes all my brainpower," he said, relief flooding him as she began to relinquish her anger. "I swear, Shan. When I see you, I can't fucking remember my name. I can barely figure out how to form words." Her expression softened, and he inched even closer, pressing his forehead lightly to hers. "You're all I see. You are perfection."

She looped her hands around his waist. Ah, sweet victory.

"I'm sorry," she whispered.

"For what?"

"For getting so pissed," she said, her tone sweet and soft now, wafting over him. "I just hate the thought of this night ending."

"Good. I'm so damn happy you feel that way, because I do, too."

She wrapped her arms tighter around him, tugged him against her in the cool, air-conditioned hallway. "I was looking forward to spending the night with you," she said in the barest voice, and it sent tremors of desire throughout his body. "And when you told me you were leaving, it made me feel like you just didn't care. Like you care about work more than me."

"I care about you so much more," he said.

"Brent," she began, bringing her hands to his hair. "Let's go to the room. I owe you a dance, and I'm going to make it so good for you."

That was music to his ears. And his dick. And his balls.

CHAPTER NINETEEN

Inside the room, she grabbed his shirt and furiously began unbuttoning it. She didn't bother to glance around the room, to take in the surroundings, to comment on the thread count or the mood lighting, or the unparalleled view of the Strip from the floor-to-ceiling glass windows. Nor did he.

He saw nothing but her as they made their way to the couch by the window, where she pushed him down as she finished opening his shirt. She stood in front of him, bent forward, and let her long hair tickle his chest.

Fire burned in his blood. He needed her. Desperately.

"Forgive me," she said. She was up to something. She had that twinkle in her eye.

"You don't need forgiveness," he rasped out as she began to sway, her hips moving seductively side to side. Oh holy hell of a hard-on. She was doing it. She was going to become his fucking fantasy. He loved nothing more than when she did her stripteases.

She trailed her fingernails down his chest. "How about a little music, handsome?"

He grabbed his phone from his pocket, and scrolled through his music at the speed of light. In seconds, Marcy Playground's "Sex and Candy" blasted from his phone.

"Perfect for you, babe," he said as he grasped her hips, and she wagged her index finger, tsking him.

"You know the rules." She spread her palms over his chest. He inhaled deeply, his body rocketing with pleasure at the feel of her touching him. She glided her talented palm over the hard ridge of his erection, setting off fire after fire inside his body.

She was an arsonist. And she was a tease. She took her hand away.

"No. Tell me the rules," he said.

"They're different tonight, since you're leaving in thirty minutes," she said, hiking up her dress and straddling him.

His cock throbbed in his jeans. What he wouldn't give to have her touching him right now. Hands, mouth, pussy —any or all of the above, please.

"What are the rules then?" he asked, breathing erratically as she moved on him, a stripper's dance, grinding and teasing to the music.

"No sex, because I can't bear the thought of you getting on a plane right after. Instead, we're going to play fantasy night," she said, swiveling around. She arched her back, her long hair spilling down her spine. Lust pinballed through him with every succulent move she made, every bump of her ass, every sway of her hips, every press of her against any part of his skin.

"Which fantasy? You're going to need to be a little more specific because I have about twenty million fantasies involving you," he said, holding tight to her hips as she moved up and down on him.

She shifted off him, and he nearly grabbed her and slammed her back down. *Contact.* He needed contact with this red-hot woman who was sending the mercury in him soaring to record highs. But she was running the show. She stood and brushed her hand from her breasts, down her belly, to her thighs. He groaned loudly, his right hand dropping to his erection.

"That one," she answered quickly, eyeing his crotch. "*That* fantasy. The one where you get off to me dancing for you. The one you told me about in your club."

He narrowed his eyes. She couldn't be serious. "You're here with me, and you want me to jack off instead?"

She nodded, and arched a naughty eyebrow. "I want to watch you touch yourself as I dance. I want to witness how turned on you get just from looking at me. I want to know how you've looked for the last ten years when you've lusted for me."

"You're a fucking vixen seductress," he said on a low hum.

"I know, and you love it."

"I do," he said in a hoarse whisper.

"Show me. Show me what I missed. Show me what I would have walked in on if I had come over some night when you were fantasizing about me," she said, her body in synch with every beat of the music.

He motioned for her to come closer. "C'mon. I want your hands on me. I want your lips on me. I want to feel *you.*"

"You will. But right now, give me this," she said in a pleading tone, running her hands along his thighs as she wiggled her ass high in the air. She unsnapped the button of his jeans, and there were no more questions. She was winning. She was having her way. His dick ached with the need to be touched. If he had to do it himself, then that was what he'd do.

He unzipped his jeans, freeing his erection.

The look in her eyes was one for the ages. Her lips parted and she breathed heavily, sighing in admiration as he wrapped his hand around his cock. Finally some relief at last from the throbbing. The chorus of the song built, and she backed away, returning to the center of the room, inching up her skirt, revealing her panties.

Moving. Dancing. Swaying.

So fucking sensual. So incredibly seductive.

Her body was a dream.

Her eyes feasted on him with each thrust of her pelvis, each sway of her hips. The way she gazed at him unleashed tremors of pleasure inside him, knowing she was savoring the sight of his hand on his cock. His fantasy—her stripping for him as he enjoyed the view—was her fantasy too.

He stroked himself, harder, faster, not needing much right now because he was so damn aroused already. She unzipped her dress, letting the straps slide down her arms, then to her waist, revealing those twin globes of gorgeous flesh.

"Bring those beautiful tits to me," he growled out, and she came to him, sinking down on his thigh, rubbing herself on him as she brought her breasts closer. In all the times he'd been with her this go-around, he hadn't seen her breasts, so lush and full. Now, they were on display for him.

"Anything for you," she whispered as she pushed them in his face. His tongue darted out, sampling a rosy peak.

"Mmm," he murmured as he licked her nipple, then drew her deeper into his mouth.

Then, she pulled away from him returning to her dance. "More," she said, tipping her chin to his crotch. "I love watching you."

"Yeah? You like knowing what you did to me when you were gone?" He shuttled his hand harder, working his fist over his dick as he had many times while picturing her. "You like knowing this is how I was? Rock hard and worked up for you?"

"Yes," she said, as she pushed her dress past her hips, showing him the top of her panties. White lacy panties. Blood pounded in his cock as he gripped himself.

"Look what you do to me. You get me so crazy with wanting you. You love turning me on. You move your hips —I'm hard. You walk into the room—I'm ready to take you. God forbid you bend down to pick up something that dropped. You don't even want to know what's going through my head."

"Oh, I do. I do want to know," she said, sliding the dress past her panties, letting it fall on the floor.

His hand tugged harder. His breathing grew unsteady. "Grabbing your hair, pushing you against a chair. Lifting your ass in the air, and sinking deep into your sweet, wet pussy."

It was her turn to moan, a throaty, feminine moan that made his balls tighten. She returned to him, clad only in her panties and the shoes he'd bought for her. "I love watching you touch yourself, knowing you're thinking of fucking me."

"I'm always thinking of fucking you, Shannon," he said, on an upstroke. His spine tingled as she resumed her lap dance, her heat mercilessly close to his dick. He was going to come soon.

All over his hand.

He let go of his grip, and grabbed her hips instead, holding her as she hovered over him. She froze mid-grind. "You stopped," she said, surprised.

He nodded. "I did."

"Why?"

"Because I'm not coming in my motherfucking hand. I'll get on the flight blue-balled and arrive in New York in the morning with a raging hard-on that hurts. But I'm not coming with you for the first time in ten years in my own goddamn hand."

A wicked grin lit up her face. She licked her lips. "We can't have that, can we?"

"No. We can't have that at all."

She leaned in, her breasts pressed to his chest, her mouth on his jaw. "Let me show you how much I've missed you."

"Show me now," he said, and she dropped to her knees and wrapped her lips around him. He groaned so damn loudly from pleasure, from the absolute otherworldly bliss of those lips. She was an angel of mercy tonight. She didn't tease. She didn't lick the tip. She drew him deep, taking him all the way, and he threw back his head and moaned.

"You did miss me," he said, as pleasure ricocheted through him. "Show me how much. Show me how much you missed sucking me."

He laced his hands through her hair, curling his fingers around her head as she bobbed up and down. The friction was intense, as her mouth sucked tight and her tongue became a wicked instrument of carnal pleasure. She was a vision, with her hair spread across his thighs, and her lips full and ripe. Only one thing would make this better right now. *One thing* would make this the blow job of a lifetime.

"You're killing me with your gorgeous mouth, but you need to get undressed now," he said, standing up quickly to strip off his shirt and jeans all the way. "Everything but the shoes."

She shot him a look that said *don't be silly.* "I know you like me to leave my shoes on, Brent," she said, standing up to hook her thumbs in the waistband of her panties, slide them down her legs, and step out of them. She dangled them on one finger in front of him, like a temptation. He grabbed them, brought them to his nose, and inhaled her honey, sexy scent. She smelled like sweet pussy, exactly as she fucking should. He threw them somewhere in the room.

She bent over in front of him, enacting another one of his fantasies. His arm shot out, and he grabbed her hair, and pulled hard. She moaned loudly and raised her head, gazing back at him, her eyes so naughty. The fucking vixen. She knew exactly what she was doing. "Like that?"

"Yes. Just like that. Now get on me," he told her as he lay down on the carpet. "Let me eat your pussy while you suck my dick. The only thing that makes a blow job from you better is when I can taste you at the same time." She obliged, straddling his face, and lowering herself to him as she took him between her lips once more.

His tongue darted out, so eager to taste her, to lick her, to savor her sweet heat. In an instant, she was rocking back into him. This was heaven. Her mouth was gripping his cock, and she was pressed naked on top of him with her delicious pussy in his face, her fantastic ass bobbing up and down. He licked her sweetness, flicking his tongue against her swollen clit. Instantly she cried out, dropping him from her mouth.

He didn't care anymore about his pleasure. All he wanted was her taste. To be smothered in it. To feel her arousal all over his chin, his mouth, his face. She was dripping on him—wetness, glorious fucking wetness everywhere. He was coated in her pleasure, and she fucked his face hard, rocking into him, grinding on him.

He loved the way she moved that gorgeous ass. He needed to touch it. To slap it. He raised his hand and smacked her rear.

"Oh," she cried out, a sexy, needy moan.

He did it again. The same gorgeous sound landed on his ears.

He ran a finger between her wet folds, sliding through her slippery paradise, and she moved faster, pumping like there was no tomorrow. Like there was only this, only this pleasure.

Her wetness was a gift, one that had to be used freely. He had no choice. He simply needed to spread the wealth. To share all this glistening liquid heat. He slid his finger across her folds once more, then pressed his wet fingertip against her bottom as he licked her. She tensed, tightening everywhere, then he slid a finger inside her rear. She screamed his name in pleasure.

She cried out as she tightened all around him, every part of her squeezing, shaking, trembling.

She bucked against his face and his finger, rocking hard and riding out the waves that crashed through her. Her cries rang in his ears like a rock song. She collapsed on him and moaned softly in pleasure.

No time to linger. It was his turn.

He gave her a few seconds before sliding from under her. He stood up. His dick was at attention.

"Get on your knees now and finish me off," he told her, in a clear and direct command.

Her eyes lit up and she obliged, crawling to her knees. She started with her thumb, spreading the drops of liquid around the tip of his cock.

"Take me in deep" he instructed. "Like you did before."

"That's the only way I do it."

"*Remind me.* Remind me how you always drove me wild." He traced his fingertip over her top lip. "I need to own that pretty little mouth of yours right now."

She looked up at him as she wrapped her hand around his shaft, her other hand playing with his balls. "Own me, Brent. You already do."

The head of his dick hit the back of her throat, and he pumped. He gripped her hair, drawing her closer, so she had to take him all the way.

"I can't hold back anymore," he groaned, as he pushed her hair away from her face, giving himself a view of her lips on him. "I'm going to fuck your mouth hard now. Can you handle it, babe?" he asked, as he began. She nodded, and that was all he needed. Permission to take over her mouth completely.

To occupy every inch of her.

This wouldn't last long. Thirty seconds, a minute tops. He was damn near there already.

"You're so fucking beautiful on your knees. So fucking perfect," he said, the words trailing off as his spine ignited, pleasure crackling through his bones as her sexy lips drew him in.

He hit her throat. Another deep thrust, and he was there. "I'm going to come so fucking hard," he whispered, his fingers curling around her skull. Lust slammed into him, tearing through every cell in his body. He closed his eyes, and the world turned black and brilliant.

It was his turn to groan. To shout her name. To throw back his head and grunt in everlasting pleasure as he gave to her what she'd given to him.

His pleasure, for hers.

CHAPTER TWENTY

He hated leaving, detested zipping his jeans, tucking in his shirt, and shoving his wallet in his back pocket. Especially since she was so snug and adorable under the white duvet on the king-size bed. She pulled the covers up to her chin, looking too cute for words. He loved how she could switch from naughty temptress to sweet princess in seconds. "Seeing as you snagged this suite for me, seems a sin to let it go unused," she said.

"You do look comfortable."

She shooed him away. "Go to New York. I'm going to enjoy this fabulous bed all by myself." She sighed contentedly, settling into the plush white pillow.

"You're killing me," he said as he grabbed his phone from the couch, patting his pockets to finish his inventory.

"Oh, I'm sure the plane will be just as nice. The only thing those first class seats will be missing is... *me*," she said, with a wicked glint in her eyes.

He jammed a hand in his hair and walked over to the bed, parking his hands on the side of the mattress. "What I wouldn't give to get in this bed with you right now."

"It's especially nice if you're naked against the sheets," she said, turning on her side, taunting him as the duvet slipped to above her breasts, exposing her bare shoulders.

"What are you doing on Tuesday? I'm back then. Spend the night with me. My first meeting Wednesday isn't till ten in the morning, so I promise I won't cut it short."

"If you don't intend to cut it short, you're going to need to get that fine ass of yours to San Francisco," she said, snaking out a hand from under the covers and grabbing his rear. "I'm there for the on-site rehearsal. At your club. I don't fly back till late Tuesday."

"Mmm," he said, stroking his chin. "I just remembered I need to visit Edge in San Francisco on Tuesday night, and then take you back here with me."

"You don't want to just meet up back here?"

"No. Because I'll leave New York in the morning so I'll see you a few hours sooner if I don't have to wait in Vegas for you to finish and catch your flight."

"Consider that a yes." She smiled broadly. "Get out of here, Nichols. You'll miss your flight."

He bent down and claimed her lips one final time, lingering on her sweet taste, hoping it stayed with him until he could touch her again in a few days.

If anyone had asked him a few weeks ago if he'd ever see the love of his life again, much less kiss her, he'd have given a resounding *no*. Fate had been teaching him a lesson up until then. *Don't walk away from the greatest thing you've ever known, you stupid idiot.*

Fate had been beating that one into his head. Relentlessly. Like water torture.

Then, he'd been granted a reprieve.

He took one last kiss for the road. "I'll see you in San Francisco then."

The little flecks of gold in her emerald eyes nearly sparkled. "When? When will you arrive?"

She sounded so damn eager to see him, too, and for the first time since he'd started chasing her again, he truly felt as if he was close to catching her, wrapping his arms around her, and holding her for always. Maybe she was on the same wavelength, too.

"I'll book my flight as soon as possible. I'll text you the details."

She scrunched up the corner of her lips. "Hmm. I wonder if I should keep making you wait more. For the thing you really want."

He grumbled in protest, then relented. "The thing I want is you. I will wait for you as long as I have to," he said, then took a beat. A pause for effect. "But preferably not much longer."

She laughed. "We'll see what kind of mood I'm in when you get to San Francisco."

"Then it will be my job to get you in the mood to spread those legs, wrap them around my back, and dig in your heels," he said, trailing his fingers between her breasts, savoring the last arch of her back as she responded to his touch.

She looked so vulnerable. So open. So ready for him. She'd given her body to him so freely during the last few weeks. And the more she gave of the physical, the more she seemed to be opening her heart to him again.

As she met his eyes, he was reminded once more of that stay of execution he'd been granted. The amnesty from his past mistakes. He couldn't let her slip away again.

He ran his thumb over her chin, and pressed his finger over her lips. "Don't say anything. It's my turn, and I want to leave you with this. I'm crazy for you. Completely, absolutely, thoroughly crazy about you."

Her eyes glittered, and on that note he walked away.

But this time, he was coming back.

He was leaving having said the right words, instead of the wrong ones. Even though they barely scratched the surface of all he felt for her.

* * *

She wasn't going to listen to his orders not to say anything.

She might have put him through his paces, made him jump through a few hoops, but she wasn't going to let him be the only one of them to take a risk.

He was changing, and hell, so was she.

"Brent!"

He stopped at the door. His hand gripped the knob. He turned to look at her. She read nervousness in his gaze, hope in his stance.

"I feel the same," she said, her heart pounding hard against her chest, trying to leap to him.

With tonight cut off at the knees, now was so clearly not the time to dig deep and tunnel all through the past to the most broken parts of them. But she could start this way— by telling him that she was falling, too. Somehow they'd shifted from him trying to prove himself, to her wanting to show she was worthy of him, too. Worthy of all his affection, of his tender gestures, of his humor, and of his heart.

She knew him well. He was easy. He was simple in the best of ways. All he'd ever wanted was to know her. To understand her past, to help her, to be the one she could lean on. When they were together before, he'd struggled mightily with her need to keep some things buried. While she'd have to find a better time—when they *had* time—to serve up the story of how her life had capsized in a London hospital, she could give him this much tonight—these words, these feelings that had raced well beyond the physical and claimed a portion of her heart.

"I'm crazy for you, too," she added.

Then she let him go, the sound of the door snapping closed sealing off the night. She'd replay it as she drifted off into bed. All of it. From the *wow* to the *crazy for you,* and every toe-curling, heart-beating, blood-pounding moment in between. Even their fight in the elevator. Because some things might change, but some would remain the same.

They were fire.

* * *

She woke up to a text message. A dirty, naughty one that sent a hot shiver through her body.

I can still taste you.

Then a sweet one. *Text me when you wake up, sunshine. I have something for you.*

She wrote back instantly. *I'm up, and glad to hear you enjoyed your dessert last night.*

As she pushed off the covers, his reply arrived. *I could have you for dessert for every meal. Every snack. Every second of every day. You taste spectacular.*

Then Brent texted her that she had an open tab at the Luxe spa to spend the day getting pampered. *Massage, pedicure, hot stones, whatever it is that happens in spas that you like—it's yours today.* That sounded like a fantastic way to spend her Sunday, so she replied, *You win. You've made it impossible not to like you again.*

She hopped in the shower, luxuriating in the hot jets of the rainforest-style showerhead, and replaying the almost-sex with the man she'd wanted to marry. He could bring it. Oh hell, he could bring it every time. There was no B game from Brent Nichols. He fired on all cylinders all the time. A game only.

She turned off the spray, dried her body, reapplied lip gloss, and freshened her breath with the hotel toothpaste. She'd slipped back into last night's dress when she heard a knock on the door.

When she opened it, she revised his grade. Make that A plus game—both in bed and in treating her like a queen.

Because, courtesy of Mr. Nichols, room service was delivering a bowl of fresh blueberries, a serving of steel-cut oatmeal, and a steaming pot of black coffee, one sugar on the side. Her favorite breakfast. Her heart grew wings and soared around the room like an animated bird.

A series of messages rained down on her screen, one right after the other.

The car service will be waiting for you as soon as you're ready to head home.

No woman of mine is cabbing it after I come in her mouth. Hard. Come hard.

Very hard.

Have I mentioned how absolutely divine your lips are?

Off to lunch. I trust your mood for Tuesday is going to be hot and bothered.

As she read them all, a rush of heat spread through her veins, remembering the night before when he'd ordered her to finish him off. She loved that commanding tone he'd used, just as it turned her on to no end when he called her *woman of mine*. She wasn't sure precisely when she'd become his woman again, but after the last two weeks, she felt like his. Which scared her and thrilled her.

In equal measures.

As she left the room, she replied. *Hot, bothered, and well fed, apparently. THANK YOU.*

She'd closed out of her text messages when an idea hit her. Something she could give to him. She leaned against the hallway wall, and found a photo-altering app she used sometimes on her phone. She opened an image from her gallery, added a few details to it, then attached the photo to the thread and sent it off to him.

Then she did something she hadn't done since college.

The walk of shame.

Her stilettos clicked loudly on the sleek gray floor of the lobby as she headed to the elevator bank that would take her to the spa level. She kept her chin up high and strolled through the hotel as if she owned the right to walk through it the morning after in the same dress, same shoes, same earrings, and a new big, fat grin.

Probably everyone there at the Luxe would be able to tell she'd had some seriously hot action last night. Come to think of it, she didn't mind if anyone knew. The after-glow from a great orgasm was a damn good look. She could market a line of skin care products in that style. *O Glow.* She chuckled to herself, making a beeline for the elevators when her cell bleated loudly from her purse. Flipping open her bag, she reached for her phone.

Ryan Sloan.

Her shoulders tensed. She shouldn't feel that way about hearing from her brother, but given their last conversation, she had a hunch what was on his mind.

"Hey Ry," she said.

"Hey. What are you up to?"

She glanced around. Okay, fine. She might not care if strangers thought she looked like a woman who'd gotten some, but her brother didn't need the details of her sex life, which would be obvious if she said she was leaving a hotel.

"I just finished breakfast. What about you?"

"Heading to the gun range for a little practice."

She shuddered involuntarily. Even though she owned one, guns were not on her list of favorite things. Ryan was in the security business though, so he needed to stay sharp.

"Aim carefully," she said, as she leaned against a nearby wall.

"Hey, remember what we talked about at Grandma's?"

"Yeah," she said with a sigh.

"I got some more info. I need to talk to you."

She drew a deep breath, her pulse skittering with nerves. "Tell me."

"Not on the phone. Let's meet up."

She glanced at the time. "You're over at Reiss Range, right?"

"Should be there for an hour."

That gave her enough time to change into something simpler. Something that wouldn't scream that she'd been licked senseless the previous night. Because whatever Ryan needed to tell her did not necessitate her wearing fuck-me shoes.

"I'll be there."

She dialed the car service number Brent had left for her. The driver told her he'd be there in five minutes.

So much for the spa. She couldn't relax now if she'd wanted to.

Soon, she slipped into the town car, savoring the cool air, and the final few moments of this cocoon—the morning-after moments, as she floated down from her high from last night. Any minute, her feet would touch the cold, hard ground again.

CHAPTER TWENTY-ONE

The head of the neighborhood association was a certified fanboy.

Alan Hughes knew all of Brent's dirtiest and filthiest bits by heart.

As he held up his fork, preparing to dive back into his steak, the man who stood between Brent and the Big Apple expansion recited more lines from memory. Ordinarily, the entertainer in him would be thrilled to have someone repeating his lines. But Brent was no fool. He knew the polo-shirt and khakis wearing, forty-something father of two tween girls wasn't quoting him to suck up at this lunchtime meeting at McCoy's over prime rib and problems.

Brent fixed on a closed-mouth smile as Alan Hughes waxed on from a comedy bit deemed too crude for his late-night show. This joke had only appeared online. Brent tensed, knowing what was coming next.

Alan punctuated the finale with a stab of his utensil in the air. "And that's why you should never shave your own balls."

The joke had been beloved by twenty-something guys. Dudes had gone ape-shit over some of Brent's bits. That one had earned him some serious guy cred online. Trouble was, that was exactly the opposite of the crowd he needed to impress now. Though Alan lived in Tribeca with his wife and two daughters, the man screamed suburbs, which meant he was the kind of guy trying to turn the city into a quiet, calm hamlet at night.

Alan pointed to himself. "Don't get me wrong. I'm a huge fan of *Jackass* and that kind of humor. I love the whole filthy, dirty, late-night Comedy Nation style. I watch it myself when the wife and kids are in bed. The problem is, you're not trying to win guys like me over."

Brent nodded. "Got it. And I'm glad you liked it. But talk to me about who I need to win over, Alan. Tell me what you see in your neighborhood," he said, inviting the guy into the conversation, letting him know he cared. Sealing the deal on New York was vital to Brent's plans, so he had to play ball. New York was mission critical for Edge, but he also didn't want to let down his friend Bob. He wanted to come through for him with the gig as manager of the club, delivering for the man who'd given him some of his biggest breaks.

But first, he had to deliver for others.

"Everyone else," Alan said crisply. "The moms. The stroller moms. The soccer moms. The—"

"The moms," Tanner barked, his coarse voice grating on Brent. He slammed his palm against the table at McCoy's. It shook. "*All the moms.*"

Brent nodded several times, then kept his tone light. "Call me crazy, but I'm getting the sense you're saying... the moms don't like me."

"Sorry to bear bad news, but they don't right now," Alan said, hanging his head. The guy truly did seem sorry.

"What can I do to win them over, Alan?"

Alan clucked his tongue. "It won't be easy. How can we say you run a classy joint when you have this kind of history? You were the bad boy of comedy. That's what your own network called you."

"They did. But let's be frank here. I wasn't some criminal. They called me that because I had a foul mouth on stage. Because I had ink on my arms. Because it was part of a character." Brent held open his palms. *Nothing to hide here.* "But at the end of the day, I was just a comedian, telling some dirty jokes. Let's move on." He tapped the table with his index finger. "Talk to me, Alan. Tell what I need to do to convince your neighborhood that I can be good for business."

Alan nodded, and held up a glass. "I like you. You're a straight shooter. So I'm going to be straight with you. You need to meet the people in the neighborhood. You need to be charming. You need to show them you're not just the guy who tells filthy jokes that Axe Spray-wearing douche-canoes watch while smoking bongs."

"I can do that. And I never use Axe body spray, so there you go."

Alan chuckled again. "See? I knew you'd make me laugh."

But laughter wasn't enough. That was Brent's stock in trade in his twenties. He'd spun laughter into gold on stage. He'd parlayed jokes into a career, moving up the ladder with each chuckle, each laugh, and each hearty guffaw. They'd fed him and made him wealthy. Now, he'd pivoted. He was reinventing himself as a businessman, and in some ways he was starting at the ground floor. He had to prove he was trustworthy, that he was reliable, and that he was worth betting on when it came to this new playground he was playing in.

Playground.

So bizarre that his days of ball-shaving and first-date waxing had been replaced by playground makeovers. Brent saw a bigger opportunity. "Don't know if Tanner told you, but I've donated some money to have some of the parks revamped in Tribeca. Happy to go further. Build a playground, too. You think the moms will like that?"

Alan nodded approvingly. "Moms love playgrounds. The only thing they'd love more would be a coffee shop in a playground," he said, and now it was Brent's turn to laugh. "Anyway, that's a nice start. And we can build on that. This is what I'm thinking. We've got a big picnic coming up in the park. Fundraiser for some neighborhood services. Let's have you at the picnic. You could come by earlier in the day and say hello. Talk to them. Let them know you're a family guy at heart. Mention your brother and his wife. Mention your mom. Your dad. Don't talk up the Vegas roots, or the comedy. I know you're not married, but is there any chance you have a pregnant fiancée or something like that? If you did, that'd be a nice slam dunk," Alan said, miming stuffing a basketball through the net.

Brent laughed deeply, and shook his head. "Nope. I'm not opposed to either, but I don't have a woman in the family way."

"That's okay. I'm sure you've got plans to have a big family some day soon since you love kids, right?" Alan said, in a leading-the-witness tone.

Brent nodded. He got Alan's drift. He got it loud and clear.

* * *

"Let me see if I got this straight. The neighborhood association only wants to approve your plans to move Edge into the space if you seem less like the guy you were on TV and more like a clean-cut family guy. So you want my daughter—my precious angel princess—to be your prop?"

Clay raised an eyebrow as he pushed Carly lightly in a bucket swing in a park in Greenwich Village. The one-year-old giggled and kicked her feet.

"*My niece* who adores her uncle," he said, stepping in to push the sweetie-pie and elbowing Clay aside.

"Watch it there. That's my baby girl."

"And she's the sweetest, cutest, most adorable baby in the universe," he said, and Carly leaned back to smile at Brent. He cooed at her and made animal sounds. First a monkey, then a duck, then a chicken, and Carly scrunched her baby cheeks and laughed, the kind of infectious laughter only a child possesses. He shot Clay a sharp-eyed stare. "Told you so. She loves her uncle."

Like a hawk, Clay swooped in and rescued his daughter from the swing, cradling her against his chest. "Clearly, she's suffering from temporary insanity. I better get her to the pediatrician right away."

Later, as they walked through the Village, the baby strapped to her father in a Baby Björn, his big brother relented. "Obviously, you can bring her to the picnic. I'll just be the guy hanging by the fence, watching my kid. Ready to grab her if I need to."

Brent clapped him on the back. "Excellent. I knew eventually you'd be good for something."

"Or maybe I won't be so generous," Clay said as they neared a bustling coffee shop, spilling over with Sunday afternoon foot traffic.

"Nah. I have faith in your generosity. And I have faith in caffeine, which I need right now. Red-eye and all," Brent said, pointing to the shop. "My treat."

Clay shook his head, and crossed one finger over another, as if he were warding off evil spirits in the cafe. "Not that one. That shop has bad luck written all over it. That's where Julia practically had my head when she found out I'd done something she wished she knew about sooner."

"I've told you, man," Brent said, because he was privy to the details of what had nearly split up the two of them before their happy ending, back when Julia had been in trouble with the mob, saddled with debt owed by an ex. "You need to be upfront with women. Just in general. Look at me. I'm a goddamn open book."

Clay stopped in his tracks, scratching his head. "Wait. I'm sorry. Did I hear that right? You're trying to give me relationship advice?" he asked, rubbing his thumb against his wedding band.

"Whatever, man. All I'm saying is women want you to lay it all out for them. Be open. You know that. Secrets are almost what ripped you and Julia apart."

His brother nodded seriously as they resumed their hunt for coffee. "That they did, man. That they did. And I learned my lesson."

"You ever hear from that guy? Charlie? The one she was forced to play poker for?"

"He called me once," Clay said as they reached the corner and stopped to wait for a walk sign. A cab blew past them on the street, and a pack of Sunday afternoon runners whipped by on the cobbled sidewalk.

"What did he want?"

"Tried to get me to come work for him. Said he needed a good lawyer."

Brent scoffed. "I bet he does. Mob bosses always need someone to bend the rules for them. What'd you say?"

Clay's mouth twitched in a smile and he spoke in a wry tone. "I told him that my client list was full. But I appreciated the offer. Always be a gentleman with men like him. You never know when they're going to reappear, and you need to make sure you haven't pissed them off."

"And you didn't piss him off, I trust?"

Clay adopted a *who me* look. "I never piss anyone off. But you? You're another story. If memory serves, you were pretty skilled in pissing off Shannon back in the day. You learned your lesson on that front? You're treating her well now?"

Brent flashed back to last night and Shannon's cries of ecstasy. To the past week, and how her eyes lit up with happiness over their lunches. To the sadness he saw in them, too, when she shared all her fears. All of it. Everything. He desperately wanted to be the man to make her happy. To give her hope.

"Like a queen," he said. "Like a queen."

"Excellent. That's the only way to treat a woman."

CHAPTER TWENTY-TWO

Shannon crossed her arms and watched her brother mow down targets with clockwork precision. Huge earphones covered Ryan's head, muffling out sound as he fired with one hand. A sure shot. She knew how to fire, too, though she rarely did. She owned a sub-compact Glock 42 that Ryan had bought her when she moved back to Vegas.

"It's your housewarming present," he'd remarked when he took her to the gun store.

"You afraid the Royal Sinners are coming for me?" she asked, joking but not joking.

He'd squeezed her shoulders reassuringly. "They're not coming for you. But you never know who is." He'd filled out the paperwork, plunked down his credit card, then handed her the weapon and said, "Welcome home."

Then he'd taught her how to handle a gun.

Sometimes she joined him at Reiss, sharing his intensity of focus, his cold concentration. Other times, she wished she'd never learned to shoot, never imagined that she might need to. Even if you were skilled in how to shoot, a gun couldn't always save you. In fact, it probably *wouldn't* save you. If her father had carried a gun, he'd still be dead. He'd been shot in the back, and never saw it coming.

Guns were useless when someone put a price tag on your head.

Ryan took aim at another black and white cardboard cutout. Shannon counted off in her head with each bullet.

One target. Two targets. Three targets. Now, four. Now, five. Absently, she crossed her fingers, hoping for a perfect six. Random, but that was the number she picked.

He landed the last one. Straight down the middle. He lowered his arm, his revolver solidly in his right palm. After he tugged off the earphones and goggles, he turned around, and flashed her a bright smile. He blew on the end of the gun, and winked.

Show off, she mouthed, watching him from just outside.

He waved her into his lane, gesturing for her to join him. "You hit half of what I did, I'll buy you lunch," he said.

She rolled her eyes, but accepted the challenge. He positioned the earphones over her head, placed the goggles on her eyes, and set the Smith & Wesson in her palm. She planted her feet wide, peered down the lane, and raised both hands, keeping the weapon steady, solid against her flesh. She peered at the target at the end of the range, a black and white sketch of a body with a bulls-eye on his chest.

She tried not to think of Stefano ending her father's life. But that trick never worked. She *always* pictured that man, that street thug, that fucking scum who took a job from her mother.

That killer.

If she didn't see Stefano at the end of the barrel she'd imagine her mom. She couldn't go there. She couldn't live in that land of hate for the woman who'd raised her, taken care of her, kissed her goodnight. If she pictured her mom, she'd be just the same as her.

Her hate was reserved for the triggerman. For the man who had shed her father's blood. Her jaw tightened, and she watched the reel. Each unlived moment played before her eyes. Her father would never know where she'd gone to college, what she did for a living, if she was happy, if she was in love. He'd never walk her down the aisle, and he'd never tuck his grandchildren into bed or take them to the park.

He'd never enjoy a day of fishing as a retired man—his dream.

He'd never celebrate his fiftieth birthday. He was eternally thirty-six, and always would be.

He'd never grow old.

They took that all away from him.

From her.

From her grandparents.

From her brothers.

Her teeth were clenched, her lips were a tightrope, and her hands belonged to a surgeon. Steady, practiced, perfect.

She fired three shots to the heart.

Adrenaline surged through her, lighting up her bloodstream with wild energy. She could lift a car, fight a man twice her size, or run down any enemy. Her chest rose and fell; her fingertips tingled. Then those endorphins were chased with a dose of red-hot anger, with the madness that comes from the black hole of loss.

She pressed her fingertip to the trigger, wanting, wishing, eager. Itching to fire again.

Before the anger consumed her, she lowered the gun. She handed it to Ryan. "I'm not hungry."

Minutes later, they sat in his car in the parking lot. The engine was off. The radio was on. The National, Ryan's favorite band, crooned about missing the one you love. Such a moody song. Fitting, too.

"What's the story?" she asked, cutting to the chase. "Is Stefano facing more charges?"

Ryan shot her a quizzical look. "No. Or not that I know of."

She rolled her hands, as if to jog his memory. "You told me your friend in the DA's office said he visited Stefano in prison about other crimes or something."

"Right, but even so, that won't change his sentence."

"I know that," she said, but then she realized—Ryan hadn't called her to discuss the latest news about the shooter. "So *this*," she said gesturing from him to her, "isn't about Stefano?"

"No," he said, forming an *O* with his mouth. "Not at all. It's about someone else. I talked to Mom."

* * *

His sister's jaw dropped. Ryan hadn't intended to shock her, but the evidence was on her face.

"She called you?" she whispered, as if she couldn't quite wrap her mind around the concept of the phone, and how people used it to stay in touch.

He nodded and scanned the parking lot through the window to make sure they were alone. No one was wandering around. He turned up the music a little more, just in case. Ryan had always believed it was best to have these kinds of conversations in person, with plenty of background noise. He'd learned to keep certain aspects of his life completely untraceable. "She called me collect the other night. She told me her lawyer came to see her."

Her eyes widened. "The same one who represented her at trial?"

He shook his head. "Nope. That guy is long gone. He went into private practice. But, the guy who came to see her is also a public defender. She said she contacted him and he went to Hawthorne."

She cleared her throat and swallowed, then spoke in a clipped, controlled voice. "What does she have to talk to a lawyer about? Is she trying again to get them to re-open the case? Is she rehashing the details over and over like the last time we saw her? The evidence against her? The phone records showing she *repeatedly* called Jerry Stefano for two months before the murder?" Shannon said, smacking the side of one hand against the other for emphasis. "The lies she told about those calls were ludicrous. The prosecution saw right through them. She couldn't even come up with a decent reason for all the calls."

He knew why his mom had lied about her calls with Stefano. The truth would have made her look guiltier. She'd gambled and lost. The lies she'd told to the prosecution didn't do the trick, but honesty would have tethered her more closely to Stefano and his Royal Sinners.

Rock and a hard place.

He knew some of those truths. She'd shared them with him, begged for his help, and he'd kept them locked up in his head. He'd never uttered a word of them. He'd learned that the best way to protect a secret was to never tell it. Seal your mouth, zip it shut, and don't breathe a word. That was the one guaranteed method, and Ryan Sloan kept secrets like a champion.

But he hadn't asked his sister to meet him so they could revisit the chain of evidence that had landed their mother behind bars. He'd called Shannon because she was the only one of his siblings who hadn't closed the door on their mom. He needed strength in numbers even if that number was two.

"Mom and I didn't talk about the phone calls with Stefano," Ryan said.

"So why did she see a lawyer?"

"She said she'll tell us in person when we come see her."

Shannon held out her hands in frustration. "See? She can't even tell you why she's talking to a lawyer. She's manipulating us into seeing her."

"She's our goddamn mother!"

"I know," Shannon hissed, and pointed two fingers back at her eyes. "I damn well know. I look in the mirror every day and see her eyes. I have her eyes. I have her goddamn cheekbones and chin, too."

"And you have nice eyes, so just focus on that. And besides, maybe it's the kind of thing she needs to tell us in person. Maybe it's important," he said softly, but in a firm voice that brooked no argument. "We need to find out what's up. End of the month. Her hours were cut, but she gets her final two hours the last day of June. We need to plan for it. Take the day, because it's an all-day thing to get to Hawthorne in the middle of god-knows-nowhere. No excuses."

She shoved her hand through her hair, yanking it back into a ponytail. "Why are you so determined to believe she might be innocent?"

His lips parted, but he took his time. His mother wasn't an innocent woman, not by any stretch of the law. She might not even be a good person. But he believed that there was a difference between the things she'd done, and the things the district attorney had said she'd done.

"Because we need to be certain."

She closed her eyes, as if the conversation pained her. Hell, it pained him. When she opened them, the look in them was one of defeat. Even so, she nodded. "I'll go with you."

"Good. I need you there," he said, and flashed a small smile.

"Now there's something I need to tell you, and if you so much as pull a big brother act, you will go alone. Is that clear?"

"Crystal."

Then, she told him she was seeing her ex again, and even though he wanted to slug the guy for having hurt her, he understood what it was like to be unable to let go of something.

* * *

She cranked up the volume on "You're the One That I Want" on the radio in her cherry red BMW as she drove home. She needed the upbeat, dancey number to reset her mind. Belting out the celebratory tune as she turned onto her street, she let the lyrics fill the hollow and angry space between the conversation with Ryan and the rest of her day.

The music was her buffer, and as she sang, she choreographed the number in her head, the dance and the movement ushering the hard kernel out of her heart. Dance had always been a way through tough times for her. Today she would lean on it even more. She had a plan for the rest of the afternoon. She'd review the video from the Edge rehearsal, take notes and tweak here and there, then that evening she'd work with her dancers.

Tomorrow, she was off to San Francisco.

Tuesday Brent would join her briefly.

Wednesday afternoon she had to fly to L.A. with Colin to meet with the reality show producers.

The busy week would keep her focus off her mom.

As she flipped her right blinker to descend into the condo's parking lot, she spotted a car she'd never seen before parked outside the gate. A Buick. She was used to Audis, BMWs, SUVs, hybrids, Mini Coopers, and plenty of electric cars at her building. This vehicle was the answer in a *which one of these things doesn't belong* game. Buicks weren't common cars. They were old. They were hand-me-downs. Though she hadn't memorized the rides of all her condo mates, she was sure she'd have remembered this earthy brown vehicle that hailed from days gone by.

She didn't remember it.

A young guy in jeans, boots and a worn black T-shirt leaned against the trunk of the car, his elbows resting on the metal, smoking a cigarette.

He was doing nothing wrong. *Technically.*

But cars didn't park by the gate. Young guys didn't smoke and wait by her building. He didn't look familiar at all. But Stefano probably hadn't looked familiar to her dad either. Her spine crawled.

Better safe than sorry.

She heeded the warning bell. The automatic gate rose for her as it picked up on the transponder in her car that gave her access. Rather than slide into her regular parking spot in the garage—a garage that someone could easily enter by foot—she made a loop around the cars on the first level and exited on the other side.

The guy was still there. She couldn't tell if he was watching her, or just waiting.

But that was precisely why she left.

By the time she slowed to a stop at a red light, her heart was hammering in her chest, and her hands were clammy.

Soon, she found herself at her studio, and she locked the door behind her, then bolted it. She spent the next few hours working before she tried again to go home.

When she reached the gate to her building, the Buick and the guy were gone.

CHAPTER TWENTY-THREE

He unknotted his green, striped tie and tossed it on the king size bed. Making quick work of the buttons on his crisp white shirt, he stripped that off next, grateful to be rid of it. He grabbed his phone, scrolled to his messages, and clicked open the photo Shannon had sent him earlier.

Best part of the day. Hands down.

Brent lay back in the hotel bed at The Pierson in midtown, and ran his thumb over the picture she'd snapped at the photo booth on Friday afternoon. She'd added a bushy black mustache to his face, and planted a purple wig on her own head. Rudimentary photo work, but he loved it all the more. His lips curved into a grin as he stared at the two of them and her comical additions to the picture.

He ran his fingertip across her face. Even in a silly shot like this, she was beautiful to him. He dropped his head onto the pillow. "I'm so fucked," he muttered.

He was more than crazy about her. He was completely under her spell, hypnotized, and he never wanted it to end. It hadn't taken much for him to fall back under. He was nearly there before he'd even started seeing her again. But then she did things like *this*—things that were so goofy, so silly, and so utterly *them*. Things that made him want to hold on tight and never let go.

Out of the corner of his eye, he caught a glimpse of pink and purple on his bicep. The tattoo she'd given him was still there.

He called her.

"Hey," she said softly when she answered on the second ring.

"Hey you. Guess what I just learned?" he said, as if he had a big surprise.

"What did you learn?" she said in an instantly playful tone.

"Those temporary tattoos last at least two days."

She laughed. "Admit it. You just haven't showered since Friday."

He heaved an exaggerated sigh. "You're right. It's because I couldn't bear to wash off the scent of you lusting over me."

She cracked up. "You're ridiculous."

"And so is this mustache you gave me. Remind me to never ever grow one because I look stupid as hell like this. You, on the other hand, are hot in a purple wig."

"Why thank you. I do have mad Photoshop skills, don't I?"

"Could be another career path for you," he said, parking his free hand behind his head, thinking how fucking epic it was to slide right back into this kind of chatter with his woman. He savored the kind of easy connection they had. It was part and parcel of why he'd fallen so quickly for her in college, and why he'd been absolutely certain he wanted to spend the rest of his life with her.

They clicked.

On every level.

In every single way.

"How was your day?" she asked, and it was such a simple question, such a *couple* question, and it made his heart nearly trip out of his chest. "How did the meeting go?"

The fact that she asked about work, especially since his work had come between them before—hell, it came between them last night—meant the world to him. He recounted his meeting with Alan, from the guy's admiration for the ball-shaving bit all the way to the fiancée comment. "If I showed up at this picnic with a pregnant woman or a baby in tow, I'd be a slam dunk," he said, with a laugh.

He was met with silence on the other end of the phone.

Dead silence. Shit. Maybe he was pushing things too far by even saying something that suggested babies, or pregnancy, or being more serious than they were. He sat up straight. "You still there, Shan?"

"Sorry," she said in a quiet voice, sounding strained. Her reaction didn't compute for him, but then he didn't have the benefit of looking her in the eyes. Besides, it was a weird comment from Alan. "Sorry they're giving you such a hard time," she added.

He settled into the soft covers on the bed. "Yeah, but what can you do? I need New York. The location is perfect, and New York is the centerpiece of our expansion plans. I just have to jump through his hoops."

"It's silly what they're focusing on. Like, that's what makes a difference in whether they approve you," she said harshly, now switching from the odd distance of a minute ago to a controlled anger. "It's your character. It's who you are. It's how you treat people. That's what matters. Not whether you have children or a wife, or whether you swear or don't swear. Or tell jokes about everything that goes wrong with shaving your balls."

"Couldn't agree more, but I need to play their game."

"Well, for what it's worth, I'm not a twenty-something guy, obviously, and I happened to think that joke was epic," she said.

His ears perked. "You did? That bit was two years ago. I didn't think you'd seen it."

Her voice turned flirty. "I might have caught up on some of your greatest hits recently. You've always cracked me up."

Pride suffused him. He'd made millions laugh, but she was the one whose laugher he craved the most. "That's awesome. I love that you have a dirty sense of humor."

"Like a twenty-something guy," she said. "Though, I'm especially glad that it's just a joke. Because you'd look silly with a Mohawk down there."

A grin spread across his face. "See? I'm telling you. You can't shave your own balls or you wind up with a comb-over or a Mr. T style 'do, and neither one is attractive," he said, and there it was—the sweet sound of her laughing once more. "So what about you? Did you spend the day getting pampered at the Luxe?"

She sighed, and in that wistful sound he sensed her *no* before she even said it. "I really wanted to, but Ryan called, and I had to see him, because…" She stopped to take another breath. "We need to visit my mom at the end of the month."

He sat up straight, pressed the phone more firmly to his ear as if that would bring him closer to her. He felt like a schmuck for having bitched about something as small as whether the neighborhood association liked him. "Tell me more."

* * *

She gave Brent the details as she paced around her kitchen table, her edginess returning.

"Why do you think she saw a lawyer?"

"I have no idea. Brent, she's crazy. Prison made her crazy," she said, as she stopped at the fridge and found an open bottle of chardonnay.

"I can't even imagine. It must be awful."

She poured half a glass. "It's gotten worse in the last few years. She wasn't like this before, though, when I first knew you. She was more together. She's become more..." Her voice trailed off as she struggled for the words to describe her mother. Dora had been a passionate and desperate woman when Shannon was younger, desperate to achieve more than the little she'd had. Once she was locked up, all that passion churned into something else—an anxious, dangerous determination, a rattled desire for freedom.

Shannon picked up her wine and took a sip. "More un-stable, but obsessive too. She's always trying to get people to listen to her. I bet she's contacting the Innocence Project. She'd do that. She'd spend her time getting up to speed on prisoner rights and wrongful convictions. She's convinced she's not supposed to be behind bars."

"Have you ever thought she shouldn't be?" he asked, a softness to his tone. She could tell he wasn't suggesting Dora was innocent, as Ryan often did. He was simply ask-ing what she believed.

"The evidence against her is pretty compelling. I know the truth. I'm sure of it, but she's still my mom, and she's still in prison," she said, heading to her yellow couch, the kind of bright yellow that made the room feel cheery, in contrast to Shannon's mood right now. "But I'll go anyway. Ryan needs me. He's always been caught up in her orbit. I need to go with him."

"I'll go with you if you want."

His words surprised her. She hadn't been expecting that. No one had ever offered to be a part of this side of her life. Then again, she'd never gotten close enough to anyone to let him or her in this far. "What?" she asked, incredulous.

"I'll go with you," he said, again, making it sound so simple. "If you want me to. I know it can't be easy. Let me be there for you."

Her mood switched in an instant, as she shrugged off the dark and heavy cloak of the day. "You're amazing. It's five hours away though."

He laughed. "I'm not afraid of a little car time. Especially if it means I can be with you."

"You can't go in though, to see her. Only pre-approved visitors like family and friends she knew before she was in prison are allowed."

"I'm not going to see her. I'm going to be there for you. I'll drive you. I'll wait for you in the parking lot or waiting room or wherever. Wait—do they even have waiting rooms in prison?"

She chuckled lightly. Only Brent could make her laugh about this. "Oddly enough, they do," she said, then let her mind imagine how much better it would be to have him waiting for her when she was done. "Brent," she said, speaking softly as she settled into the couch, "why do you do so much for me?"

"Why do I do so much for you?" he repeated, as if her words didn't make sense. "What do you mean?"

"Does it ever bother you that you've had such a normal life and I have this... *crazy* one? I have so much baggage, and you have none."

"Baggage doesn't scare me."

"It doesn't bother you that my family is so messed up?" she asked, because it bugged her. "It's so uneven between us. I mean, you just offered to take me to visit my mother in prison, who's behind bars for murdering my father for money. Meanwhile, you bake pumpkin pie for your parents every year at Thanksgiving. What could I possibly ever do for you?"

He scoffed loudly. "You have no idea what you do for me."

"Then tell me. I can't even imagine what I could ever do that would compare."

"First of all, it doesn't have to compare. You send me a selfie of us and I'm fucking ecstatic," he said, and his voice was filled with sincerity that made her heart beat faster. He was the easiest person to please, and she loved that about him. "Think of me like a cactus. I don't require much. A little water, some sun, I'm good."

"I've often thought of you as my sunflower, but cactus works too," she said, as a smile spread across her face. "I guess that means I'm a hibiscus. They need a *ton* of water."

"That's why we're right for each other," he said, and she wished she were with him right now, to see his face, to touch his cheek, to kiss those lips that said words that made her feel so much joy.

"But sometimes I worry that I don't have enough to give," she said, voicing her deepest concerns. That no matter what, she would always be the one needing him more than he ever needed her. "That all I'm doing is taking because I need so much. That you'll resent me."

"Don't you realize? I want to give what I have to you. I'm lucky. I know that. I have an overflow of luck, happiness, all that stuff. And yeah, I don't have family issues, but what I have instead is the ability to be by your side as you deal with yours."

Her heart leapt. It twirled, it skipped, it tried to jump across the country and find him in New York City. "What can I give you though?" Her voice rose with worry. She didn't want to lose him again, and she feared that all this crap in her life would be too much. Especially since there was more to come. More confessions, more secrets still to be shared.

"All I want is you. Give me you," he said, and his words warmed her from the tips of her toes to the ends of her hair.

Later. She'd deal with the rest later. "You can have me."

"Good. Now tell me what you're up to right now. Right this second. I want to picture you."

She carved out a deeper spot in her living room couch, making herself comfortable, not wanting the conversation with him to end. "Just lying here on my couch, glass of white wine in my hand, talking to the most handsome man I've ever known," she said, taking a swallow of the chardonnay, then setting down the glass on the coffee table.

"Oh yeah? Sounds like you've got it bad for this guy."

Shannon turned on her side, perhaps subconsciously shifting into an even sexier pose, picturing Brent's eyes roaming her body as if he were there, his gaze holding her captive. "I tried to shut him out, but it was impossible. He's pretty much the cat's meow."

"What's he like? This guy you're into?"

She closed her eyes, seeing him perfectly. "He's gorgeous, he makes me laugh, he loves showering me with gifts, he has a matchstick temper—"

"Hey, now."

"And he's this totally sexy nightclub owner." She was keenly aware that she was using his current job, focusing on the man he was now. Not who he used to be.

Brent played along, his deep, gravelly voice sending a charge through her as he spoke. "Sounds like this guy rocks your world. In more ways than one. Is he good in bed, too?"

"Oh, yes. He owns my body. He's always known what to do to me."

"What would he be doing to you right now? Kissing your neck, tugging on your hair, doing little things that get you all revved up for him?"

A gentle pulse beat between her legs as he began turning her on. "Kissing me all over. Making me want more."

"I bet he'd tease you. Drive you wild. Work his way up and down those sexy legs of yours, all the way to your ankles."

"He loves my ankles. Loves them in high heels."

"Bet he makes you leave them on, because it turns him on."

"He does," she said, in a purr.

"Right now, I have a hunch he'd be getting you so worked up you'd breathe hard, and your knees would fall wide open for him," he said, as if he were laying out the roadmap to her body. Her skin heated up, and that gentle pulse turned into an exquisite ache between her legs.

She let the blanket fall off her. She opened her legs. And she stopped talking about the two of them in the third person. "I wish you were here right now, Brent," she said as she unzipped her jeans and pushed them down to her knees.

He groaned, a deep, throaty rumble that gave away all his desire, too. "I want that so much. I want you so much."

"I want you even more than I did before. It's crazy how much I want you," she said, wriggling on the couch as she dropped her hand inside her panties. Her fingers slid easily between her legs, to the wetness waiting for her touch. A fresh wave of heat raced across her skin as she touched herself, gliding her fingers through all that hot desire for him.

"I don't even know how to get through the next thirty-six hours till I can have my hands on you," he said, huskily. "I have to have you again."

"You will have me. I want you to have me. All of me," she said, her breathing speeding up, her voice turning feathery. Her body tingled everywhere.

"Where is your hand right now?"

She closed her eyes and stroked her slick heat. She moaned as her fingers rubbed her swollen clit. "Between my legs. Where I want you to be."

"Fuck," he hissed. "Are they spread for me? So I can prop them up on my shoulders and take you deep?"

A rush of heat swooped through her. "Yes. I love it when you do that." She let her knees fall open wider. "You can take me any way you want."

His voice turned dirtier, harsher. "I'd like to flip you over. Put you on your hands and knees. Watch you raise that perfect fucking ass for me. Slide into you. Bury myself in you."

She could hear his breath growing faster. "Is your hand on your dick?"

"I'm doing exactly what I stopped last night."

"Don't stop now. Finish this time. Finish and I will, too," she said on a pant as she writhed into her own touch, wishing it was him, imagining he was touching her, tasting her, fucking her into blissful oblivion.

"You better finish. You better finish because I love hearing you come. I always finish you," he said, and she moaned loudly, like she was singing a hot, sultry chorus to a song.

That song was his name, and it tumbled from her lips as desire climbed faster up her spine. "I love being on my hands and knees for you. I want you to put me there. Or bend me over the couch. Whatever you want, just please do it to me. *Please*. I love it all with you," she said, as her fingers flew across her heat. She loved everything with him, every position, every moment, every touch, and every taste. Especially because he liked to dominate her, and she craved that. She hungered for the ways he needed to take her.

"Say that again. Say *please* again. I love it when you beg for it."

She arched her back, thrusting into her fingers. "*Please, Brent*. Please make me come. I want to come all over you."

He groaned, a feral sound, and she heard his breath hitch. He was close, too. "I'm going to make you come so hard. I want to feel you come all over my cock. I want you to lose control all over me, and scream my name so loud you go hoarse," he said, and she imagined his big hand flying over his cock. Gripping himself. Tugging hard and rough and fast.

And she broke. She soared. She rode her own fingers shamelessly as she screamed his name, like he wanted, like he needed. "*Brent.*"

"Yeah, just like that. Just like that," he said, then his words turned into growls that seemed to rip from his throat. The sound of his pleasure tore through her body, igniting her once more, sending her into another powerful climax, as she cried out once again.

* * *

He could picture her on her couch, all blissed out and sated, her skin glowing, her hair a wild tumble, fanned out across the pillows. There was no better image in the world. No better sound than her voice as she murmured, "Have I mentioned I can't wait to see you?"

"Yes, and you can say it again. Because I like hearing it."

"Can't wait to see you," she repeated.

"The next time I see you, I'm going to make you mine."

"I'm already yours. I swear, I am."

They were talking about sex, and fucking, but they were talking about so much more. The fact that she'd shared her worries about her family meant the world to him. She trusted him again, opening her heart to the things that were hard for her, and that was a precious gift, one he intended to always treat with care. He wanted to be there for her for all her needs—the physical, but also the emotional.

He sighed. Happily. So damn happily. "I told you I'm easy. Because you're all I want."

CHAPTER TWENTY-FOUR

The lithe, pretzel-like redhead swung upside down on the gauzy, cherry red swath of fabric that hung from the ceiling of Edge. Her hair spilled below her, like a sheet of fire, as she held on with only one ankle twisted round the cloth.

As lush music pulsed, she twirled in gorgeous split-second circles, along with three other girls. They were silvery and shimmery in their costumes, and captivating with their contortionist-esque skills.

Shannon zoomed in on the foursome with her phone camera, capturing the finale of the dress rehearsal. She choreographed custom shows for every venue, even though she knew that the crowds didn't come to Edge specifically to watch the dance. People came to the club for drinks, to meet lovers, to party with friends, to let loose and spend a night on the town. The dance show was staged to blend into the background most of the time, like beautiful art on the walls, like sensual music that thrummed through you. The dancers were part of the ambience of the club along with the smoky violet lights, the sleek decor, and the pulsing music.

But every now and then during the evening, the dancers would take on a larger role, moving from the background pedestals that framed the club, to the dance floor itself, becoming the focal point for those few minutes in time, the eye of the hurricane on a night of pleasure.

The redhead named Cassidy spun in crazy-eight circles, curving her entire body into impossible shapes. Then, along with the trio of other dancers, they slid in a wild rush upside-down to the floor. Shannon stopped recording, and clapped proudly. So did the sound engineer who was running the boards, and the nightclub manager from behind the bar. Shannon acknowledged them all, and nodded a thanks. Cassidy flashed Shannon the bright, magnetic smile of an entertainer who'd nailed it.

"You were amazing," Shannon told her. "Absolute perfection. No changes."

"Thank you, Shay. I'm so happy you liked it," the girl said, beaming as she and the other dancers took off for the dressing room.

"Wow. That was a hell of a show."

Shannon turned around to see Travis, Brent's firefighter friend, standing beside her. She hadn't realized he'd been watching. She had met him earlier in the day. He'd come by as a favor to conduct a preliminary fire inspection, given the additional lighting and needs of the production.

"You enjoyed it?"

"I'm just trying to figure out how a human being gets her body into that upside-down pretzel shape," he said, parking his hands on his hips as he stared admiringly at the scene of the finished show, and the thick ribbons of fabric that dangled from the ceiling. "That is out of this world."

"They're amazing, aren't they?" Shannon said, proud of her dancers, and her production.

"Incredible," Travis said with a big nod. He had dark hair and a sturdy fireman's build that could probably grace a calendar somewhere. She imagined he would make a lot of women with fireman fantasies quite happy indeed.

Though she could appreciate his smoldering looks, she only had eyes for one man, and she'd been ticking off the hours until Brent arrived. They had a few short hours in San Francisco, then they'd both return to Vegas late that night for meetings early in the morning back home.

"Think Edge will pass the additional inspection next week before the show rolls out?" Shannon asked Travis.

"Definitely," he said, hooking his thumbs into the pockets of his pants. "I just spent an hour going through everything, and it all looks good. I'll let Brent know for sure and then everything should be all set for the official inspection from the city. I'll be hanging around for a bit, since a buddy of mine is having a bachelor party here tonight."

"Oh, how fun. And I really appreciate that you took time out of your schedule to make sure everything is all set for Brent."

Travis waved his hand to signal it was no big deal. "We go way back. Happy to do him a solid. He's a good guy."

A light bulb went off in her brain. She lifted her phone again, and tapped the screen. "Any chance I could have you say that on camera?"

Travis furrowed his brow. "Sure. But why?"

She quickly explained her idea, and his eyes lit up. "Like I'd say no to that. Love that man like a brother."

She hit record, and asked Travis some questions about Brent and the club. After she finished, she wrote out her plan on her phone. She made a list of everything she'd need to do.

Then she looked at her watch. He would be there in about an hour, giving her plenty of time to change. She retreated to the dressing room where her dancers had been, changed into a new outfit, freshened up, and returned to the bar. In thirty minutes, Edge would open for the first trickle of early evening crowds. For now, the establishment operated at a low hum as bartenders and waitresses set up for service and the sound guys tested equipment.

Shannon knocked back an iced water as she remained glued to her phone and to Brent's text messages, savoring every single one. He told her he'd landed, then that he was on his way. Somehow, the seemingly impossible thirty-six hours had compressed into thirty, twenty, ten and now mere minutes.

A message dinged on her phone.

You better be naked or close to it. I'm walking in.

* * *

"Why would you say you aren't giving?" Brent said as he shut the door to his office on the second floor. The sound of it clicking made his dick even harder. It was the sound that signaled the start of what he'd been waiting for all day, all week, ever since he'd laid eyes on her at the Mandarin.

But his desire dug deeper than the past few weeks.

It unspooled over years.

It had grown roots into the last decade.

There was no way out of this. The only way was through it. He was finally going to have her. To take what was his—this woman he adored to the ends of the earth and back.

He locked the door without looking away from her beauty. He had never seen her dressed like this. She wore a black pencil skirt that hugged her luscious hips, a white, silky button-down blouse, and black sheer stockings that made him think only one thing—how far up did they go?

Then, there were those shoes. Those black leather pumps that he was going to have wrapped around his back so damn soon.

"Why would I say I'm not giving?" she asked, as he backed her up against the wall. His hands were already on her. He ran a fingertip over the top button of her blouse, watching goosebumps rise on her skin as he touched her.

"Because *this*," he said, raking his eyes over her, "is the best gift I've had all year. You. In my office. Dressed like *this*." He brushed his fingers along the buttons, and she trembled. That telltale sign of her lust that scorched his blood. "Like the businesswoman I intend to fuck."

She licked her lips. "That's who I am right now. For you."

He leaned into her neck, kissing her, inhaling her honey scent. He bit down gently on her flesh. "All day," he growled. "All day I've thought about this. Nothing but you. Touching you. Tasting you." He buzzed a path along the column of her throat. She made the sexiest little whimpers and sighs, her noises making his cock try to fight its way out of his pants. He pressed his body against hers, his hard-on hitting her belly.

She moaned in response.

"That's how much I want you. I've been hard for you all day long. I flew across the country like this. With my dick at attention the whole time because all I can think about is having you again," he said as he began working the buttons on her blouse.

She grabbed his tie, tugged him close. Her eyes were on his, hazy and full of heat. "You think it's different for me? You're all I think about, too. I changed my panties twice already today. I get turned on beyond any and all reason just thinking about what you're going to do to me."

He hissed. His blood was on fire. He dragged his fingers up the sheer fabric of her stockings, groaning when he reached the lacy top, hitting the soft flesh of her thighs. He didn't stop though. He was in hot pursuit of her pussy. "Let me test that for sure," he said, then slid his fingers against the panel of her panties. She was soaked all the way through. He dived in, gliding his fingers inside the black lace, sliding them across her sweet flesh that felt like heaven to his touch. He brought his fingers to his lips, and sucked her off. "You are so fucking ready for me."

Her lips parted on a sexy sigh. She looped her arms around his neck, and arched her hips against him. "Please," she said, echoing their conversation from the other night on the phone. "Please take me now. I can't wait anymore."

He scooped her up in his arms and stalked over to his desk, pushing the papers off with his elbow. He set her down, her petite frame barely taking up any space on the big oak desk. Her shirt was open, her bra still on.

She reached for him and began unbuttoning his shirt, her gaze pinned on him as she spoke in a sexy purr. "You've fucked me as a dancer and as a college girl, but never as a woman who runs her own business. So I dressed like one.

Because that's who I am now," she said, working her way down the buttons as he undid his tie and tossed it to the floor.

"That's who I want," he said.

She grasped his collar. "And I've fucked a comedian, and a big man on campus, but never this gorgeous man in a suit. So fuck me here on your desk as the man you are now."

And he'd thought he couldn't want her any more than he already did. She'd just proved him wrong. He wanted her even more.

CHAPTER TWENTY-FIVE

She was ready.

Nearly. There was something she had to say. Something that couldn't wait any longer. She'd held this in too long, for too many years, and it was aching to be set free.

"Wait."

She placed her hands on his chest, so firm and strong and solid.

He froze on her command. "What is it?"

She cupped his cheeks. "There's something I have to tell you before we have sex."

"Okay," he said, tentatively.

"Something important."

"Okay."

He sounded worried, and she was going to nip that worry in the bud. He'd shown her he'd changed, he'd become the man she wanted, and he was willing to give himself to her. She had more to tell him, which she planned to do when they returned to Vegas that night. But right then, she needed to be the first to say the words that she hoped would tether them together once more, and for always. She wanted to put herself on the line for him.

"Brent," she said, stroking his stubbled jaw, loving his five o'clock shadow. Loving his deep brown eyes. Loving all of him.

"What is it, Shan?"

She wasn't scared. She didn't need liquid courage, or a hearty dose of guts. All she felt was an incredible joy, an iridescent passion that tripped through her bones and sparked along her skin. "I have a question for you," she said, her lips curving into a grin.

He arched an eyebrow playfully. "Why yes, I'm clean, so if you're on the pill we can do it without a glove."

She laughed and swatted him. "No, that's not it."

"Then what is it, babe? Because I am dying to be inside you. I owe you several orgasms and right now I intend to deliver," he said, tilting his head to the side. Waiting.

Waiting for her words.

Words that she was dying to share. She felt so vulnerable, but so sure. He was the one true thing in her life. "Do you think it's possible to fall in love with someone in just two weeks? Especially if that person is the guy you were madly in love with before?" she asked, watching the expression in his eyes change from lust to wonder. He parted his lips, but she shushed him, pressing her fingertip over those soft, delicious lips that she'd be kissing in seconds. "Because I do. It happened to me. I'm so in love with you, Brent Nichols. I am so unbelievably, madly in love with you."

His eyes sparkled, full of a passion that matched hers. He clasped her hand and kissed her palm, and when he looked at her, he was grinning like a fool in love too. "Yes.

I believe it's possible. Because I'm madly in love with you. I never stopped, Shannon. I never stopped loving you. Not once. You are the only one for me."

Happiness raced through her veins. Hope flooded her body. Love was all she felt. Heart, mind, and body, she was all in. "You're the only man I want. Let's stay together this time. I want to be with you."

"I'm never letting you slip away from me again," he said, as he brushed his thumb along her cheek. "You belong with me."

"I know," she said on a nod. "I do. Everything feels right being back with you."

"We're going to keep it that way. I promise."

"I promise, too," she echoed as she held his face, not wanting to look away, not wanting to break the hold he had on her. "Fuck me, take me, make love to me," she said in a hot whisper.

"It is always all three, babe. I assure you when I fuck you, you are always the woman I love. You always have been. You always will be," he said as he pushed up her skirt and yanked off her panties. She ached between her legs, pulsing with heat and want.

He gazed hungrily at her. "Beautiful," he murmured on a low rumble, fucking her with his eyes, his hot stare making her wetter. He unzipped his pants and pushed down his briefs, freeing his gorgeous cock. It was beautiful— long, thick, hard—and she knew what it could do. She knew the depths of pleasure he alone could deliver. She was schooled in the way his cock could take her to heaven and back.

He trailed his fingers along the inside of her thigh, and she trembled with desire, watching the path of his hand.

He mesmerized her as he slid his finger through her folds. A current surged through her from his caress. Then she turned fever hot as he took his hand away and spread her wetness along his shaft.

"You're so fucking turned on, I can coat myself in you," he said, rubbing her slickness on his hard length.

Her mouth watered as she watched him stroke himself with her arousal. He groaned savagely as he spread her heat on the head, then back down all along his length. "I could get off like this right now. With your wetness on my cock. I want more of it. I want you all over my dick," he said, going in for a second round, brushing his fingers across her hot center then returning to his cock. His eyes floated closed as he stroked—a long, lingering, tantalizing stroke meant to tease her to the point of no return.

It worked. Oh hell, it worked. She was an inferno.

She couldn't wait. Seconds seemed too long. She had to have him inside her. "*Please*," she begged, as he rubbed the head of his cock across her now, teasing her with that first touch, tempting her with so much more. She desperately longed to feel him slide into her. To have him so deep inside her that the world faded away, that day shaded into night, and night melted into day. And that *this*—the connection between the two of them, the intensity of their need for each other that spanned years—became all that existed.

Because this was everything good in the world.

Then it hit her. "Condom," she said, crisply. "We need a condom."

He furrowed his brow. "I thought you were on—"

She didn't want to have this conversation. Didn't want to even tread near it. "I am. But can we just use—"

He cut her off. "Say no more," he said, grabbing his wallet and finding one quickly. He rolled it on. "Spread your legs on my desk so I can see those shoes."

She obliged, hooking her spikes on the edge of his desk, opening her legs wide for him.

"Mmm... these legs," he murmured, running a hand from her knee to her thigh. "In these stockings. And this skirt." He pushed her skirt all the way to her waist so it bunched up. "And this beautiful, perfect pussy just for me."

He teased at her entrance, sliding the head along her slick heat. "Take me," she said, a flush darkening her chest as her nipples hardened to tight peaks. "Take me now."

Every atom in her buzzed. Her cells were no longer made of molecules. They were comprised of desire and lust. There was no more waiting, no more time. She needed only this, only now. Mercifully, he sank into her.

"Oh God," she cried out, and roped her arms around his neck. His eyes blazed darkly at her, so hot, so full of the same raw and primal need. He stilled himself when he was all the way in, letting her feel him, letting her adjust to his size.

"It feels so good," she moaned. "I want you so much."

"I have never wanted anyone like this," he said, moving in her.

"Me, too," she said, gasping with each thrust.

"I have never been so in love."

She gripped his neck, dug her nails into his skin. "*Never.* I've never felt like this." Her world spun silver and gold. The intensity of him inside her drove her wild. Her heart beat in a frenzy.

"I fucking love you more than I did the first time," he said on a powerful thrust. Her head fell back on her shoulders and she squeezed her eyes closed. She rocked her hips up into him, chasing even more pleasure.

"The same," she said, barely able to form words anymore. The fire roared through her, her center an inferno. "I feel the same."

He grabbed her hips, yanked her up to him, deeper, harder. "Fucking you is like coming home."

Her body jolted with each delicious thrust. Her heart pumped wildly as he drove into her, burying himself. "Deeper," she panted. "More."

"Lie back," he told her, pressing a hand on her chest, lowering her spine to his desk. She lay flat, and he cast his gaze to his shoulders. "You know where I want you, babe. Show me how flexible you are. Show me how you can bend that body for me."

She grinned wickedly as she hooked her legs up on his shoulders, wrapping them behind his neck. He practically climbed onto the desk, his knees on the wood, and he took her.

He just fucking took her. Her spine dug into the wood as he fucked her. His hands curled around her head as he drove into her. His cock hit that spot inside her that sent her galloping closer to the cliff. She felt him everywhere.

Every thrust consumed her. He filled her completely, and he owned her body with his. The world rotated on its axis again, as Brent Nichols fucked the last ten years of missing, the last ten years of longing, the last ten years without him, right out of her.

Time was crushed to pieces in the way he took her.

She could barely move, and she didn't care. Couldn't care. All she wanted was to give herself to him. All he ever wanted was her. And she gave, and she gave, and she gave.

Her back scraped the desk as the friction drove her to the edge. "Please," she called out, as tremors of lust slammed into her, assaulting her with pleasure and sending her flying as her body detonated. The world slipped away into bliss, into ecstasy, into the end of missing-the-love-of-your-fucking-life.

There was no more missing. There was only having.

He held her harder, gripped her head. "I love you," he grunted as he thrust, reaching his own release. "I fucking love you so much."

CHAPTER TWENTY-SIX

Travis looked dazed and confused.

He slumped against the wall, watching a woman in red walk away. Brent headed over to him, knotting his tie after having just washed his hands in the men's room. He had to make a flight back to Vegas with Shannon in a few minutes, but wanted to catch up with his old friend.

"You hiding out here in the hallway?"

Travis blinked, then shrugged. "No. Just trying to understand a woman."

Brent clapped his buddy on the back. "Good luck with that. It's like learning a whole new language, and no one gives you a dictionary for translation."

"Exactly," he said, gesturing in the direction where the woman had disappeared. "One second she's all over you, and the next second she practically wants to slap you."

"Been there, man. I have absolutely been there. If it's any consolation, sometimes those slaps can turn into something a whole lot better."

"I was hoping it was going to turn into something better tonight," Travis said, shoving a hand through his hair, then turned to face Brent and pointed at him. "Hell, I was about ready to use your office."

He laughed. "Afraid you would have found it occupied."

Travis knocked fists with Brent. "Excellent news. At least one of us is figuring out women."

"Took a long time. You'll get there. You should talk to her though. Whoever she is."

Travis scrubbed a hand across his chin and sighed. "She might be a little pissed off at me right now. I wasn't completely honest about something."

"Then let her know you were less than honest, say you're sorry, and tell her what you want. *Her*, I presume. Women like honesty," he said, speaking the simplest of truths. Weird, that after all that had transpired he was now in a position to give relationship advice. "By the way, thanks so much for coming by today. I really appreciate you doing a prelim for me."

"Anytime. And incidentally, Shay is pretty crazy about you. Let me just say that. I chatted with her earlier, and I'm pretty sure she has it bad for you. She's a keeper."

A grin spread across Brent's face. He was sure of that, too. Being certain of how they both felt was such a gift. One he'd cherish.

Fifteen minutes later, Shannon was on top of him, riding him hard in the limo on the way to the airport, and he thanked his lucky stars the flight home was short because he couldn't wait much longer to have her again. He had a wild hunch they wouldn't be sleeping much tonight. That they'd be wrapped up in each other all night long, making up for lost time. She told him she wanted him to come back to her place, and even though he had a ten a.m. meeting with James and his real estate guys, he figured that was what coffee was for.

That was all he'd need tomorrow. For tonight, he'd have her.

* * *

The stars twinkled against the inky black night as the driver pulled off the highway, and headed to her condo. Time marched closer to the moment. To the telling. Her stomach executed a fresh series of nosedives as the town car neared her home. She reminded herself that everything would be fine. Well, maybe not fine at first. But it would be fine soon enough.

She'd tell him, and it would be hard for them both, but they'd comfort each other.

This was not the sort of news that could break them up. The loss was simply another part of the past, one she'd share now that they were finally back in the town they called home. Even though so much had gone wrong for her in Las Vegas, so much had gone right there, too. Las Vegas was the place where her grandma and her brothers lived, and it was the town where she and Brent had fallen in love again, against the neon lights, and the blinking billboards, and the spectacle of the Strip. From the fountains at the Bellagio, to the Shops at Caesars, to the darkened theater at the Luxe—this was their place, and the city of sin had given them a second chance at love.

And at truth.

That was why she wanted to tell him the story there. At home. Not in a hotel room. Not in an office. Not in a cab, or a car, or a plane. But in her house, where she could tell the story the way she needed to.

As the car wedged itself next to the curb, Brent paid and tipped the driver, then grabbed their bags.

"A sleepover at last," he teased as they walked up the three flights, the sound of their footsteps echoing in the creaky silence of the building after midnight. She unlocked the door, both grateful and nervous that the moment had arrived. She spotted a lone spare key amidst the mail she'd tossed on her table in a rush when she'd left yesterday.

"Crap."

Brent turned around, and shot her a curious stare.

She smacked her forehead with her hand. "My friend's cat. She's out of town, and I said since I was only gone for twenty-four hours that I could feed him."

"He's probably hungry."

She snatched the key from the table. "Be right back. Sorry if the place is a mess. I left in a hurry."

Racing upstairs, her heels clicking against the wood, she unlocked Ally's condo to find the silver and black tabby meowing indignantly at her.

"Hey Nick," she said to the feline.

Now, where was his cat food?

* * *

So this was her place. This was her home. He'd caught a glimpse of it on Saturday, but hadn't taken it in. Her home had an open, airy feel, even at night. The couch and chairs were light shades of yellow and beige, with gold pillows tossed on the cushions, and billowy curtains by the windows.

Her house was hardly messy at all.

As he wandered through the kitchen, he spotted that frame again on the counter. The bright sunflowers. He peered more closely at it, and wondered again what the stone was by the flowers. Maybe a garden wall?

Wait.

She'd called him a sunflower, hadn't she?

He snapped his fingers, remembering. On the phone the other night, she'd said he was her sunflower. Maybe this was her way of thinking about him when they weren't to-gether—with a picture of a sunflower. The corner of his lips twitched up. Fine, he wasn't a flowery guy, but when the woman you love says you're the sun in her life, you gladly take the compliment. He tapped the frame once, then set it back in place and strolled down the hallway. He stopped short at her bedroom door, opened wide. He couldn't resist peeking. That was where she'd spent her nights. That bed, right there, with the orange and purple pattern on the cover.

That was where she wouldn't be sleeping tonight. He could picture her perfectly, on all fours in the middle of the mattress, her back bowed, hands tied to the headboard. He'd take her like that. Fuck her hard on her hands and knees. Grip her hips and sink into her. Smack her ass as he made her cry out in a pleasure.

A barely audible groan escaped his throat as the reel played before his eyes of her naked, lithe body trembling. Ready for him. He strolled into her room and brushed a hand over the corner of her bed. A few more minutes, and he could have her like that. That was his plan. He turned around to leave, when a flash of yellow caught his eye once more. Something about it felt familiar. He walked to her nightstand. The drawer was open and a small book ap-peared to have fallen off the nightstand into the drawer.

Or been shoved in.

Some part of him knew better. But another part was intrigued. Curious. Then far *too* curious when he saw the cover.

It was a photo album, and the cover image matched the picture in her kitchen frame. Another close-up shot of a sunflower. Somewhere inside of him, a warning bell told him maybe not to cross this line. He shouldn't even be in her bedroom without permission. You don't just walk into a woman's bedroom, uninvited. And you don't take a photo book out of a drawer without permission. But when you spot a black-and-white image slip out of one of the pages, and that black and white image has a name and a date, you might not be able to control yourself.

The name *Paige-Prince, Shannon* was printed in small letters on the edge, along with a date ten years ago, and then the words that knocked him to his knees. *Highgate Maternal Fetal.*

His heart sped in his chest, spinning wildly out of control. Blood pounded in his ears, and his throat went dry.

He inhaled deeply, as if the air would steel him, but his breath still came erratically. Then he did it. With traitorous fingers that dug into her privacy willfully, he pulled out the black-and-white image. He blinked. Once, twice, then he let it register. An ultrasound picture of a baby inside the womb.

His eyes returned to the date again, and he computed quickly. This was four months after they graduated from college. Four months after they split. A strange, sick fear descended on him, and his nerves frayed like the ends of a rope as questions assaulted him. Where was the baby? Did she give up a baby for adoption? Have an abortion? Have a kid somewhere? Was her grandma raising her baby?

Their baby...?

That thought was too foreign, too bizarre. He sat on the edge of her bed, frozen, holding the image, the private medical record.

His fingers itched to open the book.

His sense of right and wrong told him to let it be.

But selfish desire won. He flipped to the beginning. The album was scant, containing only a handful of images. The first was a shot of her in a mirror, and his heart tripped back in time as he gazed at Shannon, *his* Shannon, from ten years ago. Her hair was short then and still blond, her face so fresh and young, her expression a half-hearted smile. She had taken the photo of herself sideways, capturing the small swell of her belly in a mirror.

Seeing the ultrasound was one thing. Seeing her pregnant was entirely another. It walloped him.

He turned to the next page. The words *nineteen weeks* were written in blue ballpoint on the page, and in the plastic sleeve was another shot of Shannon, barely bigger. Then one at twenty weeks. He turned another page. An image of a white baby blanket on a hospital bed. After that the photos ended, and the last several pages contained only images of sunflowers.

He didn't know what to make of the sunflowers, or of the way the story in these pictures was unfinished. The story ended, and then it became something else, told in a language he didn't understand.

Shoes clicked on the floor, and the hair on his neck stood on end. He snapped the book closed as she called out his name. He started to stuff the book into the drawer. But when he turned around, she was standing in the doorway, and he had her photo book in his hand, trying to jam it into the nightstand.

Her expression was one of shock. Then disappointment, and next came a trace of grief. Somehow, her eyes contained all three.

She swallowed, and her face seemed pinched. But her voice gave her away. A bare whisper, laced with pain, as she closed her eyes, opened them, and spoke.

"Like I said, my house is a little bit messy."

He nodded. "Is there something you need to tell me?"

CHAPTER TWENTY-SEVEN

"Yes. But why were you going through my things?" she asked again as she stood in the doorway. She wasn't sure she could move.

Maybe he couldn't either. He didn't stray from the bed as he shrugged listlessly. "There's no good answer, Shan. I saw the sunflower on the cover, and it matched the one in your picture frame."

"So you went through a photo book that you found in my nightstand because it matched one in my kitchen?" she asked, taking the time to process each action he'd taken.

"It was open," he said, his voice barren.

Her skin prickled with fear at the sound. With nerves too, because she was stumbling blindly now. She'd wanted to tell him on her own terms. Not like this. Never like this.

She shook her head, as if she could erase the last five minutes. Start over—begin at the beginning. Sit down, talk, share the whole sad story, and then feed the cat. She had never wanted him to discover the truth on his own. A part of her was mad as hell that he'd gone through her book, and a part of her was deeply ashamed at what he'd found—the evidence of all she'd withheld.

A new emotion bubbled up inside her, too. Terror. She was terrified he'd walk away.

"Were you pregnant ten years ago?"

No point lying. No point hiding. "I was," she said with a nod.

"When?" he asked in a wobbly voice, as if every word was new and foreign.

"I found out two weeks after you left."

"Where is the..." he said, letting his voice trail off.

Her heart cratered, beating a drumbeat of hurt and sadness.

Oh, this was the worst. This was harder than she'd ever imagined. She knew it wouldn't be easy to get the awful words out, but being forced to say them tasted worse. Bitter and acrid to the tongue. She drew a deep breath, and laid them out, one by one, in a row of awfulness. "I was pregnant. It lasted for twenty weeks. My water broke and I went into labor in London, and the baby was born too early. He didn't live."

"He?" Brent asked hoarsely. It sounded as if he'd been punched.

She had never seen him like this, white as snow, shocked to the bone. "Yes. *He.*"

Time crawled painfully to the next minute, then the next, and then the next. Soon, he managed to string more words together. "Was. He. Mine?"

Something inside her snapped, like an electric wire sliced to the ground from high above. "Yes. How the hell can you ask that question?"

He held his hands out wide. "How the hell can I ask? Because you just told me you were pregnant. It's normal to ask."

"No," she said, shaking her head, with some kind of dangerous cocktail of anger, shame and hurt mixing up inside her. "That's not a normal question. It's an insulting question."

He stood up from the bed, planted his feet wide. She knew that stance; it meant he was angry. Fear clutched at her heart, and she flailed for the right next words. She tried mightily to turn the knob inside her chest from boil to simmer. "Yes. The baby was yours."

Brent wobbled. The world seemed to sway for him. He crumpled onto the bed. She rushed over and wrapped her arms around him. Thankfully, he didn't shrug her off. In the smallest voice, he croaked out, "What happened? When did you know?"

She squeezed his shoulder, and ran a hand through his soft hair. "I had no idea when we split up," she said immediately, because she couldn't bear for him to even think she might have known then. "But two weeks later I was late, so I took a pregnancy test and then several more. I didn't say a word to anyone at first because I didn't know what to do. I didn't know if I was going to keep the baby, or give up the baby," she said, forcing her voice to stay even so she wouldn't sob her way through the conversation. That was no small feat. As she told the story, tears fell anyway. "I knew if I told you that you would give up your job and come rushing to my side."

He grabbed her hand, gripping tightly as he looked her in the eyes. His were full of fierce determination. "I would have. You know that I would have been there for you in a heartbeat."

"I know, and that's exactly why I didn't try to tell you right away. If you had come rushing back to me for this reason, you would have hated me. You would have resented me. You loved your work, and your career, and I didn't want to be second choice or a forced first one. And I didn't want it to affect your work."

"That's not fair. That's not fair to say at all. You don't know how it would have affected me. You don't know it would have affected me negatively. Maybe it wouldn't have made a difference."

"Nothing made a difference," she said, heavily. "The baby is gone. It's better that I never told you because it wouldn't have changed a thing."

"No, it's *not* better," he said, his voice rising. "I hate that you went through it all alone, without me."

"I tried to call you a few times. I called you before I even went to London. Your number was disconnected. I didn't think you even wanted to hear from me."

"Of course I wanted to hear from you."

"But I didn't have your number."

"I had to change phone services when I moved. It was different then. No one kept their phone numbers."

"Well, that's exactly why I didn't have it. I had to have my brother track down your new number. And I called you when I went into labor."

His face turned blank again. He didn't move. A memory seemed to flick past his eyes. He stared at the wall for several seconds. She whispered his name to draw his attention. He turned away from whatever unseen point he was focusing on and looked at her. Recognition dawned in his eyes as he swirled his finger in a circle. "*You.* This. The baby. I thought you had to have been the unknown call from London that night."

She nodded, letting the tears fall. "I called you in the taxi on the way to the hospital. My water had broken. I was losing the baby already. I'm sorry. I'm so sorry."

He lowered his head into his hands, pressing his fingertips hard against his eyes. "I was at work on the show," he said, recounting the night. "I saw a missed call from an unknown number in London. I had no way to reach you."

"There was nothing to say after that point. The baby was gone. We can't change the fact that my body failed. There is nothing that will change that. Even if we had been together, the fate would have been the same. The baby was never going to survive. The decision was made by Mother Nature."

"That's not true." He shook his head over and over, repeating the same words. "That's not true. That's not true. That's not true."

Her heart lurched towards him, and all her instincts said to comfort him. Because the man was in denial. "Brent, nothing would have changed," she said softly.

He smacked his fist into the bed covers. "I would have wanted to know. No matter what. I hate that you went through this alone. I wanted to be there for you, and you didn't give me the chance."

She choked back the tears. "I wanted that, too. But how was I to know what you wanted? You left. It was over. You made your choice. You chose work over me. You made it clear I had to go with you or we were through. Why would you expect me to think you wanted to be there for me?" she asked, her voice breaking. "Besides, by the time this happened we'd been apart for four months. Even after it happened, what was I going to say that would have changed a thing? You were gone."

* * *

He didn't see it that way.

Because he'd just learned he was a bigger schmuck. He had done something far worse than walk away from the love of his life. Turns out, he'd abandoned the mother of his child. Thanks to his epic last words, she'd thought he wouldn't have wanted to be by her side.

She had every reason to think that.

"If you don't go with me, there's no point staying together."

He pictured her in London, alone and scared, not even sure what to tell the father of her child. He stood and paced around the room. He opened his mouth, but he had no clue how to respond. He was a fish out of water, gasping for air. Everything in his life had come easily to him. He had never suffered bad news. He had never lost someone he loved. But now, he felt the sting of devastation the first time in his life. He was experiencing all sorts of things that had become far too normal for Shannon. Unlike her, he had no roadmap to navigate this new terrain.

"I don't know what to say," he muttered.

"It's okay. You don't have say the perfect thing," she said softly. She rose, too, and clasped his hands in hers, consoling him.

He couldn't let her. Not when he'd failed her abysmally. If he hadn't backed her into a corner, they'd have stayed together and he could have properly cared for her. He pushed her hands away. He didn't know how to touch her. He didn't deserve her affection. So he said the one thing he could manage. "I'm sorry I looked through your things."

She flashed a small smile, absolving him. "I wish you hadn't, because I was planning on telling you tonight. But it's okay, and now you know. I was going to tell you as soon as I came back from feeding the cat."

In a flash, his guilt vanished because that sounded awfully convenient. He arched an eyebrow in a question and shoved all his hurt on her. "Why didn't you tell me sooner?"

She stepped back. "I only started seeing you again two weeks ago. It's not really the sort of thing you say at a first meeting. '*Sorry I haven't seen you in ten years, but hey, thought you might like to know it turned out I was pregnant when you left.*'"

"That's a start," he said, even though those words felt all wrong, out of sync.

"Brent, that's not a start. That's not how you tell someone something hard."

"Okay fine, since you're such an expert. How about over dinner then at the Cromwell?"

Her eyes bugged out. "We were just starting to get to know each other again. I had no idea what we were going to become."

"Then how about at one of our lunches?" he tossed back, simply throwing things at her, barely knowing where they would land, or how much they would hurt. All he knew was that everything inside him ached terribly, and now that he'd recovered the power of speech, he was using words as missiles lobbed at the nearest target—the woman he loved.

"That hardly seemed to be the time or place either. But since you're reviewing chapter and verse and naming all the times I saw you, you should know that I actually did plan to tell you on Saturday night when we went out to Alvin Ailey."

"Why didn't you?" he asked, as if he'd caught her red-handed.

"Seriously? You're seriously asking me? You left town that night. You sprang it on me after the show that you were leaving town in an hour. That's why," she said, parking her hands on her hips.

His eyes flared with anger. "Are we going to go over this again, Shannon?" He was sick and tired of having every mistake he'd ever made boomeranged back at him. "Can you ever fucking give me break?"

She stared at him, jutting out her chin. "Excuse me. This isn't about cutting you a break. I was just saying that when you're getting on a plane would have been a really shitty time to tell you. Think about it. Is that honestly when you wish I'd have tapped you on the shoulder and said, 'Hey, I know you're off to New York for a really important business meeting, but I've been meaning to tell you I had your baby and lost your baby. Have a nice flight.' Is it?"

She had a point, but he could barely see it just then. He was filled with anger, brimming with self-loathing. He hardly knew what to do with all this horribleness, so he erected more walls. "This whole time you've been asking me to be honest with you. And I was. I was honest about everything," he said, shaking a finger at her. "And you have never been able to honest with me. It's like pulling teeth to get you to tell me anything."

"That is bullshit," she said, her voice breaking with tears and anger. "And you know that. I am more open with you than anyone in my entire life. You just expect it from day one. And I'm so sorry I'm less than perfect at finding the best moment to tell you about the tragic fucking circumstances that have trailed behind me."

He tossed his hands in the air and huffed. "There you go again. It's always about you. It's always about the shit you've been through."

A fresh stream of tears rained down her cheeks. "This is what I meant the other night on the phone. That you're going to resent me, and you already are." She swiped her hand across her cheeks, wiping away the tears. They seemed to be falling faster now, relentlessly, streaking down her face. "I guess it's nice not to have to deal with shit, isn't it? But maybe if you could think about it, you'd realize it wasn't so easy to tell you on our first date in college that my mother was in prison. That she sent me letters that ripped me to pieces. That prison made her go insane.

"And I'm very sorry that I didn't tell you at lunch last week that I had a child, and lost a child. And that I miss him terribly and I imagine what he was like, and if he would have been like you. If he'd have had the best parts of you, like your heart and your humor, and the way you love. I'm sorry that I didn't tell you that right away. And I'm sorry that one of the reasons I wished he was alive is that I would have had a part of you then. I'm sorry I didn't have the words to tell you all of that so eloquently at lunch, or in the photo booth, or the elevator, or at your club. And I'm sorry I'm doing a shitty job now. Most of all, I'm sorry that you're finding it in you to belittle the fact that you've had a perfect life and mine has been problematic." Every single word she said cut him to the bone. "But I guess now you know how it feels to lose something. It's pretty awful, isn't it?"

He nodded and clamped his lips shut. He swallowed, and the lump in his throat was like a jagged rock. It cut him to pieces, and he had no clue what he'd say if he spoke again. Words had killed them last time. He'd said the wrong things ten years ago, and he was treading dangerously close to doing it again with the cruel ones he was firing off at her now. He couldn't chance it happening a second time. He walked to the kitchen, picked up his bag, and headed to the door.

She followed him, grabbing his arm and spinning him around. Devastation was written in her eyes. "Are you leaving me?"

He took her hand, peeled it off him, then cupped her shoulders. He ached to swipe his thumb across her cheek, to tell her everything would be okay. But he couldn't because he was feeling things he'd never felt before—like his skin had been sliced open. He had no training in how to stem the bleeding.

"No. I'm not walking away," he said, taking his time with each word. "But I'm pissed that you didn't tell me, and I'm pissed that you went through something awful and I couldn't be there for you. And I'm pissed at myself for not having the right words to say. I'm leaving, because I love you, and because I don't want say another wrong thing. I need to go, Shannon. I really need to go and have some time to deal with this. You've had ten years to deal with it. I've known for ten minutes."

He opened the door, and left.

* * *

She collapsed, falling onto the floor, tears spilling into her lap. It wasn't supposed to be like this. She wasn't supposed to hurt more than she had before.

But he'd punctured a hole in her heart, and that damn organ had already been bruised too many times.

He might not call it walking away, but hell if she could tell the difference between now and the last time he'd done it.

CHAPTER TWENTY-EIGHT

She scratched Nick between the ears and the tabby arched his back. Purring contentedly, Nick rubbed against her legs, a thank you for feeding him again that the morning.

"You're a sweetie," she said as she crouched in Ally's condo, stroking the happy guy. Her voice sounded empty to her ears, a hollow noise, mirroring her insides.

Eight hours later, and no word from Brent.

She was a big girl, she could handle eight hours; she could give him the time, she told herself. Even though it felt like an eternity. Her body was keenly aware of every passing minute, and each one wore her to the bone. Running a hand down the cat's back, she wished her life were as easy as this—eat, purr, be happy.

But the universe insisted on throwing hurdles and roadblocks at her. The universe kept moving the line. Jump higher. Run faster.

Then it cackled at her and demanded she do it once more. It was so unfair, given what they'd shared in San Francisco. Making love with Brent again had been nothing short of cloud nine. It had been bliss and beauty, passion and pleasure. He had seduced her, body and soul, and she had craved every second of their intense connection. She longed for him. More than she'd ever expected to. More than she knew what to do with.

That was what hurt so much. After ten years of barely getting over him, she'd let down her guard in a few short weeks. Little good that had done. Here she was with a raw, beating heart, and no one to tend to it.

But herself.

"Be a good boy. Ally will be home later today," she told the cat, who answered her with one final silky rub of his head against her leg.

She locked the door and texted her friend. *Nick is fed, rested and ready for your return. Meow!*

She popped back into her home, grabbed her purse, dropped a big pair of shades over her eyes, and drove to the airport. At the gate, she met Colin for their quick day-in/day-out trip to Los Angeles. He was leaning against the window looking at his phone. An airline voice blared overhead. "Flight twenty-three from Las Vegas to Burbank will board in ten minutes."

Colin tucked his phone away when he saw her walking to him. "You look like hell," he said.

"Thanks. Good to see you too."

"What's wrong?"

"Didn't sleep much," she said, yawning.

"Is that a good thing or a bad thing?"

She shrugged a shoulder. "It was supposed to be a good thing, but it turned out to be a bad thing."

"Man trouble?" he asked, arching an eyebrow.

"Something like that."

"Be a nun. Easier that way."

She narrowed her eyes at him. "You be a monk. How about that?"

He shook his head. "Hell no." He tipped his forehead to a Starbucks across the concourse. "Let me get you a coffee. We can't have you yawning like that in the meeting."

On the short flight to Los Angeles, she downed her coffee, the caffeine rejuvenating her, temporarily erasing the sleeplessness. She touched up her makeup as Colin walked her through his goals for the meeting with the reality show producers who wanted her to choreograph a one-night reunion, but her mind kept wandering to the sight of Brent walking away.

He hadn't called it that, but to her it was déjà vu.

The door shutting.

The two of them on opposite sides.

"The meeting should be short and sweet, and I have some key thoughts on how to make this a good deal for you," Colin said, in his businesslike tone. The sound of his voice returned her to the present moment. She forced herself to focus, since he was in her corner, going to bat for her. "The important thing to keep in mind is that you're rising. When you worked on the show a few years ago, you were merely an associate choreographer on staff. Now you're a star, and you create your own productions. Those network guys know that, but it'll be natural for them to revert back to thinking of you as an employee. My goal is to make sure they don't treat you as anything but the star that you are," he said, and even though she was still hurting, his praise made her feel a little better. "That's why I'm going with you. Because you are Shay Fucking Sloan," he said, punctuating his pep talk by pointing his finger at her. "And if they want you for a one-night reunion, I'm going to make sure they treat you like a queen."

She wrapped her arms around him. "You're the best. Thank you for always looking out for my interests."

He waved a hand as they pulled apart. "You make it easy."

When they landed in Los Angeles, her phone was silent. No messages. No texts. No calls.

Her heart sank. Brent had been radio silent all through the night and early morning.

But she'd survive, she reminded herself, as they deplaned on the tarmac, the sun shining brightly. No matter what became of the two of them, she would survive. She always did; she always had. She knew how to keep on living, keep on moving, and keep on fighting.

She had her brothers. She had the three men who had never abandoned her. The three men who would always be by her side. She would stand by them, too, through anything.

The four of them had an unbreakable bond. They were her people.

* * *

October.

The pictures he'd seen were from October. She'd been four months pregnant then. If the pregnancy had continued, she'd have carried to March.

He'd have a nine-year-old son.

As his real estate attorney talked about neighborhoods in Chicago that were ripe for nightclubs, Brent ran his palm across his chin, trying to process the passage of time.

What grade was a nine-year-old in? Third? Fourth? Hell if he knew. The only kid he'd spent any time with lately was Carly and she was one. He knew nothing about children. Would his nine-year-old have been a sporty kid? Wanting to play catch or baseball or whatever kids wanted to play these days? Or would he have liked video games and Xbox? Would he have been a mama's boy or just like his dad?

He twirled his pen between his thumb and forefinger, a long-time habit. He stared at his hand in motion as if it were a new addition to his body. Was this part of his DNA? Was something as mundane as pen twirling at a conference table a genetic trait he'd have passed on to a kid?

Brent lifted the pen to his face and studied it. Was his son right-handed or left-handed? Would he have been a good speller, or a whiz at math? Would he have liked being read to at night? Kissed on the forehead before he fell asleep?

"So there you go. We should be able to secure the property in Chicago, and I hope that we can get this one you had your sights set on in Atlanta. Ten-four, gentleman?"

Tate raised his eyebrows and glanced around the conference table, waiting for an okay from Brent and James.

But Brent was seeing his boy before his eyes, watching Shannon tuck him in at night, planting a kiss on his forehead.

"Where's Daddy?" his kid said. "I want Daddy to say goodnight to me, too."

Brent closed his eyes briefly. The scene was too much to hold onto. Too much to let go of. Because he couldn't even put himself in the scene. He was seeing Shannon and his

phantom son, but he wasn't there. He wasn't saying goodnight to the boy he didn't have. He hadn't been there to
help his son's mother.

Guilt clawed at him. His chest ached as if it had been
carved up and hollowed out. He was left with a strange
new feeling—*missing.*

He missed someone he never knew. This kind of missing
was hard like a fist, its knuckles pushing up against skin
and bones. He missed a person he'd never met, and would
never know. A person who was a part of him, and a part of
the woman he loved madly.

Tate and James were asking him questions, but they
might as well be speaking Swahili. Hell, everyone was
speaking in foreign tongues today. Sanskrit and Latin and
Greek rained down on him. He had no clue what anyone
was saying, and he had no notion of how to speak. It was
as if his voice had been snatched away. His voice—his goddamn instrument, the tool he'd relied on when on stage,
and now in business—was gone, turned into the ash that
was coating his throat.

"Sounds great," he somehow managed to say, finding
those words deep within some primordial part of him that
remembered how to communicate.

After the attorneys left, Brent stood too, but James sat
him back down. Concern was etched in his eyes. "Never
seen you like this." James gestured heavenward. "It's not
even like you weren't here. It's like you were on another
planet."

Brent rubbed his hand over his jaw, the day-old stubble
reminding him that he hadn't even bothered to shave this
morning. He glanced down at his outfit, making sure he'd
remembered to put on clothes. The jeans and button-down

he wore were the only reassurance that he hadn't gone completely insane. He'd remembered to dress.

"Sorry," he said, because that was the only thing he could say.

James patted him on the shoulder. "Hey, no worries. I'm here for you. This is your ship, and you run this baby," James said, and Brent cringed at that word—*baby*. "You sure you're okay? Why don't you take the day off?"

Before Brent could answer, James's phone rang. He looked at it quizzically. "New York number. Let me grab it."

As James talked on the phone, Brent tuned it all out, parking his chin in his hand, and staring at an abstract piece of art that hung on the wall—a series of red, gray and yellow geometric shapes jutted across the canvas at harsh angles. He studied it, as if he could make out the meaning, but he saw nothing. He let his eyes go blurry, let the shapes melt into each other, into one jumble of colors. The one color he could still make out was yellow.

Like those damn sunflowers.

What was up with those sunflowers? That was the part he didn't get. Why did she have all those pictures of sunflowers? Where they were taken?

"Earth to Brent."

He looked up.

James pointed to his phone. "That's Tanner Davies in New York. It's on mute. He said he's been calling you all morning, but your phone is just ringing and ringing. He emailed you too, but got no response. He wanted to confirm the time of the picnic in New York," he said, then rattled off a date the next week. "Can you make that date? He wants to let the association know you'll be there and are looking forward to it. Said to bring your girlfriend if you want. You got one you want to tell me about?"

"Sure, sounds good," he said, in a dead voice. He had no clue what he'd just agreed to. He didn't answer anything else.

James finished his call, then cocked his head to the side, and waved his hand in front of Brent's face. "Where's your phone? Did someone drug you last night or something, man? I have never seen you like this."

His phone was in the dishwasher.

He'd left it there on purpose that morning before he took off for work. If he had it with him, he'd cave. He'd call. He'd text. He'd try to contact her, to make her laugh, make her smile, and turn her on. But those weren't the things that needed to be said or done right then. He still didn't know what to say. He barely knew how to operate his mouth.

"Battery ran out," he mumbled.

"I think we need to get you home. Let me call you a cab, and you should take the rest of the day off. Whatever business you have scheduled I can attend to."

"Yeah. I should cut out early," he said, blinking, trying to focus again on the world around him. Then, something James said sparked a wire in his brain. Lit a fuse. *Ringing and ringing.* Tanner had been ringing and ringing him.

What if Shannon had been ringing too? Just like when he'd moved to Los Angeles. Just like when she'd been in London. Just like when she'd tried to call him on her way to the hospital. *Shit.* He had to do something and soon. He had to figure out what to say.

He stood up, a blast of necessary energy zipping through him. "But I can't leave. There's someplace I need to be."

He went to the Allegro to find Mindy.

* * *

Colin high-fived her as soon as the glass doors to the network headquarters swung shut. The network had agreed to the terms, and her brother had just booked her a marquee contract for a quick, high-paying, high-profile gig. The best part? She wasn't madly in love with the head of the network. She hadn't been involved with him ten years ago. Working together would be a cinch. She should do all her deals with men she wasn't once engaged to. Made them so much easier.

"You are a rock star," she told her brother as they headed down the steps to the waiting car that would whisk them back to the airport, then home to Vegas before the clock struck three. Trips to Los Angeles were the best, since the city was so damn close.

"No, you are," he said.

As soon as they slid into the air-conditioned vehicle, she checked her phone, hoping for something. Surely, he'd have reached out by now.

The screen was empty. No messages from him. Nothing but a low-battery notice as her phone neared the end of its life for the day. A lump rose in her throat, but she shoved it back down. She would not cry over a lack of messages. She would not lament the radio silence.

But she also would not sit and wait for him.

She'd never waited for him before, and she wasn't going to be that kind of woman now. She was Shay fucking Sloan, and she wasn't going to let her heart sit on the sidelines. Nor was she going to hide her feelings.

She dropped a hand on Colin's arm. "Hey, you know when you asked about my man trouble this morning?"

He nodded.

"It's Brent."

He furrowed his brow. "What do you mean?"

"I'm with him again," she said, keeping her voice strong because even if she and Brent were fighting, she was choosing to believe they'd work it out. "And we're in love, and we're trying to work things out. You've always stood by me, and helped me, and that's why I want you to know."

He nodded slowly, as if taking in the news. "Is he making you happy?" he asked carefully.

"Most of the time," she said. "It's not perfect, and we have stuff to figure out, but I think we'll get there."

"I'm here for you. Whatever you need."

She rested her head briefly on his shoulder, then opened a new text message, and sent Brent a note.

I am thinking of you. I'm always thinking of you. When you're ready, I'm here.

That was it. That was all. It was time to stop fighting, and to start behaving like adults who had history and baggage, and who had hurt and pain.

But who were willing to fight their way to the other side.

CHAPTER TWENTY-NINE

Dolly Parton's "9 to 5" rang out from a nearby slot machine as coins splashed into the metal bucket. A guy in a Hawaiian shirt working the one-armed bandit shouted a triumphant *yes!*

Brent and Mindy walked through the slot machines while she made her afternoon rounds through the casino

"I get that you're pissed—" Mindy began.

Brent held up a finger. "Correction. *Was* pissed. I was pissed last night."

Mindy nodded, and pressed the Bluetooth in her ear, listening for a few seconds, then returned to the conversation. They strolled past a machine crooning "Pure Imagination" as a cartoonish Willy Wonka presided over the slots. "Fine. You were pissed last night. And now you're resentful and kind of catatonic. Am I right?"

He huffed, but nodded.

"Then get ready for some tough love, my friend." She stopped at an empty Cleopatra machine, parking her hand on the queen's golden headband. "This is what you need to realize—and none of this is to belittle what you're feeling.

But sweetie, you don't get to be angry. You don't get to own this feeling of resentment."

He narrowed his eyes and shot her a look. "What do you mean?"

"I'm not denying your role in this loss. I'm not saying it isn't painful, or shocking, or sad. I get that you lost something you didn't even know you had lost," she said, speaking in a thoughtful, teacherly tone. "But I'm giving you a couple hours, maybe a day, to feel all those things on your own. And then your job is to be there for her. You don't get to own this hurt. It is *hers*. She went through it."

Mindy's words were iced water splashed onto him. They were the stark reminder that he couldn't co-opt Shannon's grief or pain. His was a fraction of hers.

"So what do I do?"

"Be the man she needed you to be ten years ago. The man who doesn't walk away when you hear that shit didn't go in your direction."

"I didn't walk away," he said, trying to defend his actions. "I told her I needed time to deal with it."

Mindy nodded a few times, acknowledging him. "Fine, you needed time. You needed space. I understand. It was a shock. Well, you had your time and you had your space. Now man up, and be who she needs. That's all you've wanted," she said, slugging his arm. "You have wanted her to need you. You've wanted her to want you back in her life. Now she does, and you walk away at the first bit of bad news?"

"I didn't—"

She held up her palm. "Talk to the hand. You can say you didn't walk away, and maybe you didn't, but I bet it feels like that to her. Think back to Boston. Rewind to ten years ago. You hated it when she wouldn't give up her career for you," she said, her voice rising as she sent him back in time. "And what did you do in response then? You walked away from her. Now, you hear another thing you don't like, that she lost a baby, and you do the same. You walked away again. You can finesse it all you want, and say you needed space, but the net effect is the same."

Her words shamed him. They knocked him out of his stupor of self-loathing. He had wanted so badly to be everything she needed, but when push came to shove, he'd let pride, and fear, and a million other things stand in the way last night.

"Shit," he said, heavily. "I've fucked up."

"No. You haven't fucked up," she said, pressing her fingers to his cheeks and turning his frown upside-down. "You just took a step back. Now, take some steps forward. This time, instead of walking away, walk back to her. Be there for her, and for yourself. I know it's hard and I know you're feeling this loss too in a new fresh way. But feel it with her, not against her. Talk to her about it. Don't run away. Don't hide. Face your fears with her, and tell her how you feel," she said, squeezing his shoulder. "And move through it together."

"I need to see her right away."

"You do."

Brent cycled back to their last few conversations, trying to figure out where she might be. "I think she's on her way back from L.A. Should I, you know, do that thing where I show up at the airport with a sign that says 'I love you?'"

Mindy clutched her belly and laughed deeply. "God no. That only works in the movies. Besides, you know she's a private person. She wouldn't like that. All she wants is you.

Not a sign. Not a gift. Not some cheesy love song dedicated to her. Strange as it may be, she wants *you*. So give her you."

"Can I borrow your phone for a second?"

Mindy dug into her pocket, and handed it to him. He dialed Shannon's number. It went straight to voice mail.

* * *

Her grandmother slid a mug of tea across the counter. "Have some."

"I don't even like tea, and you know that. But you always try to give me tea," Shannon said, but she said it with a smile. She knew why her grandmother was offering tea. It was Victoria's comfort beverage.

"It cures all troubles," she said in an over-the-top wise woman's voice as she picked up her mug of green tea and knocked some back. Shannon was parked next to her on a stool. She'd stopped by on her way home from the airport, grateful that she was always welcome and didn't have to call first. Besides, her phone had chirped its last breath in Burbank. She was snagging some juice for it at her grandmother's in an outlet on the wall.

"Then I better drink some after all," Shannon said, and took a hearty gulp. "Because I have a lot of trouble."

"Tell me what brings you here."

Shannon didn't mince words. She was straightforward, revealing the key details of her epic argument with Brent, laying it out for the woman who had been her parent for the last eighteen years. "I guess I never thought it would unfold like that. I imagined a million other scenarios but not that one. And I know I should have told him sooner, or tried harder to find him. And I understand why he'd be upset," she said, running her finger absently along the mug. "I just wish there was something I could do. I left him a message, but I haven't heard a word from him all day." She took a beat then asked the hardest question of all. "Is it over?"

"Is he dead?"

Shannon flinched, taken aback by the question. "Grandma!"

"Well? Is he? Answer the question," she said sternly.

"No. Of course not."

She shrugged happily. "Then find him. Talk to him. Say you're sorry for not telling him sooner, say you love him, say you want to be with him. As long as he's not gone, you can keep making up with each other. We live and we love and we hurt each other. We don't always say the right thing, or do the right thing at the right moment. Sometimes we need space, and distance, and sometimes words fall from our lips that shouldn't have been said. Sometimes they seem untenable, and sometimes they are," she said, then reached across the counter to take Shannon's hand. "And we always hurt the ones we love most. If we didn't love so much, it wouldn't hurt so much. But you keep going. You keep loving. You keep working on that love every day. The only time you won't have a chance at making up is when one of you is gone. Since he's still here, it's not over. Not in the least. So love him. Show him that you love him."

"I do. I do love him."

Victoria parked her palms on the counter, and gave Shannon a steely-eyed glare. "Then go get your man back."

"I will," she said, and a small grin formed on her face as the words *show him* echoed in her head. She didn't have enough time to show him what she'd started working on for him yesterday in San Francisco, but she could line up the pieces. As her phone lit up again, she opened the list she'd made.

Then she saw a notification for a voicemail.

CHAPTER THIRTY

He waited.

For an hour.

Then another.

Outside her building, with a bouquet of sunflowers in one hand, his phone in the other. He'd stopped by his house to grab it from the utensil holder inside his dishwasher, then he made a pit stop at a flower shop on the way. He'd been taught never to show up empty-handed for a woman.

In some ways, flowers were just flowers. They were an ordinary, average gift. But since Shannon had photos upon photos of sunflowers in a personal and private album, they obviously meant something important to her. They were more than flowers to her. He hoped this bouquet was more than just an average *I'm sorry* gift.

That it said he was trying to understand the woman he loved.

Since he'd arrived and parked his bike at the curb, he'd sat on the steps and answered emails from earlier in the day. He'd called her again, and encountered her voice mail once more. He'd paced back and forth in front of the building. At this point, he probably looked like a stalker, and he hoped her neighbors wouldn't call the cops or neighborhood watch on him. Nobody seemed to care though that he was hovering around the entrance. A hipster with huge headphones had nodded hello on his way upstairs. A brunette with a yoga mat had walked by on her way into the lobby. Some dude in a Buick parked by the curb had even glanced over at Brent a few times, giving a cursory *hey there* nod.

Brent paced up and down the block to kill more time, his phone clutched in his hand. He reached the corner, turned around, and headed back. The guy was still in his car, his arm hanging out the passenger window, watching Shannon's building.

A bit too closely for Brent's taste.

The guy had been there for twenty, thirty minutes now, looking like he was reading a book, but he kept glancing up, scanning the street as if he didn't want to miss anything.

It reminded him of a cop on a stakeout, only the guy didn't reek of cop. Something about the guy rubbed Brent the wrong way. It was hard to say what it was, but as he neared the Buick again, he held up his phone as if he were answering a message. Instead, he snapped a few pictures of the license plate and the car, and then zoomed in on the guy's arm, covered in ink.

He tucked his phone away as he reached the open window. "How's it going?" he said casually.

"Good," the guy grumbled. He had a baby face and looked young enough to be carded if he were at Edge. Brent continued along the block, and turned around again at the corner. As he returned, the Buick was no longer idling at the curb. The guy had pulled out into traffic, and was driving away.

Probably just some neighborhood guy. But Brent didn't like the idea of anyone hanging out outside Shannon's building for too long. Except for him. Call him a hypocrite, but he knew his own motives. Trusted his own motives.

Then he stopped thinking about anyone but Shannon when her number flashed across his screen.

At last.

He answered in a nanosecond.

"Hey, babe. I'm at your building. Hanging out outside. Looking like a stalker, or maybe like a caged lion in a zoo pacing back and forth. You want to put me out of my misery and make me just look like a man who's waiting for his woman so he can tell her how much he loves her?"

She laughed, and he savored that sound, the sweetness of it, the way it threaded through him. He wanted to bottle it up and keep it close to him forever. "I can definitely make you look that way. And I got your message. My phone died after my flight, so I didn't pick it up till a few minutes ago. But I'm glad you're there because I'm on my way to see a stalking lion who I love, too."

* * *

After she hung up, she listened to his voice message one more time on speakerphone as she drove. "My phone is in the dishwasher, so I'm calling from a friend's phone," he'd said. "I just want to say I love you madly. And I'm on my way over to your house because I'm not walking away. I'd never walk away, and I did a bad job saying that last night,

306 · Lauren Blakely

so I'm trying again right now, and I want you to know that I've meant everything I've said to you in the last few weeks. I will do whatever it takes for you."

Best. Message. Ever.

As she neared her street, she made one more call to a friend of his, the guy who ran the Luxe. He agreed to help with her project, and so she had everyone lined up. She ended the call as she turned onto her street, the kernel of hope expanding inside her, blooming into something bigger, something full of possibilities. She kept her eyes on the road, but peered up ahead, so damn eager to see him. She spotted him, outside her building, his tall strong frame coming into view. He was pacing as promised, aviator shades on, brown hair glinting in the late sun, and that grin she adored flashing at her. Her heart was fighting its way out of her chest, racing to him, knowing they'd somehow fix the mess they'd made.

Because he was waiting for her.

It was that simple.

She yanked the wheel in a sharp right, the tires squealing as she pulled along the curb and cut the engine. In seconds, she was out of her car, and rushing over to him. He held a bouquet of sunflowers in his hand, and the sight of them made her breath catch.

"Hi," she said, as he took off his shades and met her gaze.

"Hi."

Then he wrapped his arms around her, and she did the same, grasping his waist. The flowers pressed against her back. His sunglasses clattered to the sidewalk. "I'm sorry I left last night."

"I'm sorry I didn't tell you sooner," she said.

"I'm sorry I wasn't there for you when it happened."

"I'm sorry you had to find out like that."

He lifted her chin with his fingers, raising her face. "I guess we're both sorry."

She flashed a rueful smile. "We say that a lot don't we?"

He nodded, but kept his arms around her. She was glad he didn't want to let go. She wanted him to hold her.

"Maybe because we fight a lot," he said softly. "Maybe that's just too hard a habit for us to break."

"I think it might be. I just want us to keep coming back together."

He sighed into her hair, and tugged her close again. "Me, too."

"I'm glad you didn't walk away," she said, looping her hands tighter around his strong waist.

"I came back. I told you I would. I meant it, Shan. I'm not ever walking away from you. As long as you'll have me, I will always be here."

She wrenched back to look him in the eyes again. "You," she said, as she ran her hands along his shirt, "are all I want. When you left, all I wanted was to see you again. For you to come back. To open the door and find you. And here you are."

He set the bouquet on the ground, then cupped her cheeks in his palms. He gazed at her, his brown eyes full of passion, full of love. "I told you I won't make the same mistake again. I won't lose you twice." He brushed his thumb along her jawline. "Last night floored me. You have to know that. It shocked me to the bone, and I didn't know what to do. I still don't know how to feel about everything, but one thing I know is true is that I am in love with you.

That's never going to change, so whatever happens, I want to figure it out with you."

His words tugged at all her heartstrings. His hands on her face were the reassurance she'd always sought. They were comfort and protection all at once. "I want that too. I want you here with me. Life is better with you, even if we're dealing with something hard. I don't claim to have all the answers, but I've been through enough to know that whatever comes our way we'll get through it. And hey," she said, her lips quirking into a small smile, "that's my specialty. Maybe that's what I can help you with. Getting through things."

He nodded solemnly. "I'll take it. I need it. I barely knew what to say last night. I left so I wouldn't say something else that was wrong. Last time I said everything wrong."

"So let's say the right things now. It's my turn. When we started seeing each other again, you said you weren't going to let me go. You were damn insistent. You made it clear I was yours, come hell or high water."

He grinned proudly, and nodded. "I did."

"I feel the same about you. I belong with you, and you belong with me. You and I are fire. We always have been. And sometimes we burn with how much we love. Sometimes we hurt each other. But I will do whatever it takes for you. Just as you will for me. I lost you once, and there's no way I'm going to let that happen again. Got it?" She poked him in the chest. "You are mine."

He smiled wide and broad like the sun. "And you're mine."

She cast her eyes to the bouquet. "I see you brought me something."

He bent down and picked up the flowers. "I had this plan to get a skywriter and say *King Shmuck says he's sorry and please take him back,* and then have a Mariachi band play 'You're the One That I Want' after you came through security. It was that, or the flowers." He made a nervous face, one that was clearly deliberate. "Did I pick okay?" he asked.

She laughed and grabbed his arm again, not wanting to let go of him. "I think you did okay, Nichols. You did more than okay. You noticed I like sunflowers, and yellow, and sunshine."

He held his hands out wide. "Help a man out. I have no idea what your sunflower obsession is, but I know they matter to you, and you matter to me, so I want to know."

Her laughter erased itself and so did the smile on her face. She turned serious. "You want to know? Even if hurts? Even if you won't know what to say?"

"Yes. I do."

She tipped her forehead to her car. "Take me for a ride. I'll show you." She handed him the keys, and let him drive.

CHAPTER THIRTY-ONE

The grass was spongy under his feet, and the early evening sun cast golden shadows across the headstones.

The oaks and elms rose stately and green, their lush leaves forming canopies. Flowers burst to life everywhere, some wild, many in bouquets laid on the ground. It was an odd juxtaposition—all that verdant life in the midst of those markers of death. But that was what cemeteries were for—for the living to remember the dead. With her hand in his, they neared her father's grave.

As the simple stone came into view, he saw yellow. So much yellow.

"My grandma was here this week. She brought those," Shannon said gesturing to the sunflowers along the headstone.

He read the etching. *Thomas Darren Paige. Loving father.* His throat hitched, and he swallowed it away as he wrapped an arm around her shoulder.

"I bring them here, too," she continued.

"They're beautiful," Brent said softly, as they stopped a few feet from the grave. "It's a beautiful way to remember him."

"They're not only for him," Shannon said, looking up, meeting his eyes.

"Who are they for?" he asked, but he knew the answer. In a flash, everything made sense. He inhaled sharply, walloped once again by something unexpected.

"I like to think he's with my dad. Somehow. That my dad is looking out for him. That they keep each other company in the great beyond."

He swallowed roughly, and spoke softly. "I believe that."

"I started to bring the flowers when I came back from London. I was struggling and I needed to find a way through all that sadness. I'd been pregnant and utterly confused, and then in mere hours, I became not pregnant and completely empty. I wasn't just sad. I was hollow, and aching. I felt the loss every day for the first few months. I felt it like it was this hole inside me. I didn't know what to do," she said, holding her hands out wide, showing the helplessness she must have felt. "I talked to my grandma about it, and it's not as if I was trying to compare what I lost to what she lost—she lost a son she'd raised and loved for thirty-six years. I lost a son I never knew. But she told me that remembering the person who was no longer here was what helped her the most to heal," Shannon said. Huge tears welled up in her green eyes, and he couldn't help himself. He bent his head to hers and kissed them away.

"And so I did the same," she said, sharing more of the story. "I thought it would just help me deal with the initial awfulness. That kind of grief upends your daily routine. It makes it hard to get out of bed. This helped though," she said, and her voice was soft, but steady. He could hear her strength in it. He could sense all her resilience, all her survival. "And soon, the pain lessened. Time did what time is supposed to do. The pain didn't feel so raw or so new or so fresh anymore. I was able to do my job, and live my life, and not be seized with sadness every second. But I'd still come here when I was in town, and I'd leave more sunflowers, and soon I realized I wasn't leaving them for the baby anymore."

"You weren't?"

She shook her head. "They were for you," she said, and a new shock reverberated in his system. But it wasn't the horribleness of last night; it was something else. It was shock mixed with a strange sense of hope. "They reminded me of you and how I felt for you. I was leaving them here as a way to remember that I wasn't alone. That even though you didn't know, you were a part of it, too. Sunflowers always reminded me of you."

"Why?" he said, his throat dry as the desert, choked with emotion.

She didn't answer with words at first. She answered through touch. She pushed up the sleeve on his right arm, revealing his ink—the black sunburst he'd had done with her in Boston, when she'd told him it fit his sunny disposition. "Because you were like the sun to me. You made my days better. You were my warmth and my happiness. And I wanted to remember that the baby was as much you as he was me. That we were in it together, even if we weren't together."

His heart stopped. His breath fled his chest. His life narrowed to a before and an after. To that moment in time. It marked the man he was, and the man he was becoming. The man he could be for her. That second, those words became the epicenter of his life. "I never knew how far and deep it went when you said I was like the sun to you."

She ran her fingertip over his sunburst, her touch electrifying him, even in the intensity of this kind of admission. "You were all my sunny days, Brent. You were always so happy, and so upbeat, and you never let anything get you down. And you gave all that to me. You turned my days around when I met you."

He closed his eyes and swayed closer to her, trying to take that all in, to digest the enormity of what she was saying. Of how she'd never let go of him through all the years. Of how she'd included him in her life, the good and the bad, even when he'd had no clue where she was and vice versa.

"I thought you hated me," he said softly, trying to process this.

She shrugged, happily. "I thought I did, too. But I never stopped loving you."

"I never stopped either. Not once. Not once through all the years."

Then it hit him, with the clarity of a thousand suns. There was life and death, and the thinnest thread separated the two, by the edge of a razor. Life was for the living, and for the loving.

He dropped down to one knee for the second time ever. He had no ring. No plan. No speech. He grasped her hand in his. "Marry me."

She blinked, a look of utter disbelief on her face. "Are you proposing to me in a cemetery?"

"I am," he said. Hoping. Praying. Wanting that yes.

"You're crazy," she said, but she was grinning wildly.

"Am I?"

"You might be. You did put your phone in a dishwasher. Was it dirty?"

"Yes. It was full of my filthy, dirty messages to you. It was about to combust from the hotness."

She laughed loudly, clasping her free hand on her belly. "Brent, you're ridiculous."

"And that's what you always say when I make you laugh. You say I'm ridiculous. That's another reason why you should marry me now. Because I make you laugh, and I always will. Because I make you happy, and I promise to make that my greatest mission for the rest of my life. Because you make me so damn happy. Loving you is the best thing I've ever done. I love everything about you—your body, your heart, and your mind. I have been in love with you for more than a decade and I've barely spent any of those years with you. Let's pick up where we left off and spend our whole lives together. Let's do what we were supposed to do ten years ago. Let's do it now."

"Now?"

His eyes lit up with mischief. "Vegas, baby."

She arched an eyebrow.

"Think about it," he urged. "Everyone comes here to get married. We live here. This is our town, babe. This is our place. Let's make it ours."

She held out her hand and tugged him up. "Vegas, baby."

Chapter Thirty-Two

There were no flowers. There were no rings. And the bride didn't wear white.

Neither one of them changed from what they already had on—her green dress, his blue shirt and jeans. It was a hell of a lot more fun to race over to the marriage license bureau and snag the paperwork. The bureau was open until midnight every day, and plunking down IDs was nothing short of thrilling.

He pulled up in her car to a drive-thru chapel, its orange neon sign lit and flashing. The officiant came to the window. Brent had called earlier to book a quickie ceremony, and that's exactly what they got. No Elvis impersonator, no Johnny Cash stand-in, no Vegas theme package of mobsters, or starlets, or showgirls. At the end of the two-minute ceremony, the officiant said the words Brent had longed to hear years ago. "I now pronounce you man and wife. You may kiss the bride."

No one needed to tell him that twice. He laced his fingers through Shannon's hair, and dropped his mouth to hers, kissing her softly at first, savoring the sweet taste of her lips, memorizing every second of the first kiss with his wife.

Mrs. Shannon Nichols.

The name played in his head, and it was so fucking perfect, so damn sexy, and so everything he'd ever wanted in his life. In mere moments, the kiss climbed the heat scale as he kissed her furiously, and she tangled a hand in his hair, consuming his lips with her fire too.

He kissed her harder, even as the officiant clapped and cheered and wedding music played from the chapel.

Click.

Click.

Click.

He opened his eyes to see her cell phone held in one outstretched hand. He broke the kiss.

"I know you love selfies of us, so this is your first wedding present from your bride. Our first picture as husband and wife."

"I love it, Mrs. Shannon Nichols," he said in a low dirty growl in her ear. "Now, I need to fuck my wife for the first time."

"Then put on your seatbelt, handsome. I see a parking spot over there that's got our name written all over it."

"Mr. and Mrs. Nichols?"

"Yes. Those names," she said, wiggling her eyebrows.

"Love those names."

A minute later, he pulled into the farthest spot in the lot, away from other cars and lights. In a quick tango they'd practiced years ago in college, he moved to the passenger seat, lowered it, and lay back, bringing her on top of him.

He reached into his back pocket and proffered a condom. "Now I get why you're so particular about them."

"Some day I won't ask you to use one."

"Maybe someday soon. But for now, you should really ride your husband hard. Because we have ten years of lost sex to make up for."

"We're going to be pretty busy," she said, her eyes sparkling with equal parts naughtiness and love, then with heat and want, as he hiked her skirt to her waist.

"My beautiful wife," he said, as he brushed his fingertips along the front of her white panties. She trembled into his touch. He traveled lower, his fingers on a luxurious path to her center. Her mouth fell open in a sexy gasp as he felt the first evidence of her desire. "Hmmm. Seems marrying me turns you on."

"Nothing has turned me on more," she said, her breath already coming fast.

He unzipped his jeans, yanked her panties to the side and handed her the condom. "Put it on me," he told her, as he held tight to her hips.

She opened the condom and rolled it onto his erection. He couldn't believe it had only been twenty-four hours since he'd been inside her. It felt like forever. But as he lowered her, he savored both the intensity of sliding into her gorgeous body, and the sweet, blissful knowledge, that he had a lifetime ahead of him to be with her like this.

His wife.

She took her time, rising up and down, and swiveling her hips in a way that drove him wild. He watched her, raking his gaze over her face, her body, her hips. She was his now, completely his. He reached for her hair, threading his fingers into her strands, pulling her on top of him.

"Closer," he said on a groan. "I need more of you."

He dropped his hands to her ass, and gripped her tight as he moved her up and down, the friction, the heat, bringing them both to the edge. She rocked faster, harder, her hands grappling with his hair, her breathing turning frantic.

She said his name in the most desperate, ecstatic voice he'd ever heard, and it sent them both over the edge.

After, he wrapped his arms around her, her heart beating fast against his chest, her cheeks flushed. "Come home with me tonight, Mrs. Nichols."

"Tonight? Just tonight?"

"Every night," he said, as he smacked her ass. "Get your stuff. You're moving in with me."

She shot him a pouty look. "Why your home?"

"Why not my home?" he countered.

"Actually, I don't care if it's your home or mine. I just want to be with you. Plus, I hear you have a pretty good dishwasher."

She went home with him. It had only taken him more than a decade to carry her over the threshold, but all those years of missing her were worth it that night.

CHAPTER THIRTY-THREE

One week later

Shannon kissed Brent goodbye at the door to his house. Now, it was their house. "I'll see you late, late, late tonight in the Big Apple," she told him.

"I'll be counting down the hours till you knock on the door dressed as a sexy room service French maid."

She furrowed her brow. "Just exactly what kind of hotels do you stay at, Brent?"

He winked. "The kind where my wife shows up at midnight." Then he kissed her. "Have a great rehearsal." He swooped in for one more kiss. "See you tonight."

She shooed him out the door. "Go. You'll miss your plane. You need to be fresh and ready to impress the ladies of Tribeca tomorrow."

"With you by my side, it'll be a piece of cake," he said, then left for the airport.

She finished getting ready for work, pulling on a pair of black leggings, a tunic tank top, and high heels, then tossing her favorite scarf around her neck—the silk, blush pink scarf that Brent had given her. A thin, wispy thing, it was perfect for the summer heat. She had a final on-site rehearsal today with her dancers at Edge. The San Francisco debut had been a smashing success, and with the show set to launch at Edge in Vegas next week, Shannon wanted to make sure everything was perfect. She'd catch a late afternoon flight to New York and land in the Big Apple at midnight. That would still give her plenty of time to go to the picnic with Brent tomorrow, and support him in this key business deal. Tribeca was making him jump through some crazy hoops, and though she might not agree with the neighborhood association, she was ready to stand by her man, and to show, too, that his wife supported him. More importantly, she wanted him to know that his job mattered to her. That it wasn't a source of friction as it had once been, and that they were in this together now.

The weekend was packed and was sure to fly by in a whirlwind. After the picnic tomorrow, they'd visit with Julia and Clay in the evening. Shannon was thrilled and a bit nervous to meet her brother-in-law's wife for the first time. She wondered if they'd give her and Brent a hard time for "eloping," just as her brothers and grandma had done. Of course, that hard time lasted all of five minutes because her grandma then declared she'd start planning a wedding celebration party with barbecue and beer for both families. The menu pleased her brothers, and the party planning pleased her grandma. Julia and Clay were coming to the party in a few weeks, but Shannon was eager to see them tomorrow night, too. Then she and Brent would fly back Sunday morning in plenty of time for Shannon to visit her mom on Monday when Ryan returned from his own weekend business trip. Departure was slated for the crack of dawn on Monday to allow for the five hours of desert driving between Vegas and Hawthorne, a small town with a big prison.

Whew.

She was exhausted just thinking about everything on the agenda. But maybe she was mentally drained, too, in advance of the visit with her mother. As she finished applying mascara, she fast-forwarded to visiting day at the Stella McLaren Correctional Center. Her stomach churned as she heard her mom's voice in her head, as she imagined that desperate, manic look in Dora's green eyes—the same damn shade as Shannon's. Surely she'd be trying to convince them once again of her innocence. But not just *convince*. Dora wanted to prove she should be a free woman. That had been her mission for some time now. The fact that she'd met with a lawyer gnawed at Shannon.

It was that little detail that twisted her gut. That made her worry. Her mom was losing touch with reality, but surely a lawyer wouldn't have come to have his ear bent with her mother's latest obsessive claims. If a lawyer had visited, something was up, and Shannon needed to know what that something was.

As she slung her purse over her shoulder, her phone bleated from inside the bag. She fished it out to find an incoming call from an 800 number, one she didn't recognize.

"This is Shay Sloan."

The phone was silent, and Shannon was ready to hang up when she heard a tinny voice say, "This is the operator. Will you accept a collect call from the Federal Bureau of Prisons?"

Her stomach plummeted. She managed a yes, and five seconds later her mom was on the line.

Cooing.

Her mother actually cooed when she heard Shannon say hello.

Her mother launched into rapid-fire chatter. "I can't wait to see my sweet babies. Are you and Ry-Ry on your way? Will I see you any minute? I've been waiting all morning for my babies. I even put on lipstick today. I can't wait to see you. I'm so excited I had to call. I hope you don't mind."

Shannon sighed, a sad, wistful sound. Her mom couldn't even get the date right. "Mom, it's Monday. We're coming on Monday. When Ryan is back in town."

Her mother gasped. "No, no, no. It's today. Did he tell you Monday?"

"You did, Mom. You told him and you told me in your letters. Last day of the month. That's what you said."

"I meant today. It's today. Last Friday of the month," she said, with the speed of an express train. "Today, today, to-day. They gave me my final two hours today. Mondays are bad. No one likes Mondays. It's today. By five p.m.," she said, her voice turning into a low wail. "There's so much to say, baby. So much to say. I have to see you and Ry. It's urgent. You have to come, you have to come today, you have to come today. It could change everything."

Everything.

There was no way this could change everything.

Her mouth tasted bitter. Her skin felt clammy and cold.

But that desperate, frantic tone clawed into her. She pressed her palm against her door, holding on firmly. *What if? What if? What if?* That question echoed in her mind, in the house, across the whole damn expanse of time. Shannon didn't believe for a second that anything had changed, and yet...

What if it had?

She glanced at her watch. It was eight-thirty. She could rush over to Edge for fifteen minutes since it was on the way out of town. The valets could babysit her car so she wouldn't lose much time there. She could be on the road by nine-fifteen and at the prison by one-thirty, two p.m. at the latest.

"Mom, I need to put you on hold for one second."

She set the phone down, snapped open her laptop on the kitchen table, and opened a browser window for her airline. She tapped in the destination and the date—today —at cheetah speed. She waited for the beach ball to turn, and spit out the results. She pumped her fist. There was one seat left on the Red-Eye to New York. If she spent an hour at prison, she'd be back on the road by three or four, then pulling up to the airport with time to spare before the midnight flight.

She could still make Brent's picnic.

She picked up the phone. "Yes, Mom. I'll be there," she said, then switched her flight, and paid the change fee.

* * *

With the crackle of gate announcements overhead, Brent fired off a few, quick emails to James and his real estate attorneys on the various expansion plans. The Chicago club was coming together more quickly than expected, and all the approvals were in place.

He wrote back. "*Great. If only New York would go so smoothly.*"

But that was what this weekend was for. To seal the deal. To say hello to the families of the neighborhood, and let them know he was good for business and ran a tight, clean ship. He was flying in ahead of Shannon to finish up some key paperwork with Tanner and meet with some potential vendors for the club in New York.

Five minutes later, the boarding had begun and as he walked down the Jetway, he called Shannon. "Hey, babe. I'm about to get on the plane. Can't wait to see you tonight."

"Actually," she said in a heavy voice, "I won't be there till first thing in the morning. I had to change my flight to the red-eye."

Something inside of him tightened with worry. "What happened? Is everything okay?"

"My mom called. The date was wrong. I'm going to see her today."

His spine straightened. "You are?"

"Yeah. She was pretty worked up that I wasn't there today with Ryan. I guess there was a mix-up with the date. She said she has something to tell me that will—" She paused and he could practically see her sketching air quotes as she said, "*Change everything.*"

"Shan," he said softly as he neared the plane. "You can't go alone. Ryan's not even in town."

"It's okay. I can handle it," she said, in a cheery voice. "Seriously. Don't worry about me. I'm sure it's nothing new. Nothing I haven't heard a million times before."

"Hmm," he muttered.

"Hmm, what?"

"I don't think you believe what you're saying."

"Brent, it's fine. I've got it all under control. I will see you as planned. It'll just be a little later."

But he didn't like the idea of her driving five hours through the desert on her own. To a prison. Then five hours back. Then flying five hours on a plane to New York to be with him. To help him. This was not sitting well with him at all.

"Shan—"

From her phone, he heard a car horn honk in the distance

"Let me call you back. Traffic to Edge is getting dicey. Need to pay attention. Bye."

She hung up, and he stared at his phone with narrowed eyes, as if there were an app to reveal how she really felt, and whether she could truly handle this meeting with her mom all by herself. Well, of course she *could*. But should she? The things her mom had been saying lately seemed to suggest the woman had uncovered some key piece of evidence. What if it was the kind of evidence that turned on its head everything Shannon and her brothers had ever believed about their mom's conviction?

He stopped dead at the plane door.

"Good morning, sir."

He met the chipper expression of the flight attendant, who flashed a bright smile. His opportunity.

"Hey, I was hoping you could help me with something," he said as he stepped into the galley.

"Of course. What can I do for you?"

"I need to switch flights. Get on a later flight, as it turns out. My wife was on the four p.m. and she just changed to the red-eye. Can I get on that flight with her?" His evening meetings would need to be cancelled so he could accompany Shannon. They'd still make it in time for tomorrow's picnic.

"Let me just check with the gate. Why don't you take your seat, and give me a few minutes to look into this?"

Five minutes later, the flight attendant found him in the second row and her mouth formed an apologetic *O* as she dropped a hand on his forearm. "I'm so sorry. The Red-Eye is full. We just sold the last seat."

Shannon's seat.

He exhaled deeply, taking in the knowledge that she'd switched her plans to be with him, and now there was no way he could do the same.

* * *

"Go," Shannon's assistant Christine said, pushing her arm playfully. Or maybe not so playfully. Christine was trying to shove her out the front door of Edge.

Shannon held up her hands in surrender. "I'm going. I swear."

"I have this under control," Christine said, gesturing to the final rehearsal. The dancers were glorious, moving like waterfalls, lush and sumptuous, the music playing loudly overhead at Edge.

"You go take care of things," Christine said. Shannon hadn't given Christine the details, and she was glad her second-in-command wasn't nosey enough to pry.

Shannon took a deep breath and nodded, then waved to the scene unfolding in front of her in the empty club. "You're right. Everything looks amazing."

"I will text you and keep you updated. I can even send you pictures and video," Christine said, as she continued to shoo her away.

"Yes, please do," she said, and then walked out of the club.

Along the way, she spotted James, Brent's key investor and advisor. "Hi James," she said with a quick wave.

"Hey, Shay. How's everything going? The dancers look great, don't they?"

She gave him a double thumbs up. "Thank you. So glad you feel that way. And thank you for your time earlier in the week."

"It was nothing. Brent's great. Glad to help out, even if it means my mug is on camera."

She race-walked past the shops of the Luxe and threaded her way through the slot machines and card tables on her way to the exit. She handed the ticket to the valet, and tapped her foot as she waited for her car. She lowered her shades, and grabbed her phone from her purse. She had several missed calls from Brent.

Shit.

She hadn't heard her phone when she was inside Edge and the music was playing.

Quickly, so she could get out of Dodge in a jiffy, she called up the GPS app on her phone, plugging in the address of the Stella McLaren Federal Women's Correctional Center in Hawthorne, Nevada. Four hours and thirty minutes away, the app predicted. That was doable. Very doable. She plugged in her headset and dialed Brent.

"You looking for me?"

She stared at the screen. The voice didn't seem to be coming from the phone. It was coming from... she looked up and saw the valet shutting a town car door, then her husband walking over to her.

She parted her lips to speak, but he went first as another valet pulled up with her little red car.

"I'll take it from here," he said. "I'll drive."

"But..." she said, sputtering.

"No ifs, ands, or buts about it. No wife of mine is driving five hours in the desert, then five hours back to catch a flight to be by my side. I'm going to be by *her* side," he said, his eyes fixed on her, his gaze so strong, as he opened the passenger door for her. She slid into the car, the surprise of seeing him still working its way through her.

He walked behind the vehicle, tipping the valet, then got in on the driver's side. After adjusting the seat and the mirrors, he pulled out of the Luxe's portico.

"Did you just literally walk off the plane?" she asked, still trying to compute that he was there, and not flying across the country to New York. "Stand up and leave? Like in the movies or something?"

He nodded as he flipped on the blinker to turn right. "I did."

"So we'll take the red-eye together?"

He shook his head. He was grinning wickedly.

She scrunched her brow. "I don't get it."

He dropped a hand to her thigh and squeezed. "The red-eye was booked. No room on it. Turns out my wife got the last seat, and I'm having none of that. I missed the chance to be there for you in the past. This is important. You're not going alone. I'm going with you. Every step of the way. I called Tanner and said I wouldn't be able to make it."

She brought her hand to her chest, overwhelmed by what he'd done. How he'd chosen her. How he'd walked away from work to stand by her. "What did he say? Was he angry?"

"He wasn't too happy about it. I said I had to be here for you. Case closed."

"But you'll lose New York if you don't go to the picnic tomorrow."

He flashed her a million-dollar smile. "Sometimes you win. Sometimes you lose. And sometimes you decide there are more important things than a business deal. Like you. Always you." He pointed to the radio. "Now, let's crank up some tunes. You got a desert driving playlist? We need something to rock out to."

She raised an eyebrow. "Would 'Folsom Prison Blues' be too ironic?"

"Irony is my middle name."

She turned on Johnny Cash and held her husband's hand the whole way through the desert as the sun rose high in the sky, blazing through the windshield, the road unfurling before them in a slate ribbon, her heart fuller than it had ever been.

CHAPTER THIRTY-FOUR

The air conditioning hummed, blasting out sheets of cool air in the stark visiting room. Shannon rubbed her bare arms, wishing she'd brought a sweater. She didn't remember it having been so chilly the last time she was there. Perched on the edge of a hard plastic chair at a table inside a small room, she waited.

She tried to conjure up an image of her mother, tried to remember how Dora had looked at Christmas, but the images that paraded before her eyes were older ones, so much older. Sewing Shannon's leotard, the corner of her lips screwed up in concentration as she threaded. Placing a Band-Aid on Shannon's knee when she'd skidded on her bike. Holding her hand as she walked her to school. So young, so vibrant, so blond. Just like Shannon. She'd had the same bright blond hair. Absently, Shannon raised her hand to her now-brown hair.

Someone opened the door.

Shannon rose. Nerves skittered across her flesh. The corrections officer appeared first, a tall, sturdy woman with dark hair in a braid. Holding the door open, the guard nodded and grunted a curt hello.

"Hello," Shannon said, the word feeling strange on her tongue. Even after all these years, it still never felt normal to be conversing with a corrections officer.

Her mother entered, and Shannon did her best impression of a sealed-up box. Otherwise she'd fall to pieces. Keeping her chin up, her muscles steady, she managed a simple, "Hi, Mom."

Her mother was a shadow of the woman she'd once been. Her bright blond hair was the color of dishwater, her cheeks were sunken, and her green eyes were a shade of sallow. Even so, she smiled. Her lips, with their cracked red lipstick, quivered as she held out her arms for a hug.

"My baby," said the woman in orange.

Shannon walked into her arms, embarrassment and shame smacking her from all directions. She wasn't ashamed this woman was her mother. She was ashamed for Dora, for what she'd become, for the choices she'd made that led her to this. Thin arms wrapped around Shannon, arms that had once been strong and maternal. Her mother clutched her.

"Oh, baby. My baby. It is so good to see you again," Dora said, her mouth closer to Shannon's neck than she would have liked.

"It's good to see you, too, Mom," Shannon said, lying, but knowing it was only a white lie. It wouldn't hurt anyone for her to say that.

"I'm so happy you're here." Another firm grip, then she felt the first drop from her mom's eyes. A tear had fallen on Shannon's bare shoulder as Dora embraced harder and tighter, as if she could graft her body onto Shannon's and escape as a growth on her kid.

"All right, Prince. That's enough," the CO said, her command clear.

Shannon's mom pulled away, and shot the woman a contrite look. "Sorry. I just missed my baby girl so much. She's a dancer. Isn't she lovely?" Her mom held out her arms to Shannon as if she were presenting her on *Wheel of Fortune.*

"Mom, stop," Shannon said, embarrassed now for a whole new reason. She glanced at the woman. "We're fine. We'll sit down now."

"Behave, Prince," the woman warned as she shut the door, leaving Shannon alone with her mother. They sat at the gray plastic table, like the kind in a cafeteria.

"Baloney," her mom said.

"Baloney?"

"That's what they fed me the other day. Baloney on white bread. Can you believe it? Baloney." Her mom brought her hand to her eyes, covering them, as if the memory of the cold cuts was too much to bear. "I hate baloney."

"Tell them you hate it."

"I tried. I asked for turkey. They don't think I deserve turkey."

"Did they say that?" Shannon asked.

Her mom raised her face. "They don't have to. I can tell. They don't like me here. They don't like me at all."

"Mom," she said, doing her very best to sound comforting and caring, because that was all she could do. "Why would you say that?"

"Because." Her mom clamped her lips shut, as if she was refusing to speak.

"Because why?"

"Because."

Shannon held up her hands in defeat. "It's okay. You don't have to tell me."

"Because of what happened," her mom snapped out, like a wild dog.

"Because of why you're here?" she asked gently, as if she were talking to a child who'd been caught skipping school.

Her mom shook her head, whipping it back and forth so rapidly she was a cartoon character in fast forward. "No. Not that. Not that at all. It's because of the—" She stopped talking and jammed her fist in her mouth, biting hard on her knuckles.

Shannon cringed and reached for her mom's hand, trying to remove it. It wouldn't budge. She tried again. Her mom bit deeper. "Mom, stop that," she said in a harsh whisper. "Your CO will come back and you'll have to go. You're making a scene."

Her mom crunched, digging her teeth into the flesh of her hand.

"You're going to draw blood. Stop!"

The door swung open.

"Enough, Prince," the corrections officer barked.

Dora dropped her fist from her mouth, her shoulders sagging, her body going limp. The big woman held up her hand and raised her index finger. "One more shot, Prince. One more shot."

"Okay," her mom muttered.

Shannon dared to look. Her mom's hand had deep grooves from her own teeth. Red and raw, on the cusp of bleeding. "What was that all about?" she asked, bewildered.

"Nothing," her mom mumbled. "Just nothing."

Shannon nodded, trying to digest everything that had gone wrong so far. Baloney obsession and gnawing her own fist in the first three minutes. Steeling herself for another painful visit, she fixed on her best happy face, and asked, "Are you still watching *General Hospital*?"

Dora's eyes lit up. They sparkled with a mad kind of glee as she began rattling off couples, and plot lines, and twists and turns. Shannon let her talk, and let her share every spoiler, because that soothed the savage beast inside her mother.

After fifteen minutes of mindless chatter about TV and the meatloaf served last night, her mom asked about Shannon's work, and Shannon told her the latest about her shows. Then, after they'd settled into a peaceful rhythm, Shannon broached the topic of the phone call. "You said earlier you wanted to talk about something that would change everything," she said, then swallowed. Her throat was dry. Her mouth was sawdust. She had to do this though. She had to know. "Is the case being reopened?"

Her mom sat up straight, like a puppeteer had just pulled up her marionette strings. "Is it?"

Shannon sighed. "Mom, I don't know. I thought that's why you wanted to talk. You told Ryan on the phone, and you told me earlier today you had news that would change everything." She placed her hands on the table, knowing her mom would take them, knowing the woman who gave her life would want to hold them. Her mom shot out her hands instantly, gripping Shannon's. Inside, she cringed, not wanting that kind of connection to the woman. But she let her mom do it anyway. Because it was the compassionate thing to do. That was where she could be different from the woman in orange. "Tell me. Did someone find new evidence? I heard the DA was talking to Stefano. Is there something going on? Tell me, Mommy," she said, hating to use that term, but it was the way to get her mom talking.

"I don't know anything about Jerry," she said, using the shooter's first name.

"What did you see your lawyer about then?" Shannon squeezed her bony fingers, urging her to speak.

Her mom's chest rose and fell. She breathed heavily. Then, faster. A lone, silent tear streaked from her eye. "It's about Luke."

Shannon flinched. She hadn't heard that name in years. Hadn't thought it much either. There had been no reason to. Luke Carlton was long gone. The local piano teacher her mother had had a brief affair with when Shannon was thirteen was ancient history. The police had questioned him, but it was perfunctory. He was never a suspect. He'd had no connection at all to the crime.

"What about Luke?" she asked carefully. She wasn't wild about the man, not by any stretch, but there was a big difference between being a cheater and being a killer. There was no evidence to show her mother's lover was involved in any way, except loving the wrong person at the wrong time. "The police cleared him, Mom. In just two days he was cleared of any knowledge."

"I know. He didn't do it. He's not that kind of man. He's a gentleman and a saint. He's not the one who shot your daddy in the driveway. And it wasn't me either. It was a robbery gone wrong," she said, sticking chapter and verse to her age-old defense, as if the open wallet and stolen bills missing from it proved her innocence.

Shannon sighed deeply, her heart cratering as her mom toed her own party line. "Then why are you bringing up Luke?"

Her mom peered to the door, making sure it was shut, then back at Shannon. She lowered her voice to a feather of a whisper. "He said he'd wait for me. He promised he'd wait for me."

"You're in for life. He's going to be waiting a long time."

"Not if they find the real killer."

"If they were going to, it would have happened already. It's been eighteen years," she said, reminding her mother that time was not on her side. She didn't bother to bring up the powerful evidence that had put her there in the first place, including the shooter's own testimony that Dora Prince had hired him. That didn't need to be said, because it didn't change this interaction.

"Oh, it'll happen. They'll realize."

Shannon bit back all the things she wanted to say. All the truths she wanted to remind her mother of. She didn't want to rehash the case. She didn't want to play courtroom trial again. "What does this have to do with Luke?"

Her mom leaned across the table, coming as close to Shannon as she could, and said in a fast breath, "Because he promised to wait for me. He swore he would. And I just found out he's remarried. One of my girlfriends on the outside told me. Baby, he married another woman. He was supposed to wait for me. For me, for me, for me. And now he's with someone else, and I'm all alone." She dropped her head to the table, tears spilling like summer rain from her eyes.

Shannon brushed a hand over her mother's limp hair. "That's what you talked to your lawyer about?"

Her mom nodded her head against the table as she sobbed. "Yes. Because it proves something. And lawyers need proof. So I told my lawyer."

"What does it prove?"

"It proves that Luke lied to me," she said, her voice breaking like waves. "He lied when he said he'd come back."

"And that changes everything?"

"Yes. It changes everything for me. Everything." Her mom cried more, a river of tears rolling down the plastic as Shannon stroked her hair, some strange kind of relief washing over her even in the midst of all this hollowness, all this hurt for the woman her mother had become.

Through it all, one fact remained starkly clear.

The case was closed. Her mother's fate was irrevocably sealed eighteen years ago, and now she was paying for her crime in so many ways. With her life, with her health, and with her sanity.

Dora Prince lived in her own land, and she'd done it all to herself.

CHAPTER THIRTY-FIVE

"Skittles? Salt and vinegar chips? Twizzlers?"

Brent plucked the snack foods from a dusty shelf, wiggling each bag in front of his wife.

She crinkled her nose. "I'm not that hungry."

"Yeah, these might be stale." He lowered his voice to a whisper. "I don't think many people come around here too often." He peered at the expiration date on the Skittles. "Whoa. These Skittles were past their prime two years ago."

She laughed half-heartedly as he dropped the unwanted snacks on their shelves.

"I'll just get a soda," she said, pointing vaguely in the direction of the fountain drinks at the Lucky Seven Gas & Go somewhere in the middle of the desert. As far as he knew, they were halfway between Hawthorne and Vegas, which meant two and half more hours of cruising south on the highway to home.

"Shan, you need to eat. You haven't had anything all day."

"Maybe just some pretzels then," she said. "Pretzels taste expired anyway."

He grabbed a pretzel pack with gusto, as if his enthusiasm for potentially out-of-date road trip snacks would somehow buoy her spirits. She walked to the soda fountain, grabbed a cup, and pressed it against the Diet Coke spout. She leaned forward slowly, as if she was starting to tip over, then rested her forehead against the dispenser. She'd slept the whole ride back so far, slumping against the passenger seat with her shades on after she'd left the prison and given Brent the cliff notes as they drove out of Hawthorne.

Crossing the distance in a second, he took the cup from her. "I'll do it."

She rested her head against his chest. "Thank you."

It was only a soda. That was all he was doing. Filling a flimsy paper cup at a rest stop in the middle of nowhere. But it was something he alone could do for her right now. And she needed it.

He finished filling the cup and popped a lid on it.

"I'm sorry I made you drive me all the way here for nothing," she said.

"Hey. You did not make me do anything. I chose to. And it was not nothing." He set the cup down on the counter, and lifted her chin. "It was *not* nothing."

"But you missed your meeting and it's just the same old stuff with my mom."

"Then that's something. That's exactly what you needed to know."

"The same old stuff?"

He nodded. "The same old stuff. Because now you know. Now you know that nothing has changed. Now you can stop worrying that something is going to change. This is the same stuff she did to you in college," he said, running a thumb along her jawline as he held her gaze. "She tried to work you over. She tried to get you to believe her madness. And you are good, and loving, and you did the right thing by seeing her, Shan. You visited her; you listened to her. You did a loving thing without compromising who you are. And now, you can let it go. The past is the past."

* * *

She leaned her cheek into his hand, so strong, and so soft at the same time too. "How did you get to be so wise?" she asked softly.

"My wife taught me how," he said, planting a kiss on her forehead, then rubbing her belly. "Now I need to go pay for this stale nourishment I'm procuring for you."

He picked up the soda and pretzels and walked to the cash register to pay. As she watched him, she couldn't help but feel an unexpected pang of guilt over the day, and what he'd miss tomorrow. The Tribeca club had been his single-minded mission for expansion, and he'd worked his ass off to please the neighborhood. He'd come so close, and she'd even made the video to show them at the meeting this weekend.

Then it hit her. Like a bag of obvious smacking into her. The answer had been under her nose and on her phone the whole time. She didn't know if it would make a difference to the neighborhood association, but she had to try. As Brent finished paying, she fired off a quick text to James, grateful she still had his number from the first night they'd met.

Ten minutes later, she had an email address for Alan Hughes, and the video she'd made was on its way to him as they pulled back onto the highway.

A few miles down the road, a sign rose into view, the rays of the dipping sun illuminating the battered wooden billboard. GATEWAY TO DEATH VALLEY, BEATTY, NEVADA. ESTABLISHED 1903. POPULATION 1000. It stood proudly amidst the sand and rocks, the dryness and dust.

Twenty feet away, there was a sign for a Motel 6.

Shannon touched Brent's arm and pointed to the sign, then wiggled her eyebrows.

He cut the wheel at the exit, and they checked into a fifty-nine dollar a night room at a hotel that boasted a coin laundry, free local calls, and morning coffee on the house.

As well as a bed that squeaked, she learned as she pushed down on the springs of the mattress inside room number fourteen, on the first floor with a view of the parking lot.

"Are you tired?" he asked.

She shook her head. "I don't want to sleep."

"What do you want to do?"

She ran her fingers along the silky fabric of her scarf. "I want you to fuck the day away."

His lips quirked up. "That is my specialty," he said, and soon he'd stripped her naked and tied her hands with the scarf, knotting the ends to the headboard of the creaky motel bed. "I knew this gift would come in handy."

"It's a multi-use scarf," she said, squirming, as he began to kiss her.

No, he didn't just kiss her.

He worshipped her.

He caressed her breasts with his lips. He nipped her throat with his teeth. He adored her belly with his tongue, working his way across the landscape of her body, marking the territory of her with his lips, and his sighs, and his groans. As he traveled across her with his tongue, she let the day fall away. She gave herself over to passion.

Her hips shot up, seeking more of him, begging with her body for him to work his magic.

But it was more than just magic. He was more than just her sweet drug as he consumed her and sent her soaring into a state of ecstatic bliss that had her singing his name to the heavens.

He flipped her over, her wrists still bound to the headboard, and sank into her. She cried out, louder than she'd ever been, more aroused than she'd ever been, there on her hands and knees in a Motel 6.

Yes, it was so much more than mere intoxication. Sex with Brent flooded her brain with endorphins, filled her body with pleasure, and freed the past.

He wasn't just fucking the day away. This connection, this deep and abiding love, was part of the letting go. As they came together in a mad carnal frenzy, the past crumbled to dust.

There was no more past.

It was done. It was over.

There was only the present, only love, only life. Her life together with her man.

* * *

As he lifted his fork for a final bite of scrambled eggs and hash browns at a truck stop diner an hour outside of Vegas, Brent's phone rang. It rattled on the table, blinking Tanner's name across the screen.

Brent groaned. He showed the screen to Shannon, and she simply shrugged. "Maybe it's good news?" she suggested.

"Ha. Ha. Ha. I knew you were funny," he said as the ringer sounded again. "I'm sure he's calling to tell me I'll never get a club approved in New York."

Brent slid his thumb across the screen and answered. "Hey Tanner."

"Congratulations," the man barked.

Brent narrowed his eyes. Waiting for the *sucker* to come. *You've been punked, you jackass.*

A waitress in a starchy pink diner uniform stopped at their table, holding up a pot of coffee.

"Thanks. But for what?" Brent asked carefully, holding up his mug for a refill. It was early in the afternoon. They'd slept in late that morning, then extended the shower by a few orgasms, and didn't hit the road until noon.

"They fucking loved your wife's video. They loved it," Tanner said, as if he were licking each word like a lollipop.

"What video?" Brent asked, though the word tickled a distant memory. Shannon had said something once about making a video of the Edge rehearsal in San Francisco. "Of the dancers in San Francisco?"

"That. But it was mostly all the soundbytes. Something from James. Something from some chick who's known you forever. Mindy, I think. A few nice words from that hotel guy. A bunch of others, too. But I think they liked your wife and her note most of all."

Brent caught Shannon's gaze as she brought her mug to her lips and drank some coffee. Her eyes were full of mischief.

"What did my wife's note say?"

Tanner cleared his throat. "It said, and I quote. 'Please accept my apologies that my husband was unable to attend your picnic. I was very much looking forward to joining him and meeting you as well. I had an urgent family matter to attend to here in Nevada, and needed to visit my mother. My husband wanted to be by my side, so he chose to come with me. I hope this video I made of his work, and his friends, colleagues, and family will show you that he's not only the man on stage telling dirty jokes. He's a man with a heart of gold.'"

Brent's heart raced. It tripped out of his chest and leapt into Shannon's hands. "She did that?"

"She did. She's a keeper. Hey, I'm here with Alan. He'll tell you officially."

Alan took the phone, and spoke. "The neighborhood association is firmly behind you."

After the call ended, Brent switched sides and moved in next to Shannon on the sky blue, cracked vinyl booth. "Seems like you were up to something," he said with a smile. "Want to show me the video of this guy with the heart of gold?"

She rustled through her bag for her phone, opened a video file and hit play. He watched, filled with awe and astonishment that she'd found all his friends and family and asked them to say a few words. Nate appeared on screen to talk about Brent's business skills, then Travis said some kind words about how long they'd been friends, and how he'd trust him like he did his firefighter buddies. Mindy batted next, his dear, sweet friend saying, "Brent is the one of the greatest guys I've ever known. We help each other. He's helped me through some sad times, and I've helped him, too. He's like a brother." Brent parked his chin in his hand as he watched his brother talk about how he'd helped him plan a proposal for his wife, then Julia shared a story about how Brent had helped her out when she'd run into some trouble. Even Bob at the Comedy Club talked about how Brent had done everything he could to find a job for him when his had ended.

Finally, Shannon showed him the note she'd written to Alan. This time she read it out loud to him, and he loved the sound of it in her voice, especially the final words.

"Do you like it?"

"I love it. Madly," he said. "You didn't have to do that at all. But I'm thrilled you did."

"You once made a video hoping I'd see it and know you were still thinking of me. It seemed only fitting that I should make this for you, and help you get what you wanted."

"Babe," he said, cupping her cheeks and moving in for a kiss. "I already have everything I've ever wanted."

EPILOGUE

The delicious scent of barbecue wafted through the summer air. Shannon's brothers manned the grill, flipping burgers and chicken breasts, and turning cobs of corn.

Music played from an outdoor speaker. A string of red pepper lights hung along the wooden posts of the fence. Her grandparents had insisted on a wedding celebration, and everyone was there—his parents; his brother and his wife, and their daughter; Mindy; Ally; Nate and his wife; James and his family; Shannon's brothers; and her grandmother's daughter and her kids.

Everyone who mattered deeply to the bride and groom.

The first three weeks of marriage had been bliss, and Brent was confident the next thirty, forty, fifty years and then some would be too.

As he took a long swallow from a bottle of beer, his eyes found his wife. She relaxed in an Adirondack chair on the deck, bouncing Carly on her knee and making cooing sounds to his niece while chatting with Julia. The sight of his Mrs. Nichols holding a baby tugged on all his heartstrings, reminding him both of the loss in the past but also of a bright, possible future. They'd need to get working on that soon.

Very soon.

He felt a hand on his arm and turned to see Mindy. "You checking out Shannon's brothers?" he teased.

She rolled her eyes. "Oh yeah. Totally. Just standing around, staring at the eye candy."

He laughed, then lowered his voice. "Did you ever find out anything about that guy? The pics I showed you?"

"Brent," she chided. "We're at your wedding celebration."

"This is important, though," he said. He'd given Mindy the pictures he'd taken of the guy in the Buick a few weeks ago, and she'd agreed to show them to some of her friends on the force to see if the plates or the car or the tattoos revealed anything. He couldn't dismiss the notion in the back of his mind that the ink meant something.

"Truth be told, I don't have anything yet. They're pretty swamped, and can't really do license plate checks anymore for privacy reasons. But one of my guys said he'd take a close look and see if the ink looks familiar. I promise to let you know as soon as I hear."

Out of the corner of his eye, he noticed Shannon handing the baby to Julia, then blowing him a kiss. He returned it, and watched as she headed inside the house, her brothers in tow. They'd told him they had a special gift for Shannon, and he suspected they were giving it to her now.

He lifted his beer and tapped it to Mindy's. "Thank you."

"Anytime. Now celebrate. Don't worry about the pictures. Have a great time with everyone here."

That sounded like a damn fine plan.

* * *

Her grandmother was in the kitchen refilling a pitcher of iced tea. Michael swooped in behind her and grabbed something from the counter.

"Told you we'd get you a wedding gift," he said, holding up a small white box with a silver bow tied daintily on it.

"I wrapped it," her grandma chimed in. "That's why it looks nice."

"Because you boys don't know how to wrap gifts," Shannon said as she reached for the box. "Yet another reason why you all require further domestication," she said, taking her time to give each of her brothers a steely-eyed, yet playful stare.

"Good luck on that front. Pretty sure I'm not trainable at all," Ryan said, tucking his thumbs into the belt loops of his shorts.

Shannon patted him on the cheek. "There, there. Every dog can learn."

"All right, funny girl. Open your gift," Michael said.

"You know I don't need anything, right? I hope you didn't get me a blender," she said as she removed the silver bow from the box.

"The world's smallest blender," Colin joked.

Peering inside, she found soft tissue paper laid on top of something metallic. She folded back the tissue paper to uncover a gorgeous platinum bracelet that matched the rose gold and silver ones she already wore.

"Oh, it's so pretty," she said, admiring the simple and elegant design. When she spotted the date engraved in the center, she brought her hand to her heart. "My wedding date."

"Look at the inside, too. It's also inscribed," Michael said, nudging her with his shoulder.

Turning the slender bracelet on its side, she read the engraved script. "*To our incredible sister on her happily ever after. We love you, always. Michael, Ryan and Colin.*"

A lump rose in her throat, fighting its way free. She clasped a hand over her mouth, as a tear slid down her cheek.

That tear was a declaration. An announcement of their love, their bond, their unbreakableness. Her boys—her men. She wrapped her arms around Michael and Colin, and Ryan jammed his way in, too, for a big group hug.

"I love you guys. So damn much," she whispered in their huddle.

"We love you," they all said in unison.

When they pulled apart, Shannon wiped the tears from her cheek, and shot them a wild grin. "Hmm. Now who gets to go next? Michael, Ryan, or Colin?" she said, counting off her brothers as her grandmother laughed. "I have a feeling the next one of us to fall in love will be—"

The doorbell rang, cutting off her prediction.

"I'll grab that," her grandmother said, heading to the front door, a few feet away. "Probably my neighbors. I invited them too."

When she opened the door, there were two men on the front step. One wore a light blue button-down. The other sported a gray striped shirt. Both had ties, loosely knotted, and badges at their waists.

Her spine straightened and her smile erased itself. Shannon did a quick inventory of people, even though she already knew the answer—everyone she loved was safe and sound in the house. Still, her pulse doubled as she and her brothers moved closer to the door, flanking their grand-mother.

The guy in the blue button-down spoke. "I'm looking for Victoria Paige. Is she here?"

Her grandmother nodded crisply and held out a hand. "I'm Victoria. What can I do for you?"

He shook her hand. "I'm Detective John Winston with Metro. This is my partner," he said, but Shannon barely heard the other man's name as blood pounded in her ears. "We wanted to let you know as the family of the murder victim, that due to new evidence in the homicide of Thomas Paige, the investigation is being reopened."

THE END

Stay tuned for SINFUL DESIRE, book #2 in the Sinful Nights series, now available for preorder across all retailers! SINFUL DESIRE releases in September and tells the story of Ryan Sloan as he falls in love with the glamorous and brilliant Sophie Winston against the backdrop of the re-opened investigation. If you'd like to receive an email when SINFUL DESIRE and other new titles are available, please sign up for my newsletter:

laurenblakely.com/newsletter

A brief excerpt of
SINFUL DESIRE follows.

SINFUL DESIRE

Book 2 in the Sinful Nights series

Chapter One

The light was playing tricks on him.

The golden haze of the late afternoon sun, and its halo glow, was some kind of illusion. No way, no how—it was not possible for anyone to be so gorgeous that she practically shimmered.

Mirage was the more plausible answer to explain the platinum blonde stepping out of the Aston Martin at three o'clock in the afternoon on a Friday in July, looking like she belonged in a gangster movie. The woman they all fought over. The woman who brought the men to their knees.

From the pinup dress, to the pouty lips, to the gleaming car that nearly stretched a city block—or so it seemed—she was...

Glamorous. Sultry. Voluptuous.

His fantasy woman.

No question about it.

This was lust at first sight. Pure, unadulterated lust knocking around in his chest and threatening to make matters in his charcoal gray slacks harder than he needed them to be right now.

But he was willing to deal with that problem because the woman could not be ignored. A groan rolled around in Ryan's throat as he stared shamelessly over the top of his aviator shades. He walked along the palm-tree lined sidewalk that framed police headquarters, cycling through his best opening lines, even though he had a hunch a woman like that—a woman who wore a black dress with a cherry pattern and bright white sunglasses—had heard them all. Busty and bold enough to pull up to Vegas' municipal building at midday looking like sin come to life, this woman wasn't going to be wooed by lines.

With one hand on the car door, she glanced to the left, away from him. In her other hand, she held a phone, a notepad and a pen. She bumped her rear against the car door, shutting it with her ass.

What a lucky car door.

He half wished she'd drop a pen, just so he could swoop in and pick it up. Bend down, grab it before it rattled to the street, and gallantly present it.

Then get her number with that pen. She'd be the type to push up the cuff of his shirt-sleeve and write it on his arm.

He scoffed to himself. As if that would work. But something had to, because the clock was ticking, and he was ten feet from this heavenly vision. Checking his watch, he saw he had two minutes to spare before he met with the detective. He could do this. He could meet her in 120 seconds.

The sun pelted its hot desert July rays at him, radiating off the sidewalks, as he ran a hand along his green tie and cleared his throat. She looked up from her phone and instantly they locked eyes. Hers were blue like the sea. As she caught his gaze, she arched an eyebrow.

This was it. No time for lines. Just fucking talk to the gorgeous creature. "Seems I've been caught staring," he said as he reached her and stopped walking, claiming a patch of concrete real estate a foot away.

"I'm afraid I'm guilty on that count, too," she fired back, her voice laced with a torch singer sultriness, her words telling him to keep going.

She had a pen in her hand and twirled it once absently.

He tipped his forehead to the pen. "Incidentally, I'm astonishingly good at picking up pens that beautiful women drop outside our fine city's government buildings."

Her lips twitched. Red. Cherry red and full. He wanted to know what they tasted like. How they felt. What she liked to do with them.

She brought the pen to her lips, danced it between them, raised her eyebrows in an invitation, and then let it drop. It clattered to the sidewalk. "Is that so?"

The pen was like a promise. Of something more. Of flirting, and then flirting back. Of phone numbers to follow. And then some. Oh yeah, so much and then some.

"That is so," he said in a firm voice, bending down to pick up the writing implement, just as Sinatra's 'Fly Me to the Moon' crooned from her phone. He rose, and she was tapping her screen, sliding her thumb across it. "Must answer this. But thank you so much for the pen. By the way, I like your tie," she said, reaching out to trail a finger down the silky fabric, her hand terribly close to his chest. Then she held up that finger asking him to wait.

Oh, he could wait for her. He could definitely wait for her.

"So good to hear from you," she said into the phone, keeping her eyes on him the whole time. "I can't wait to see you tonight at the gala at the Aria," she said, arching an eyebrow at Ryan as she emphasized that last word. "It's going to be a fabulous event and we'll raise so much money. My only hope is there will be some gorgeous man there in a green tie who can afford a last-minute ticket."

He shot her a grin, a lopsided smile that said yes, the man in the green tie could absolutely afford a ticket.

He nodded his RSVP to the gala. She waved goodbye, and walked down the street.

Suddenly, Ryan had plans that night.

SINFUL DESIRE is available
for preorder across all retailers!

Check out my contemporary romance novels!

The New York Times and USA Today
Bestselling Seductive Nights series including
Night After Night, After This Night,
and *One More Night*

And the two standalone
romance novels, *Nights With Him* and *Forbidden Nights*,
both New York Times and USA Today Bestsellers!

21 Stolen Kisses, the USA Today
Bestselling forbidden new adult romance!

Sweet Sinful Nights, a new high-heat romantic
suspense series that spins off from Seductive Nights!

Caught Up In Us, a New York Times and
USA Today Bestseller! (Kat and Bryan's romance!)

Pretending He's Mine, a Barnes & Noble and
iBooks Bestseller! (Reeve & Sutton's romance)

Trophy Husband, a New York Times and
USA Today Bestseller! (Chris & McKenna's romance)

Playing With Her Heart, a
USA Today bestseller! (Davis and Jill's romance)

Far Too Tempting, an Amazon
romance bestseller! (Matthew and Jane's romance)

Stars in Their Eyes, an iBooks bestseller!
(William and Jess' romance)

My USA Today bestselling
No Regrets series that includes

The Thrill of It
(Meet Harley and Trey)

and its sequel

Every Second With You

My New York Times and USA Today
Bestselling Fighting Fire series that includes

Burn For Me
(Smith and Jamie's romance!)

Melt for Him
(Megan and Becker's romance!)

and *Consumed by You*
(Travis and Cara's romance! August 2015)

ACKNOWLEDGEMENTS

I am grateful to so many people who helped make this book possible. First, thank you to my husband and amazing daughter who helped shape the plot, and who whiteboarded it with me one weekend. You two are brilliant!

Thank you to my father, who tipped me off in the first place. Thank you to Kelly for brainstorming the series concept. Abiding gratitude to Tanya Farrell for reading each chapter as I wrote, to Jen McCoy for her spot-on beta feedback, and to Kim Bias for her overall eagle eye. My line editor Lauren McKellar made sure I stayed on track, and my copy editor caught all those swivels!

I am, as always, in awe of the talent of my cover designer Sarah Hansen. She is the bomb. Helen Williams creates gorgeous graphics and design work and I am lucky she is mine.

A special thank you to the talented RE Hunter for her expertise in legal details, and to Jill Ciambriello for shaping the dance backstory, as well as Brian for his insight. Gale, as she always does, provided her choreographic brilliance.

Violet Duke lent her big brain for key plotting. Crystal Perkins made sure I did right by Vegas.

Big thanks to Kelley for running the social show, to Michelle for fighting the battles, and to Jesse for making the books.

I am lucky to lean on so many talented author friends – CD, Laurelin, Kristy, Monica, Marie, Jessie, Corinne, Violet and more.

Thank you to all the bloggers who have enjoyed my Seductive Nights series. I am so grateful for your amazing support and big, bold voices!

Most of all, I am thankful for my readers. You make my world go round.

CONTACT

I love hearing from readers! You can find me on Twitter at LaurenBlakely3, or Facebook at LaurenBlakelyBooks, or online at LaurenBlakely.com. You can also email me at laurenblakelybooks@gmail.com.